I0817828

The Accident

ALSO BY DONNA M. ZADUNAJSKY

Novels

Broken Promises

Not Forgotten

Books in Series

Family Secrets

Hidden Secrets

Twisted Secrets

Novellas

HELP ME!

Talk To Me

Children Books

Tayla's Best Day Ever!

Tayla's Best Friend

Tayla's New Friend

Tayla Goes to Grammies House

Tayla Takes a Trip

Tayla's Day at the Beach

Tayla's First Day of School

The Accident

By Donna M. Zadunajsky

ISBN: 978-1-7240-1916-5 —Paperback
ISBN: 978-1-938037-76-4 —Hardcover
ISBN: 978-1-938037-77-1 —eBook

Book Cover Design by: Travis Miles
Interior Format by: Donna M. Zadunajsky
Edited by: Deborah Bowman Stevens

Connect with the Author:
http://www.donnazadunajsky.com
http://www.facebook.com/donnamzadunajsky
http://twitter.com/AuthorDonnaMZ

For those who have loved and lost, but yet,

are still looking for their one true love...

1

The Morning of the Accident

The roads and highways were left wet and slick from the rain that had come and gone just hours ago. The sun played a game of peek-a-boo through the wispy layers of clouds, shining rays of sunlight down to the ground. The light from the sky created a beautiful prism effect atop the vehicles stopped on the Ohio Turnpike. The view on the ground compared to the sky wasn't as attractive, as the people sat inside their cars staring at the horrifying scene around them. No one left their vehicles to help the injured, most likely afraid they would get hurt if they got out of their cars, although with all the vehicles already piled up on the highway, there wouldn't be anywhere for an oncoming car to go.

The phones at Franklin and Edon Police Stations rang off the hook after the accident occurred on the Ohio Turnpike. Officer Adanya Moore from Edon arrived at the scene moments after the calls came pouring through. She and a few others jumped in their vehicles and raced to the accident with lights flashing and sirens blaring as they ran through stoplights to get there. Officer Moore and the others from her district weren't the first to arrive at the scene. There were already firetrucks and the state highway patrol surrounding the accident.

Adanya Moore cautiously drove her way around the parked cars congested on the highway with nowhere to go. She stopped when she found a clearing near the accident. She put the truck in park and stared out the windshield with her mouth agape. It was the kind of jaw-dropping reaction you'd have if you walked in on your boyfriend or husband sleeping with another woman, and that woman was your sister or best friend. She was in a state of utter shock. The highway looked like a mass murderer had went on a shopping spree. Some vehicles were flipped over; others were smashed with their engines sweltering and smoking. Oil and gas leaked from the vehicles, mixing on the black pavement. The mess would take half the day to clean up, and still there would probably be pieces left on the side of the road.

As Moore scanned the scenery, her eyes stopped on two motorcycles, with no bodies lying nearby. The thought of them being buried under all those vehicles made her feel sick to her stomach. The drivers of the motorcycles didn't have the protection a car or truck had. The chances of them being alive were slim to none.

~ ~ ~

The scent of gasoline hit her nose the moment she opened the door of her truck and stepped out. Glass crunched under her combat boots as she exited the police SUV. She took in the sight of broken glass scattered on the road; it was everywhere. Her eyes skimmed over the scene, counting the vehicles. There were at least ten.

A fire ignited at the rear of a black sedan. Moore watched as a firefighter raced over with an extinguisher and put it out. She watched as other police officers parked their cars around the accident with their lights strobing to keep out other cars and to direct traffic off the highway to nearby streets. People who were waiting to get off the highway sat in their vehicles and stared at the gruesome scene around them. Some of them were on their cell phones, either filming the accident or calling their loved ones to tell them what had happened and that they were okay. After 9/11 this seemed to be the first thing people did, always filming things that were happening around them.

Helicopters from news stations all around the area hovered above, recording the scene from both eastbound and westbound. The state police were able to get the traffic moving on the eastbound side of the highway, which was stopped due to a male body in the road. Officer Moore overheard two firefighters, standing twenty feet in front of her, talking about the man on the other side of the highway. Their theories were that the man had been ejected from his vehicle on the westbound side where Moore stood and flew into the grille of a semi-truck on the eastbound side.

The radio secured to Moore's shoulder chirped as one of the other police officers from the scene started talking. She bent her neck so that her ear was pressed against the speaker part of the radio and listened to the conversation.

The male officer stated, "The truck driver said that he had been driving at the speed of 75 mph and didn't have time to stop when the man came headfirst into the grille of his truck. He said he could see the man's eyes watching him, as if pleading for his life, before the impact. The driver said that it happened so fast there was nothing he could do. He couldn't stop the truck in time."

The image of the scene made Moore's stomach turn. *What a horrible thing to witness,* she thought. The poor man wouldn't be able to un-see the accident that had unfolded in front of his eyes. She shook her head in disgust.

Moore drew in a breath as she focused back on the scene at hand. She knew by everyone standing around talking that it would be hours before the chunks of twisted metal and plastic were removed from the scene, allowing traffic on the westbound side to move. The turnpike would be closed until the horrific accident was cleaned up and all the survivors were taken to the hospital, which from the look of things would be multiple hospitals in the area.

Edon Hospital was older by twenty years and had fewer rooms available, especially in the ER. Franklin Hospital, on the other hand, was newer and had three times the rooms, but there would be no doubt that both hospitals would accommodate all the people from the accident.

Nearly two hours had passed as Officer Moore stood near the overturned vehicles with her hands on her hips, watching several firefighters move pieces of car parts away, looking for anyone that might be buried underneath. She was told that there were twelve people injured in the wreck. So far, only two of the twelve were pronounced dead at the scene. Officer Moore wasn't sure how the accident happened, but she knew there had to be someone who saw something and maybe even filmed it. Other officers, including herself, would later be sent to the hospitals to talk to the victims once the highway was clean.

After the firefighters cleared the area and were packing up their things, Officer Moore decided her work here was done too, not that she'd done much with the State Police taking over the highway. They always seemed to take jurisdiction when it came to the turnpike. Granted, she was a local cop in Edon where nothing ever happened, but they called her station out here, not the other way around.

She scanned the scenery one last time; she was sure every officer in both Franklin and Edon was here along with the State Police. "Tax dollars at work," she mumbled. She was about to turn and walk back to her patrol car when she heard a faint cry for help thirty-to forty-feet in front of her. She held a hand on the duty belt wrapped around her waist as she semi-jogged toward the sound.

She stopped when she came to what once looked like a red crotch rocket, now mangled and torn into pieces from the other vehicles smashing into it. She looked past the motorcycle and saw a dark blue car lying on its hood. The scene looked different from afar, but now that she was up close, she felt queasy. She swallowed as the acidic taste of bile rose up and into her mouth. She pinched her nose and took in another breath. Her heart pounded as panic flowed through her body. "Come on Moore; you can do this. Don't show those guys your weakness," she mumbled to herself.

She blocked the thoughts from her mind and moved around the vehicles. She stopped when she came to the side of a blue Ford Focus flipped upside down. She had seen with her own eyes that the firefighters had already removed the male driver from the vehicle. She scanned the area, looking for any signs of a body or body parts just in case someone was trying to wave, but saw no one. Maybe she had imagined the sound of a person yelling; with all the commotion around her she couldn't be sure if it were real or not.

She stepped back and was about to head to her car when she heard the cry for help again. It was more of a moan than a yell coming from in front of her, but where? All these cars had been checked and evacuated, hadn't they? She was sure the firemen had just been in this area and had even taken a person to the hospital. She heard one of the firefighters yell, "All clear." Had they missed someone? Surely they had, otherwise she wouldn't be hearing someone call out for help.

She moved closer to the wreckage. The smell of gasoline became stronger; this wasn't a good sign. Twenty feet to her right, a car ignited. Flames shot several feet into the air. She knew once it hit the gasoline leaking out from the cars, wherever the gas was, there'd be an explosion. An enormous explosion, and she didn't have much time to waste. She had to act fast and find this person before it was too late.

"Hello," Officer Moore yelled. "Is anyone there?"

"Help," a voice said, sounding muffled by the helicopters still circling above.

She wished the helicopters would leave so she could hear the person calling for help. Moore moved around the pulverized vehicles. She couldn't run like she used to if this place decided to blow. Now that she reached the ripe age of forty-five, not that she was old, but her body would tell her otherwise.

Officer Moore was careful not to snag her clothes on the sharp metal sticking out from the wrecked cars or to slip on the oil that leaked out from under them. She needed to find the person trapped and get them help. "Whoever you are, keep talking to me if you can!" she yelled over the noise.

"I'm under here," the voice replied. "It's dark, and I think I smell gas. I…I think my leg is caught on something."

She was sure the voice was male. “I’m coming!” Moore shouted as she peered inside the cars that were empty just in case they had missed someone. Maybe they were pinned in the backseat? She knelt to the ground, looking between two vehicles, a Chevy Malibu and a Dodge pickup, when she saw him. The door to the Chevy had been torn off, but she wasn’t sure if it was due to the crash or the firemen. But wouldn’t they have seen the man stuck under the truck? This she didn’t know. Maybe it had been too dark, and they just hadn’t seen him. Perhaps he was unconscious at the time and couldn’t holler for help? These were things she didn’t know but also didn’t have time to contemplate.

She stood and yelled, waving to one of the firemen ten yards away. “Over here. I found someone. He’s trapped under this truck,” Moore said, pointing down at her feet. “Hurry, I smell gas!” she yelled, cupping her hands around her mouth. She had to shout louder than the noise around her.

Two firefighters raced over to where Officer Moore stood and looked under the capsized vehicle. “We need a hydraulic ram to lift the truck up and try to slide him out,” one of the firemen ordered. “Get the fire extinguisher too. We need to stop this fire before it spreads.”

A short and stocky firefighter ran back toward the firetruck and shouted orders to a couple of other firefighters, telling them what was needed. Three firefighters ran back and began working on lifting the vehicle. Within minutes, they had the truck raised high enough to drag the man out from underneath. His clothes were saturated and reeked of gasoline. They had to get him away from the fire spreading toward them.

"Put that fire out!" one of the firemen yelled as he pointed to the flames coming their way.

Officer Moore stood back, watching the firefighters work fast and efficiently. The hydraulic ram gave out and the truck fell to the ground, nearly missing the already injured man's leg. A firefighter signaled to an EMT that he needed their help and ran over to them, carrying an emergency bag.

The paramedic dropped to the ground and checked the man's airway and placed a brace around his neck. "Can you tell me your name?" the female EMT asked.

"I…," the man croaked, fading in, out. Blood covered half his face, making it impossible to identify him.

"Stay with me, sir. You've been in a serious accident and may be suffering from head trauma. We'll get you to the hospital and get you some help." The female paramedic radioed for her partner to bring a stretcher. They carefully lifted the man and loaded him onto the stretcher and into the back of the ambulance. The ambulance lurched forward before speeding away from the scene with its lights flashing and sirens blaring. Another ambulance drove off behind the one that had just left, both going to the hospital.

Officer Moore placed a hand on her stomach; she still couldn't shake the nausea she had been feeling all morning, along with a few sharp pains in her abdomen and lower back. But that had nothing to do with the accident here today.

In all her years as a police officer, she'd never seen this many people in an accident at one time, especially as bad as this one. There were so many casualties with head traumas, broken limbs, and external bleeding. These images were never going to leave her mind for as long as she lived.

Moore closed her eyes, clearing her mind of the memories of her past that came rushing in and reminding her of what she had left behind.

The past was always a reminder of what she did back then, but today it hit her harder than before. She had always wanted to become a police officer just like her dad, and she wasn't going to let anything change that. Change the dreams she dreamt of her whole life. Only she alone had to make the choices she made so many years ago, and every day she regretted what she did. That year was nothing but pain and regret; things she couldn't take back or change once she had walked away. She wasn't sure why this accident reminded her of that moment she tried so hard to forget or at least put in the back of her mind. Maybe it was because life was a mystery. No one knew when their time was up. How it could all vanish in the blink of an eye.

The sirens around her sounded near and loud, causing her to snap out of her thoughts. She took a step backward, looking down at the ground, almost tripping. She noticed something under the debris at her feet and bent down to pick it up.

It was a black leather wallet. She wiped it off and opened it. Inside was a driver's license, money and a couple of credit cards. She slid out the driver's license and looked at the picture. It looked exactly like the guy they had just taken away.

2

Two Weeks Earlier

"Kaitlyn, get back here!" Ben yelled from the bedroom, his temper rising. He did not have time for her bullshit this morning. Why of all days did she have to start a fight when he had to be at work? Couldn't she wait until the fucking weekend? He'd make her pay for walking away from him during a discussion; he always made her pay. Why did she insist on pissing him off? What was the purpose of arguing over something he had no control over? Or did he? His job at work was to travel from state to state each week. He had been doing it since he graduated from college and it was only for a day, sometimes two at the most. It all depended on where he had to go. He never flew, always drove to Indiana, Iowa, or Ohio. Those where the main states, but on occasion, he'd have to go to New York.

When Ben stomped out of the bedroom, Kaitlyn was standing near the far corner of the kitchen by the patio door. Ben didn't walk toward her; instead, he got another cup of coffee, always keeping his composure. He'd make her think that she was going to get away with it and then pounce on her like a cat on a mouse. "Seriously, why do you start something when you know I have to get ready for work? You know how irritating that is to me!" he growled. "Do you know how disrespectful that is? Do you think that the world revolves around you, my dear sweet, Kaitlyn?"

"I also know that you'll follow me," she mumbled under her breath, too low for him to hear.

He tilted his head toward her to hear what she said, but he hadn't caught the words. "I have to leave for work so standing here discussing my traveling for work isn't going to get me dressed and out of the house," he said. Ben removed his cup and placed another ceramic cup in its place for Kaitlyn. He added two sugars, stirred and held it out to her as if they hadn't been arguing. *As if he were going to let her off the hook.* This thought made him chuckle inside. *Kaitlyn didn't deserve to be let off the hook. No, she needed to learn to watch her mouth before speaking. Hasn't she learned a thing these past four years? Apparently not!* he thought.

He watched as her shoulders fell back, her face relaxing, which told him that she thought he wouldn't hurt her for causing this argument first thing in the morning and on a weekday, making him late for work. He hoped that she was done nagging him about when he was going on the road again. What did it matter to her?

She stepped forward, reached out a shaky hand, and took the coffee cup from him. He watched as she hesitated before bringing it up to her lips. In one swift move, Ben swung his arm in the air, knocking the coffee cup from her hands. The ceramic cup flew into the air, then fell to the floor, shattering into numerous small and large pieces and spraying coffee everywhere. He grabbed her by the neck and pushed her up against the cabinets. His hand squeezed her throat, cutting off all oxygen from entering her body.

He felt a satisfaction as he watched her struggle to breathe. Her hands grabbed at his, but he clutched harder, making it more difficult for her to suspire. Her body went limp and she started to melt to the ground. He pulled her back up to a standing position.

"Don't you ever start shit when I have to leave for work!" he spat in her face. "Now I'm going to be late. I hate being late! Next time I won't be so kind. Actually, there better not be a next time; do you hear me, bitch?" He flung her head back, slamming it hard into the cabinet door, and then released his hand from around her neck. "Now clean up this fucking mess!" Ben turned and walked into the bedroom, slamming the door behind him.

Fifteen minutes later, he came back out dressed in a polo shirt and khakis. He walked up to Kaitlyn, who was wiping off the counter, and whispered in her ear, "I love you." He placed both hands on her hips, feeling her tremble beneath them; this made him feel warm all over. He turned her around, kissing her lips. "Have a nice day, honey," he smiled. He loved knowing that she was afraid of him.

She smiled back at him.

The argument was dissolved just like that. He knew she'd get over it and forgive him. That's what she did after he taught her not to ever talk back to him. At least for another week or two. She'd screw up like she always did and say something she shouldn't, and he'd have to show her another lesson. When was she ever going to learn?

Kaitlyn was the world to him, and he wanted nothing more than to make her happy. She had been his life since the day he'd met her in college, but it was her fault that he must hurt her like this. If she'd just keep her mouth shut and do as she was told then none of this would happen. He wouldn't have to hurt her. Did she think he liked doing this to her? Did she think he loved damaging her body and marking it with bruises?

For once he was glad that she didn't bring up wanting children again, something he didn't want. Children were like leeches that sucked the life out of you until you were dried up old prunes. When they became adults, they would still live with you, sucking money from your pockets because they were too lazy to work. He saw other people's kids. He watched them on their phones instead of socializing with other kids their age. He wanted to snatch the phones right out of their precious little hands and make them talk like normal people. Besides, he knew what children did to women's bodies, and there was no way his Kaitlyn would look like a fat and hideous cow with saggy boobs and a belly that hung over her pants. He kissed her one more time, turned and walked out the front door.

~ ~ ~

Since Ben had left later than usual, the traffic on I-55 was bumper to bumper. He glanced at the clock on the radio, 8:31 a.m. He'd probably be late, which was something he never was, and it infuriated him. He was an on-time kind of person. He never cared for the people who had no sense of time or direction. He told people that if he was ever late, then something must have happened to him, and as usual it was Kaitlyn. He didn't need to think about her right now and listened to his music.

Twenty minutes later, he was driving through the streets of downtown Chicago with taxi drivers who had no respect for other drivers on the road. He wanted to hit them because they sure didn't care if they cut you off, making you stomp on your brakes and almost hit another car. He honestly hated the city. He was only here because Kaitlyn wanted to live in Illinois. She wanted to be close to her family and friends. Although he made sure he was in control of what her did, he on occasion let her have her way. But not always.

He entered the parking lot near Willis Tower where he worked and parked the car. The drive exhausted him more each day, but he'd never admit that to anyone. It was probably from the argument this morning or just a cold coming on, making his head feel dizzy and his eyes blurry. He took in a deep breath and grabbed the steering wheel, squeezing until his knuckles turned white and let go. It was his way of releasing the remaining anger that brewed deep inside of him like a ferocious monster, which seemed to get worse over the last few years.

Once in the elevator, he rode to the fiftieth floor. He hated elevators too, and how they shook and sometimes jerked, making you think that the cables were going to snap, and you would plummet to your death. Unfortunately, he had no control over what the elevator was going to do, and there was no way he was taking the stairs. The moment the elevator doors opened, he immediately stepped out, his ears filling with the sounds of people talking and phones ringing. It wasn't music to his ears; maybe that's why he loved being on the road so much. It gave him a chance to get away from the noise of the office. No, mostly he liked traveling because he honestly hated people. He hated being around them. They made him sick the way they talked and acted, thinking they were always better than everyone else. Talking about their stupid lives that he could give two shits about. He didn't come here to listen to why their cat puked on their brand-new rug or that their teenage daughter was seeing a guy in college. There always seemed to be competitions between all the women too. Couldn't everyone just live their own lives and stay the hell out of everyone else's? An image came to him. He saw himself walking out of the elevator with a rifle and shooting every one of them—now that would make his day.

He walked past several of the cubicles and stopped when he came to his. He set his briefcase beside the desk and sat down. He placed his head in his hands, pressing his palms into his eye sockets to help relieve the discomfort. God, his head freaking hurt. He opened the drawer next to him and pulled out a bottle of Advil, shaking four into his palm. He hated taking pills, but he hated pain more. He never let Kaitlyn see that he was in pain. He hid it from her the best he could. He hated doctors as much as he hated people, and if he could help it, he wouldn't go see one. He'd try to do the best he could to make the pain go away on his own.

"Hey Ben," Gary said, as he peered around the side of the next cubicle. "Running a little late this morning?" he snickered. "That's not like you. Everything oookaay?"

Ben hated how Gary always stretched the last word he said out like he was singing a song. Ben tossed the pills in his mouth and washed them down with a bottle of water on his desk that had been sitting there for two days. He was never a big water drinker, mostly Vodka or Gin, but he couldn't have that here at work. *Though it'd probably make the day more interesting.* He chuckled inside at the thought.

Ben didn't look up at Gary. He didn't feel like talking to him, but he had to acknowledge the man or Gary would keep bothering him. He just lifted his achy head, nodded and smiled. "I'm fine." Then he turned his chair away from the guy and clicked on his computer. He knew that Gary would get the hint because it was what all the people around the office did when Gary was around. Gary would be at the top of his list if he was to ever go postal on this place.

Ben wasn't in the office five minutes when his boss, Tom Butka, called his desk phone to tell him that he needed to talk to him in his office pronto. It was as if he knew telepathically that Ben was in the building. Ben stood and walked to the far side of the room, looking straight ahead at his boss's office. There was no way for Tom to know that Ben was here because all the blinds were closed, and the door was shut.

"Don't overthink it," Ben mumbled to himself as he walked. "Tom won't fire you for being late one time." He raised his hand to knock on the door, but Tom had somehow known he was already there before he had the chance to touch the door.

"Come in, Ben," Tom shouted through the closed door.

Ben opened the door and went inside.

"You feeling all right? You look a little ill, my friend," Tom said, looking up and then back down at the papers on his desk before Ben had a chance to enter the room.

Ben waved a hand in the air "I'm fine, really." No, he wasn't fine, but confiding in Tom wasn't something he did. Besides, Tom didn't give a crap how you felt as long as your work got done.

"Great," Tom replied without giving it another thought. "I need you on the road tomorrow morning."

Ben let out a breath of relief. "Where am I going?" It hit him at that moment. He would rather be out on the road than in this place. He had the freedom to do what he wanted, go where he wanted, and no one would know. No one would be there to annoy him, even his wife. He felt like his own boss being out on the road, though he hated being away from Kaitlyn. He couldn't watch her like he wanted to and make sure that she was obeying his every wish, but that was why he had cameras and trackers placed around the house. All he had to do was go onto the app on his phone and see what she was doing and where she was. She might think she was smart and could hide things from him, but she couldn't. He knew everything.

"I need you to drive to Iowa and talk to the bosses over at the central bank. They're hiring some new people to help run the Loans Department, and I need you to be there for two days. Make sure they're well cared for," Tom said.

Ben nodded. He knew the routine. Make sure that they were up and running with no flaws. He also knew that Kaitlyn wasn't going to be happy when he told her tonight that he had to leave again. She would miss him, that's for sure. She always told him when he arrived home or on the phone that she wished he was home. Maybe it was time that he stayed in the office and went home every evening. Maybe it would make her a better wife? For one, he could control her better and keep her in line if he were home every night. But as the seconds ticked by, his chance was slipping out the door and *poof,* it was gone. He didn't know what to do. Make his wife happy or himself? Would he be considered a bad husband if he chose to travel?

"Great! Here's some things you'll need to read up on and I'll see you on Thursday," Tom said and went back to work.

Ben grabbed the folder, turned and walked to the door. He stopped and did a half-turn, looking at his boss who didn't even seem to notice who he was still in the room. He opened his mouth to say something, but stopped himself and left the office, closing the door behind him. He wasn't feeling in the mood to talk to his boss about it yet. Besides, he needed to think about things and decide what was best for him, not Kaitlyn.

Instead of heading back to his desk, Ben walked down the hall and into the restroom. The dizziness was coming back, and he felt as if he might fall over. Maybe he should tell Tom he didn't feel up to the drive and to find someone else this time. Or maybe he should collapse and be taken to the hospital, so Tom wouldn't think that he was faking it. No, he hated hospitals just as much as doctors and people.

Tom didn't like excuses and certainly wouldn't take *No* for an answer so what other choice did he have? Ben had to go to Iowa, sick or not. He threw some cold water on his face and dried it with a paper towel. Then left the restroom and went back to work.

By the time lunch came around he was feeling better. It must have been his nerves from this morning. He hated when Kaitlyn picked a fight during the week. He decided he'd take the trip and come up with a plan to talk to Tom when he got back—that was, if he decided to stop traveling. Ben would tell his boss that he wouldn't take *No* for an answer. He wished that he could show everyone here that he was in charge like he did at home.

But it was better to hide behind this person he had become since he was young. This person that had control of his wife. The people here needed to see him as a kind and thoughtful person, especially if Kaitlyn needed to be put in her place. He couldn't lose everything he had worked so hard to achieve these past eight years. If Kaitlyn ever found out about what he had done nine years ago, he knew she'd be furious with him and he couldn't have her finding out the truth. He'd need to hide the envelope in a safer place, maybe at the bank or in a safe. He couldn't take the chance of losing her. Losing his Kaitlyn. Maybe he would try and have a baby with her. The thought made his insides turn. *Hell no!* He would not cave into having a child. He couldn't even picture himself holding one and the baby crying. God, it made his head hurt worse than it already was. He'd make sure that she never had one of those because then there would be another him, and he couldn't let that happen.

What *if* Kaitlyn decided to leave him because she wanted to have a child? He doubted this would ever happen.

She was **afraid** of him…

He **controlled** her…

He **owned** her…

She'd never be that stupid because he'd **find** her…

3

Adam sat up in bed and like he did every morning and every night, he looked at the woman in the photo sitting on the nightstand. He loved her so much and missed having her next to him.

He raked a hand through his hair, something he had always done when he was having one of his headaches. Not that he had headaches all the time, just the last couple of months, along with some dizziness. He figured that the headaches were from the war and the explosion he'd been in back when he was in the Army, but that was years ago. The doctor had told him it might take months, even years before side effects would show after a head injury. Or, he might not have any at all. He wasn't so lucky.

He climbed out of bed and walked to the bathroom, closing the door behind him. After a quick shower, he felt like himself again. He got dressed and went into the kitchen. The coffee pot that was set on a timer sputtered, bursting steam from the top before coming to a stop. He grabbed a coffee mug and poured himself a cup, his black chrome ring hitting the side of the cup and echoing through the room. The ring was a gift from an old girlfriend that he refused to let go of. The same one from the photo. He loved her more than anything and wished she hadn't said goodbye.

He went to the fridge and took out eggs and bacon. Although he preferred the bacon cooked on the stove in a frying pan like his mom had always done, he didn't have the patience for that and bought the microwavable kind.

Today, he made two eggs over-easy with a slice of toast and three slices of bacon. He placed the plate on the table and grabbed his coffee cup before sitting down at the kitchen dinette, a table he'd found at a consignment store here in the town of Edon. Actually, he'd found most of his furniture at the consignment store. They were practically brand new, which surprised him because someone else had owned them before him and had taken great care of the furniture.

One thing about Edon, it wasn't an overly populated town. There weren't many stores aside from the ones people needed to survive in this town. A small grocery store and gas station were all they had, and a few other small stores, like the consignment store where he'd bought his furniture. If you needed more than a few groceries, then you would need to drive into Franklin, where there was a Walmart, Target, Home Depot, and a Best Buy, etc.

He'd grown up here and had decided to stay and call it home. Besides, his mother lived close by and he wanted to be near her. His father, on the other hand, had left after Adam graduated high school. Neither Adam nor his mom had known that Adam's father was cheating on his mother—some younger woman from the office where Adam's father worked. Said he didn't love Adam's mom anymore and it was time to move on. His father moved to North Carolina and Adam hadn't seen him since. That was nine years ago.

Adam cleaned his plate and silverware and placed them in the strainer to dry. He was never one to leave dirty dishes lying around the house. His mother had taught him better than that. For a man, his home was neat and clean. Not a thing out of place and he would know if it were; the Army had taught him that.

He poured another cup and went outside and stood on the back porch that over-looked Lake Erie. He loved the breeze that came off the lake in the mornings, but come winter time when the snow fell, it was a bitch to get around in this part of town. Lake effect, they called it. Would throw over four feet or more at your doorstep and you'd be trapped for a day or two. Most people around this area closed their homes and went south for the winter or someplace away from the lake. But Adam stayed because this was his home and would always be his home.

Adam inhaled the fresh, warm air. He was thankful for the long weekend. Adam loved his job as a teacher. Ninth graders were at times hard to teach as they entered teenage life. This was what he loved the most about his life. Teaching was something he had dreamed of since he was a teenager, although his father thought that it was a stupid career to have. "There's no money in teaching," his father had once told Adam. But Adam didn't teach for the money, he taught because it filled his heart with joy. Besides, his father wasn't around and didn't get a say in what Adam did with his life, and that was just fine with Adam.

He didn't have any plans, except to see his mom on Labor Day that Monday. Maybe he'd go for a ride on his motorcycle before the weather got too cold. He remembered the weather man saying that September was looking to stay in the low eighties to high seventies. *Great riding weather*, Adam thought.

Adam went back inside, washed out his cup, and grabbed his keys, sitting next to his wallet. He was out the door and on his motorcycle within five minutes. He went slowly through the streets around his neighborhood, careful to watch for children who might be playing near the road; something he'd never let his kid do if or when he had one. Adam had time to have a family, but he'd have to be in a relationship first and that was something he wasn't ready for.

Once he passed the stop sign, Adam turned and drove toward the highway where he could ride fast and feel the wind through his hair. He wasn't one to wear a helmet. Never felt comfortable with something pressing against his head. At least not since he had fought in the war and the explosion had knocked off his helmet and embedded metal fragments into his skull.

Most times he rode with his best friend Scott, but today he wanted time to himself. His mind was on the woman he once knew and loved with all his heart. He shifted into third gear and accelerated, speeding onto the ramp. He passed several cars and rode in the middle lane until he entered Indiana. He took the second exit and drove through the country roads, his mind feeling at peace as the wind ruffled through his brown hair that looked lighter in the sunlight. He needed this escape—to clear his mind and not think about her.

~ ~ ~

When Monday arrived, Adam stopped at the grocery store, picked up a few things to throw on the grill and drove over to his mother's house. He wasn't there five minutes when she started asking if he was seeing anyone special. He wasn't. It wasn't like he didn't have the time to go out on dates, but more like he just hadn't met the right woman. Well, he had, but that was nine years ago when he was in the Army. She had captured his heart the second he'd seen her and he had never forgotten about her. He had looked her up after he left the Army and came home. She probably thought he had died over in Afghanistan after he stopped writing her. Well, actually she had sent him a Dear John letter, ending it with him. He knew that she wasn't single anymore and positive that he never crossed her mind like she did his. He came out of his thoughts when his mother snapped her fingers in front of his face.

"What are you thinking about?" his mother asked.

"Nothing, just a lot on my mind lately," he replied, taking a sip of lemonade that his mother had freshly squeezed this morning. His mother Rose was an old-fashioned kind of lady, sweet to everyone she met. Never once had he heard her raise her voice—well, only if Adam disobeyed her. She was a stern woman with high expectations for her son, and he was okay with that. It just meant that she loved him even more.

"I was asking you about dating, and you zoned out."

He nodded. "I will date, just busy right now that school started up again."

"Maybe someone at the school?" she asked.

He shook his head. Never date someone you work with, just in case it doesn't work out. Though his father had done just the opposite and see how that ended? Granted, he would have to go out on dates to meet a woman, but when it was the right time, he'd do it. There was just too much going on right now. "What about you?" Adam asked, changing the subject. "When will you start dating again? It's been almost nine years." Nine years since they both lost the love of their lives. Adam knew what her answer was before she even said it.

"Why waste my time on men when they'll only hurt me in the end?"

"But you can't think like that," Adam replied. "They're not all like Dad, you know. They won't hurt you like he did."

She nodded.

"Does that mean you agree with me?" Adam asked.

"How about this—if you start dating, then I'll put myself out there. I'll go to singles clubs or maybe I'll join some of the events around town," she said.

He knew what she was doing. If he expected his mom to get out of the house and meet men then he should take his own advice and do the same, but he wasn't in any hurry. There wasn't any rush to settle down. He had his whole life in front of him.

4

Kaitlyn triple-checked the kitchen before she changed for work. Usually Ben was out of the house by seven-thirty, but not today. Today, Kaitlyn had to open her big mouth and mention his traveling. She wasn't even sure why she brought it up. She didn't care that he traveled. No, she loved that he went out of town every week for a couple of days, leaving her to do what she wanted without any repercussions.

Kaitlyn had to beg Ben to let her work as a teacher, something she had always dreamed of since she was a child. He knew when they met in college that it was her dream, but once they got married he had changed and controlled what she did. Of course, like today, she had opened her mouth to find out if he was going out of town and he had thought she was complaining about him being gone all the time, but she wasn't.

The minute Ben went to get dressed she texted Judy, her friend and co-worker at the school, and said that she'd be late for class this morning. This was another thing Ben didn't allow. God forbid she had any friends in her life. She was glad that there were a few extra assistants to help in other classes. The principal would just have them fill in until she arrived. She'd just have to make sure there were no marks showing on her neck.

Three years ago, Kaitlyn had opened her own checking account and had a P.O. box for all her mail, which was next to the grocery store that she shopped at. For three years she had been taking money from her paycheck and placing it in her secret account. She didn't want to know what he'd do to her if he found out she was hiding money. He'd probably kill her and drive out to the desert and bury her body. But then people that she worked with would know that she was missing and come looking for her. He'd never get away with it. The police always suspect the husband first. Maybe she'd do a *Gone Girl* on him and have him arrested for her make-believe murder and she could start a new life without him. She had plenty of money since she'd been working all these years.

Kaitlyn was dressed in five minutes and out the door in ten, scanning the landscape for Ben's car when she walked out the front door. Since the beginning of their marriage, after he had started hitting her, she was always looking over her shoulder. She could never be too cautious of him lurking in the shadows. She had to keep herself on guard at all times. She learned to do this as time went by, with Ben coming out of nowhere and hitting her, threatening her, hurting her.

She wasn't as stupid as he thought she was—well, maybe a little stupid because she still stayed with him. But it wasn't because of love—no, that died the moment he laid a hand on her. The moment he pledged that he'd never hit her again and did. She stayed because she was afraid for her life. He'd threatened multiple times that he'd kill her parents if she ever left. If she ever told someone of their life and what he did to her, then he'd kill her.

Kaitlyn backed out of the garage and headed in the direction of the school, thinking of what life would have been like if she and Adam were still together, a guy she was dating when she started college nine years ago. She was sure he would never have hit her like Ben did. Adam was too kind and loving, something Ben was not.

The light was green as she drove through the intersection. Out of nowhere a car smashed into her car. She pivoted forward, then sideways, her head hitting the driver's side window with a *thud* as her car came to a stop. She touched the side of her skull, sharp pain slicing through her head. She sat back in her seat, dazed for a few seconds, and then she began to panic. Ben would kill her or at least badly beat her for wrecking the car.

"Oh, shit. Oh, shit," she muttered. She opened the car door and slowly stepped out. She gripped the driver's seat as dizziness swam through her head. Once it passed, she could see the other car had hit the rear driver's side. There was no way to fix it herself. She'd have to get it repaired.

"Are you okay, Miss?" an old woman asked. It was the same old woman she saw walking down the sidewalk with her dog as she drove down the road.

Kaitlyn nodded or at least she thought she was moving her head. She was still trying to focus on what just happened. It wasn't her fault, was it? No, she had the right of way and the other car blew the stop light. She looked at the vehicle and saw that the person inside wasn't getting out of the car. In fact, their head was resting on the steering wheel.

She used the car to make her way over to the driver of the other vehicle. "Excuse me, are you okay?" Kaitlyn asked as she knocked on the window. The person didn't move. She peered through the glass. She could tell that it was an old man by the white hair on his head. She opened the door and cautiously nudged the man's shoulder. Nothing. *Oh my God, is he dead?* she screamed in her head. "Sir, are you okay?" she asked again. Still nothing. She gently lifted his head and pushed his body back against the seat, so she could see if he would open his eyes. Still nothing.

"Ma'am, do you want me to call the police?" The old woman was now standing beside her.

Yes, the police, she replayed the woman's words in her head. "Yes, call the police," Kaitlyn said. She wasn't sure how to help this man who was unconscious or possibly dead.

As the woman beside was making the call to 9-1-1, Kaitlyn turned and scanned over the damage done to her blac Audi. She stepped back and moved toward her car with a purpose. She stared down at the ground, unsure of what she was looking at. She knelt and picked up a small black box off the ground.

She turned it over in her hand, trying to figure out what it was. She remembered seeing something like this once, maybe on TV. It had a magnet on the bottom and a red light was flashing and then went out.

"Oh my God!" she mumbled. "It's a tracking device." Ben had placed a tracking device on her car. She began to panic as her mind flashed back to every little thing she had done for the past four years. She was sure that she'd been cautious regarding what she did and where she went. Fear coursed through her entire body and she began to tremble. She felt stupid that she didn't think about him doing this. He had always been one step ahead of her, watching her. Why did she not think to check her car?

Flashing lights strobed around her as the emergency vehicles appeared at the scene. Kaitlyn placed the small device in her jacket pocket. She'd have to think of something. Ben would know that the tracking device wasn't working. In that instant, she heard her phone ringing from inside the car.

5

Two hours after the Accident

The ambulance pulled up in front of the emergency entrance of Franklin Hospital, which was located outside of Edon. It was the sixth ambulance today, coming from the accident on the Ohio Turnpike. All ambulances were ordered to go to either Edon or Franklin, due to shortages in the emergency room.

The backdoors of the truck sprang open and a male EMT jumped out. The driver appeared around the side and both paramedics wheeled the stretcher through the automatic sliding doors. Beds were lined up along the walls as patients waited for treatment, though the most serious ones were sent in right away to be treated.

Nurses wearing stethoscopes around their necks stood near the counter, shouting out orders. Doctors in white coats passed through closed curtains, helping injured people, most likely from the accident. A dark-haired nurse hustled over to the patient that was just brought in. “Anything you can give me on this patient? Name? Age?” the nurse asked.

The paramedic shook his head. “I got nothing right now. Once the accident gets cleared, someone should be able to get you the names of the victims brought to the hospital that are incoherent," the male EMT said. "I had to do a tracheostomy on the way here. I don't know how much longer this one will live. Seems to be in bad shape. He was at the bottom of the wreckage."

The nurse nodded and started checking the vitals. The man from the accident was unresponsive. "We need to get a CT scan done on him. Check for possible hemorrhaging in the brain, then send him to x-ray and see if there's any broken bones," the head nurse ordered to the other nurse standing beside her.

The head nurse wheeled the man to another bed and transferred him, then the man was wheeled down the hall and through another set of doors. The radiology technician cut away his shirt and pants, getting rid of any metal that might be hidden within his clothes. All materials and personal items were placed in a bag under the bed. It took three people to help place him on the table, careful not to move his neck, and prep him for the CT scan.

Once they were finished, the unknown man was taken to x-ray and then back to the emergency ward until a room became available within the hospital. Several minutes later, the doctor in charge read over the results of the x-rays and CT scan, shaking his head. "We'll need to prep him for surgery, stat."

~ ~ ~

After six and a half hours in surgery, the attending nurses wheeled the unidentified man to the ICU ward. White gauze covered half his head, making him almost unrecognizable. He not only suffered from burns on the right side of his face and head but had internal bleeding of the brain due to the crash. The unknown man had two broken bones in his left femur, one broken ulna bone in his right arm and four broken ribs. The outcome didn't look good.

"Doctor?" Nurse Leah was unsure why she was even going to ask such a question. "What is his prognosis?" she asked, holding her long, slim brown arms behind her back, like a solider reporting to her officer. At least that's what it felt like whenever she was around Dr. Amal. He always seemed to be in a sour mood—well, at least whenever she was around.

Dr. Amal looked up from the chart in his hand, his face set in a hard stare, almost as if she annoyed him. "The patient is brain-dead. I stopped the bleeding in his brain, but there was extensive damage done from the crash. There's nothing more I can do for him; besides, he was dying anyway."

"What do you mean?" Leah asked.

"Although the accident didn't do him any favors, he has a glioblastoma multiforme tumor (GBM). I couldn't remove the tumor because of its location near the frontal lobe. The tumor is pushing against the wall of his skull and would have killed him sooner rather than later."

Leah's mouth started to drop open but she closed it before Dr. Amal saw her expression. Her dark brown eyes, which accented her caramel-colored skin, looked from the doctor to the man they were calling John Doe, lying in the bed. "How long do you think he'll be on life support?"

Dr. Amal's eyes dropped down to the chart in hand. "Until a family member is notified and decisions are made," Dr. Amal replied, sounding irritable, then added, as he looked up and into Nurse Leah's eyes. "I know you're new to my ward, but the rule is not to get too close to the patients. You'll only be left heartbroken in the end. Brain-dead patients, unless a miracle happens, don't leave here alive. He's already dead," Dr. Amal concluded before turning and walking out of the room, ending their conversation.

Nurse Leah couldn't believe how heartless Dr. Amal had been. She hoped that he wasn't always like this or she'd have to find another floor to work on. She turned and stared at the man lying in the bed. She hated to refer to them as John Does because really everyone had a name. She wondered what she could do to help him. Well, she couldn't save his life, but she could help by trying to find his family. If he even had a family? She knew nothing about him and there was no identification with him when he was brought to the hospital so how was she going to find out who he was? She wasn't sure, but she'd figure out something. It wasn't her job to find the patient's family, but in her heart, she wanted the family to have the chance to say goodbye, something she didn't get with her father after she killed him.

6

Across town at Edon Hospital, as one ambulance drove away, another one pulled up. The doors to the back of the ambulance flung open and two EMTs jumped out, rolling the unconscious man into the emergency room that was crowded with other injured people from the accident on the Turnpike.

"I got a broken femur and possible concussion," the woman paramedic yelled out to the attending nurse.

"Any idea who he is? Name, age?" the nurse asked.

"No identification was found on the victim. A white male approximately twenty-five to thirty years old. He was coherent at the scene, then passed out before we got him in the ambulance. I asked him his name but that's when he went unconscious."

"Let's get a CT scan and some x-rays on this man," the nurse shouted orders to another nurse several feet away. "If there's any swelling or bleeding in the brain, I want him taken into surgery, stat." The other nurse nodded. The unknown man was transferred to another bed and then wheeled down the hall to radiology and imaging.

Several hours later the unknown man was wheeled to ICU on the fourth floor and into a room of his own. Other than a small metal object lodged behind his right ear, the CT scan came back normal, showing no signs of bleeding or swelling to the brain, but the doctor wanted to have the man watched for the night before moving him to a different room. The man was still unconscious, most likely due to the concussion he suffered from the accident.

~ ~ ~

Officer Adanya Moore arrived at the hospital later that afternoon. She talked to several of the nurses in the emergency department, showing them the photo of the man from the wallet she'd found, only to find out everyone that was working the morning shift had gone home for the day.

"I'm not sure," said the nurse. "Shift changed at eight this morning. There were a lot of injured people here and we are understaffed as it is. Have you tried the ICU? I overheard that a couple of the victims were taken to the fourth floor."

Officer Moore nodded. "Thanks, I'll go there now." Moore turned and walked to the elevator, taking it to the fourth floor where she talked to several more nurses.

"Hey Moore, how are you doing?" asked a slim, dark-haired nurse.

"I'm good, just looking for a man who was involved in the accident this morning."

"Do you have a photo of him?"

Moore handed the nurse the driver's license.

"I think the guy you're looking for is in here," the nurse replied.

Officer Moore was escorted to a room that fit the description of the man she was looking for. Although half of the man's face was covered in gauze from a deep cut and some minor burns, Moore confirmed that the man was indeed Ben Gordon from the driver's license.

"Has he woken up at all? Has anyone come to visit him?" Moore asked.

"As far as I know, he hasn't. Do you want me to get the doctor?"

"No thanks. I'll stop by later and check on him," Officer Moore replied and handed the nurse her card. "Please call *if* and *when* he wakes up. I'll need to talk to him, you know, ask him some questions." Moore wasn't sure why she said *if*. What good would it do *if* he didn't? You can't talk to a person when they're unconscious.

"Sure, no problem. I'll leave this at the nurse's station just in case he does wake and I'm not here."

"Of course," Moore replied. Now she would need to go back to the station and do a search on his name and see if he had any family, maybe a wife that needed to be called. She had searched his wallet and had found no photos or information about a family before coming to the hospital; otherwise she would have already known. Although, it was best to confirm that the victim was indeed Ben Gordon before making any such calls.

On the way back to the station, Officer Moore grabbed a bite to eat because she knew it was going to be a long night. It all depended on how long the search took to find a family member of the man in the hospital. She also had others from the scene but was grateful that the Franklin Police Department would be helping, along with Edon, since there were so many involved in the accident. Sergeant Miles from Franklin would contact her if he needed any help with the case.

By seven-fifteen that evening, Moore had found a relative of a Ben Gordon and was dialing the number for a Mrs. Kaitlyn Gordon. After several rings, the call was answered.

"Hello?"

"Hello, Mrs. Kaitlyn Gordon?" Officer Moore asked.

"Yes, this is Mrs. Gordon. May I ask who is calling?"

"Oh, sorry. This is Officer Moore. I'm with the Edon Police Department."

"I'm sorry, Edon Police Department?"

"Yes, ma'am."

"May I ask what this is about?" Kaitlyn asked.

"I'm afraid there's been an accident involving your husband Ben Gordon," Moore said before continuing, "I'll need you to come to Edon hospital."

"I'm not sure where Edon is," Kaitlyn said.

Moore glanced back down at the license in her hand and saw that Ben's address read Illinois. Of course, Mrs. Gordon wouldn't know what she was talking about. "We're located in Edon, Ohio."

"Ohio?"

"Yes, Ohio." Officer Moore was exhausted and didn't feel like sitting here discussing where Edon was freaking located on the map. God knows it probably wasn't found on any map she owned. It'd been a long day and she was beyond tired. "Ma'am, I need for you to come to the hospital and identify your husband for us."

"Oh my God, is he dead?" Kaitlyn screamed into the phone.

"No, Mrs. Gordon, he's not dead, but he is unconscious at the moment."

"Oh," Kaitlyn replied.

Oh? The woman just got news that her husband was in an accident and all she said was *oh?* Was she happy that he was injured? Well, it wasn't her business to know what was going on, and she wasn't about to make it hers. Moore filled Mrs. Gordon in on what had happened and told her that she should come to the hospital as soon as possible.

"I'm coming from Illinois," Kaitlyn replied. "I should be there in a few hours, according to my GPS."

"I'll be here when you get here. Just call my cell number." Moore rattled off her number and then said, "I'll meet you at the hospital." Moore gave the woman the address to Edon Hospital and hung up the phone. She'd have to keep herself busy for the next three hours, which wouldn't be a problem since she had paperwork to complete on the accident.

Moore looked around the room filled with several other desks. Besides her, there was no one else in the room. Where was everyone? She knew at least three officers worked the night shift so where were they? Then she heard laughter coming from the direction of the lunchroom. It figured that they would be in there instead of out here doing their jobs. She was sure there had to be something they could work on instead of doing nothing. There was a ten-car pile-up and they had nothing to occupy their time? No one to call? Had all family members been notified of their loved ones that were injured in the accident? This she wasn't sure about but decided that she needed to focus on her work and deal with those morons in the lunchroom later.

Officer Moore looked up at the clock positioned above the Captain's door. It was only nine at night. Maybe she'd run home and change her clothes before meeting Mrs. Gordon at the hospital. She had finished all her work and was tired of listening to the men in the next room, who, by the way, were still doing nothing but bullshitting all night and probably shoving donuts in their mouths. She wanted to say something to them but decided to just go home for now. She was too tired to argue with anyone. She'd mind her own business and deal with those assholes tomorrow, after she talked to the Captain.

She clocked out for the night and got in her truck and drove toward home. She lived in the opposite direction of Edon Hospital, off a side road just past the center of Edon. The houses were spaced every couple of acres, not close, but also not far from one another. Neighbors watched each other's homes out here, not that the town was unsafe to live in.

She turned into her driveway and parked the truck. The truck was one of the station's vehicles. She didn't have a car of her own and since it was a small town they didn't care if she drove the vehicle home. Besides, she'd worked at Edon Police Station for almost twenty-two years; she should be able to drive the truck anywhere she wanted.

She unlocked the front door of her house and went inside. It still smelled of her dad—nothing she was ashamed of; it just made her miss him all the more. She hadn't even found the time to go through his things or his clothes and give them to Goodwill. It was the only thing she had left of his besides the house and she would never get rid of the house. She'd die in it herself if that's what it came down to. As for Moore's mother, she had died from ovarian cancer when Moore was three years old. Moore didn't get the chance to know her mother, but her father made sure she knew that her mother had loved Moore more than anything.

She kicked off her boots and padded to the kitchen for something to drink. She grabbed a bottle of water and went into the bedroom down the hall to change. Several minutes later she settled herself down in her father's chair and turned on the television, flipping through the stations.

She must have dozed off because the next thing she knew, her cell phone was ringing next to her on the end table. She answered the phone, it was Mrs. Gordon. Minutes later she was out the door and, on her way back to Edon Hospital to meet the spouse.

7

Twelve days Earlier

Kaitlyn sat in the waiting room of her OB/GYN, flipping nervously through a magazine. She wasn't really reading it, more like looking at the pictures and passing time until they called her into the room.

The door opened, and she looked up.

"Brandi," the nurse called out.

A woman from across the room placed her magazine down on the table beside her and carefully stood. The woman's belly protruded out as if she were about to explode at any minute. Kaitlyn thought for sure that the woman had more than one baby inside her and part of her envied that woman.

She'd always dreamed of becoming a mom, whether it was one child or two. It didn't matter to her, but it wasn't her that made the decisions. Ben had told her no children and if he found out that she was here and might be pregnant… God, she didn't want to know what he'd do to her, again.

Kaitlyn blinked away her thoughts and watched the woman, Brandi, waddle to where the nurse stood and then they were gone. She went back to flipping through the pages of the magazine. She licked the tip of her finger, turned the page. Licked the same finger again and turned the next page. Flip,

flip, flip. This seemed to go on for several minutes before she was at the end of the magazine and swapped it out for another one.

She looked at her watch; fifteen minutes had passed. The door opened, and a different nurse, this one with blond hair, looked down at the chart in her hand, then lifted her head. It looked as if the nurse were talking in slow motion, mouthing the letters slowly as they slipped through her parted lips before finally forming the word. “Kaitlyn,” the nurse announced.

Kaitlyn didn’t have to look up from what she was doing because she’d been staring at the nurse the whole time but hadn’t moved. It wasn’t as though she was glued to the chair. Her mind was somewhere else. Thinking of the torture. The beating she’d get if Ben found out about the baby, but she wasn’t sure if she was pregnant; that was why she was here now.

“Kaitlyn,” the nurse announced again, stepping back through the doorway. The door started to close.

“I’m here,” Kaitlyn spoke as she stood, placing the magazine down on the coffee table and walking to the partly opened door. She was certain that her life was about to change once she walked through this door. She didn’t want to get her hopes up that she was pregnant. The last time had ended in tears and sadness from the loss. This time she wanted to be sure before making her next move.

She followed the nurse to a scale, then went into a room across the hall. She had gained one pound, not that it meant she was pregnant. Usually in the early stages you didn't gain much weight at all. No, those pounds came later, after the second trimester. She'd have to lose that one pound before Ben weighed her at home. He was stern when it came to her body weight, her figure. They worked out together, so he could see that she was *actually* working out and not sitting on her ass watching TV, something she never did.

The nurse checked her vitals and then gave her a gown. "Undress from the waist down," the blond-haired nurse said before leaving the room.

Kaitlyn did as she was told and sat down on the table covered with a single sheet of paper. She felt vulnerable sitting here in only a paper gown, waiting for the doctor to tell her that she was wrong. That she wasn't pregnant. Kaitlyn hadn't done a pregnancy test at home because she feared that Ben would find the box and start asking questions. Then, just to be sure, he'd punch her in the stomach like before and make sure she wouldn't stay pregnant. Kaitlyn's thoughts were quickly interrupted when she heard a knock on the door and Dr. Karen Williams came walking in.

"Good morning, Kaitlyn," Dr. Williams said with a smile.

"Hi," Kaitlyn replied, nervously.

Dr. Williams looked down at the chart in her hands, then said, "So, you think you might be pregnant?" The doctor smiled. “How have you been feeling since the last time? Any problems? Complications that I need to be aware of?”

“No. I haven’t had any abnormal pains or bleeding. I feel fine.”

“Great! When was your last period?” the doctor asked.

Kaitlyn replied, “A couple of months ago. I’m three weeks late…” she paused. “I know I’m probably overthinking it, but I’m not *usually* late and the last time I was late, I was positive. So that’s why I’m here,” she rambled, something she seemed to do when she was nervous.

Dr. Williams replied, “I see. No reason to be jittery. Pregnancy is a part of life. Did you do a pregnancy test at home to confirm?”

“No.”

“Okay, let’s have you give us a urine sample and we’ll test it here,” Dr. Williams concluded. “Just because you had a miscarriage the last time doesn’t mean it will happen again.”

“I know,” Kaitlyn replied, although she didn’t sound convincing. If only the doctor knew what really happened. How she really lost the baby.

“Before you get all worked up and stress yourself out, let’s make sure that you’re pregnant, okay?” Dr. Williams smiled, placing her hand on Kaitlyn’s arm. “Everything will be fine.”

Kaitlyn nodded, although she felt as if she might puke because she knew it wouldn’t be fine.

“I’ll do an exam, then I’ll have you get dressed and we’ll get that urine tested,” Dr. Williams said as she placed the chart on the counter and started washing her hands before putting on latex gloves. “Lean back and put your feet in the stirrups. Try to relax your legs to the side.”

Kaitlyn knew all too well how this procedure went, and where did they come up with this concoction? Probably by a man. No woman would think that this was comfortable and enjoy it. Men didn’t know how uncomfortable these procedures could be.

~ ~ ~

Twenty minutes later, Kaitlyn sat in the same examining room waiting for the results of the test. She tried to keep herself calm and not get anxious about something she couldn’t do anything about. If she weren’t pregnant, then she had nothing to hide from Ben, but if she were, she’d wait until he was on one of his business trips and pack her things and leave. She wouldn’t lose this baby. She wouldn’t let him beat her like he did the last time.

Kaitlyn heard the knock on the door. She swallowed and sat up straight, closing her eyes for a second. Time seemed to slow down as the door slowly opened and Dr. Williams came into the room. In Kaitlyn’s head, she heard the *tick tick* of a clock, but there wasn’t one in the room. She knew this because she’d looked for one already. It was her mind imagining the sounds or maybe it was coming from the other room beside her. The walls in these places were paper thin and you could hear people talking as if they were in the room with you.

Silence filled the air around them as the temperature rose several degrees in the room, making it unbearable to breathe. The click of the door sounded far away when it closed. Kaitlyn tensed with anticipation, not knowing what the doctor was about to tell her. She couldn't take the silence much longer, but to her it meant that she wasn't carrying a baby inside her and her eyes began to tear up. Why did she even come here? Being pregnant was her only way out.

8

The Day of the Accident

Kaitlyn parked her rental car in the lot on the side of the school. It had been two weeks and she still hadn't gotten her car back from the Collision Center. They had called two days ago and said that they needed to order more parts for the trunk. Good thing for her because Ben couldn't track her like he had been doing. She had checked under her car every time she left for work, which meant he didn't know about her going to the doctor. She didn't know how long he'd been tracking her, but at this point, she didn't care. She was finally going to leave the asshole. He'd never lay another hand on her again. She had stayed on her best behavior, so he didn't have a reason to hit her. She wasn't losing this baby!

She gathered her things from the backseat and went inside. She was glad that it was Friday and needed the break that the weekend would bring her. Working as a teacher had its perks: holidays, weekends and summers off. Who wouldn't want that?

Ben was on the road again, but he had told her before he left this morning he'd be home that evening. She, of course, was hoping that he'd call and say work needed him to stay longer like always, and she'd pack only the things she really needed and leave. It wasn't going to be easy to get time away from him, but she had to try. She'd have to change her name and go somewhere far away, where he wouldn't find her.

Kaitlyn opened the door to her classroom and walked to the desk at the front of the room. She loved that the room was filled with posters of historic poets and writers, hoping that one day if she ever got around to writing her own book, it would be known around the world like those of Hemingway and Mark Twain.

She had been teaching seniors at Lakeport High School for the past three years and loved it. At first, she wanted to teach the younger children, but her passion was English Literature, so she decided to teach older students instead.

She placed her bag on the desk and opened it, taking out the lesson plans for today. She felt a slight pang in her lower abdomen but knew that it was the baby starting to grow. Ben couldn't find out about the baby. She had to come up with a plan to run away, to hide from him before she got too big. The thing that made her the saddest was leaving her job that she loved so much. After finding out about the baby, she had written a letter to the school, letting them know that she had left and wouldn't be returning. She kept the letter in a sealed envelope inside the top drawer of her desk here at the school, so Ben wouldn't find it.

Kaitlyn quickly went online before her students entered the class and reserved a table for two at 6 p.m. Ben said he wanted to spend the evening out with her and talk, which surprised her since they didn't go out much for dinner. The last time didn't end well. He didn't like it when other men looked at her, as if it were her fault. Ben made it seem like she provoked the men to *check her out* as he called it. When they got home, he took it out on her.

She could still visualize it as if it happened yesterday. "You're such a slut, Kaitlyn," he had yelled the moment they arrived inside the privacy of their home. "I saw you looking at him. It makes me sick to see you undress men with your eyes," Ben yelled and punched Kaitlyn in the stomach. His temper was worse than she'd ever seen it before. Sure, he had gotten mad over little things while they were dating, but he had never physically hit her. He had never even yelled at her. Three months into their marriage and it was like he was a changed man. He was different and mean. He was abusive and acted like he owned her. He controlled everything she did. Before she could react and move out of his way, Ben came at her and body-slammed her against the wall. Her head flew back and hit the wall hard, knocking her unconscious.

The bell rang, snapping Kaitlyn from her thoughts. Students in her first period class entered the room. She clicked off the website and was about to close her laptop when she saw the news flash come across her Yahoo screen. She saw helicopters flying over a multi-car crash. She read the caption and saw that the accident was in Ohio and closed the laptop. It didn't concern her because she lived in Illinois. What could she do anyway? She was a school teacher, and as far as she knew, the crash didn't have anything to do with her.

She waited until everyone took their seats before beginning her class. Kaitlyn felt another jolt in her lower belly, but this time it was different. It felt as though something in her had changed. Was there something wrong with the baby? She was only eight weeks along. It was possible that she could miscarry, but she hoped that she wouldn't. She had never been this far along before, so she wasn't sure what to expect. Seconds later, the pain was gone, and she was fine, but she would stop at the nurse's station and talk to Ellen and see what she thought.

~ ~ ~

"I'm sure it's nothing but your body getting ready to change," Ellen said. "When do you go see the doctor?"

"I was there less than two weeks ago, but I felt fine. I'm sure you're right. It's probably my body changing or my nerves about telling Ben," Kaitlyn replied, wishing she hadn't said the last part.

"You haven't told him yet?" Ellen asked, surprised.

"No, I wanted to be certain and then he had to go out of town again. Besides, I want it to be special," she lied. *It'll be special when I finally leave him,* she thought.

Ellen nodded and sat back in her leather chair. "I'm sure he'll be thrilled!" Ellen smiled.

Kaitlyn left the nurse's station and walked back to her classroom, feeling better than she had this morning. By the end of the day, she was back to herself again. She grabbed her things and left the school, walking toward her car.

Usually, Ben would text her when he arrived at work and when he was on his way home, but the last time she heard from him was early this morning. It wasn't strange for them not to talk when he was on a business trip; besides, she didn't want to panic, thinking something was amiss. When Ben was working, **you did not call him!**

She didn't need to start overthinking about something that probably wasn't wrong to begin with. Maybe he had gotten busy and it slipped his mind. But that wasn't something that happened with Ben. He was always aware of everything and never forgot a thing.

She'd felt more uncomfortable since finding the tracking device. She was always looking in her rearview mirror to see if he was following her instead of at work or out of town like he said he was. Part of her wondered if he hired a private detective to watch her when he couldn't, but she hadn't seen anything out of the ordinary. No cars were following her, and there were no parked cars outside their home that weren't usually there. She was just being cautious but was still scared of what he might do to her.

She sent Ben a text before leaving the school parking lot and by the time she arrived home fifteen minutes later, he still hadn't replied. It was almost four in the afternoon and she wondered if she should try calling him, willing the thought to call him away because she knew she shouldn't and didn't want to give him a reason to hit her later. She went to exit out of the app, but her finger accidentally dialed his number.

"Shit, shit, shit," she mumbled, but then was thankful the call had gone straight to voicemail, which told her he was most likely either in a meeting or on his way home. It wasn't like him to be on his phone while driving. In fact, it was another thing that made him furious with her and other people. Especially other people, and she would get the beating because of someone else's wrongdoing. His temper would flare and for some reason, unlike most people, he couldn't control his anger and had to hit something. That something always seemed to be Kaitlyn.

She arrived home and gathered the mail from the mailbox. She hadn't noticed before how quiet everything seemed to be when she came home from work. No one was mowing their lawns or raking their grass. Even her neighbor Angie wasn't outside tending to her flower garden like she did every late afternoon. Maybe it had to do with the worry in her mind about Ben? He'd taken many trips in the past so why was this one any different? Why did she have such an uneasy feeling just because he didn't answer his phone? She should be thrilled that he didn't. She was always on edge when they talked, afraid she'd say something, and he would take it out on her when he got home. Ben not answering the phone made her more on edge because not knowing where he was, scared her to death.

Before closing the garage door, she looked around the yard and down the street but didn't see anything unusual. Why did she have this feeling like someone was watching her? There was no one on the street. *You're being silly,* she thought, not that she didn't have the right to feel this way. She needed to be careful; Ben wasn't someone to be trusted. She pushed the button, closing the garage door. The chains rattled as the door slowly descended, closing off all signs of life. Kaitlyn opened the door and went inside.

~ ~ ~

The next twenty minutes passed by quickly as she drove to the restaurant to meet Ben. Kaitlyn was full of nerves, and she felt sick to her stomach. She was anxious to see what Ben wanted to talk to her about. Did he know that she was pregnant? She was sure that he didn't. She hadn't told anyone but the doctor and Ellen at work. She hadn't done a pregnancy test at home in fear he would go through the garbage and find the box. Nope, it couldn't be about the baby, she was sure of it.

After parking her car, she stood outside and scanned the vehicles already in the parking lot. She didn't see Ben's blue Chevy Malibu anywhere. She wanted to laugh at herself because she was being paranoid that there was something wrong, though she had reasons to be scared. She should've packed her things and ran instead of coming here. Her bones ached at the fear she was feeling about the unexpected dinner plans, or was she more afraid of what he would do to her when they got home? She put a hand on her belly. What could he have to talk to her about?

She walked to the front of the restaurant and went inside, taking a seat at the table instead of waiting in the lobby. She told the waiter that she was waiting for someone and asked for a glass of water. Minutes ticked by and she glanced at her watch, 6:45 p.m. and still no Ben. She pulled out her phone to see if he'd called and left a message. Sometimes when her phone was in her purse she couldn't hear it ring. There was nothing. Not even a text. Where was Ben?

9

Kaitlyn told the waiter at the restaurant that there was an emergency and she had to leave. She was panicking when she left the restaurant. Part of her was afraid to go home. What if he had planned this and when she arrived home and went inside he'd beat her to a pulp? But why? She'd been on her best behavior since the fight two weeks ago when he tried to strangle her in their kitchen.

Once outside the restaurant, the fresh warm air enveloped her, almost choking her. Thoughts of Ben with his hand squeezing her throat came at her. She looked around to see if anyone was looking at her, then hurried to her car, checking her phone as she ran in fear.

Ben still hadn't answered any of her calls or texts. Ben always told her to answer her phone when he called, but how was it different when she called him? She was sure that something had to be wrong, right? Who could she call? It was Friday and after seven in the evening. There would be no one in the building where Ben worked downtown. She was sure of this.

She arrived at her car and climbed inside, her body shaking. A spider of tingles ran down her spine. This wasn't the first time she'd felt this scared, terrified of what was to come. She had to keep calm for the baby inside her. She had to stop and think. “Calm down and think,” she mumbled into the empty car.

She took in a deep breath, resting her head back against the headrest, and exhaled while closing her eyes. Her mind was whirling like a finished film on a reel as she tried to think what could’ve happened to him. Should she be worried when she got home? Would he be there waiting for her? If she saw his car in the driveway, she would just keep on driving. She wouldn’t stop until she was someplace safe. Yes, that was exactly what she’d do.

She drove toward home, still trying to contact her husband, although she wasn’t sure why because the phone kept going straight to voicemail. Kaitlyn knew it wasn’t safe to be on the phone while driving, especially in the state of mind she was in, but today was different. Today she hadn’t heard from her husband since he’d left this morning, and it scared the shit out of her not knowing where he was. *Maybe this is a good thing,* her mind quipped. *Stop worrying over nothing. So what if he isn’t answering his phone. Just go home and pack your things and get in the car and drive far, far away from this place and never look back.*

A loud ringing filled the car, making Kaitlyn swerve into the other lane, horns blaring. Her mind was not on her driving. She needed to pay attention before something terrible happened to her, and the baby. The ringing sounded again, and she quickly pressed the green button on her steering wheel. "Hello," she answered, feeling the panic flow through her body as she waited to hear Ben's voice.

"Hello, may I please speak to Mrs. Kaitlyn Gordon?" the woman asked through the car speaker.

She heard a woman's voice coming through the speakers, not Ben's. She exhaled the breath she was holding. "Yes, this is Mrs. Gordon. May I ask who is calling?" Kaitlyn asked.

"Oh sorry. This is Officer Moore. I'm with the Edon Police Department."

"I'm sorry, Edon Police Department?"

"Yes, ma'am."

"May I ask what this is about?" Kaitlyn asked. She listened as the officer on the other line filled her in on what had happened.

Kaitlyn sucked in a breath. The signs were there. All day she'd felt that there was something not right, but thought it was the baby. Now she knew. Listening to this woman on the other end of the phone telling her that there'd been an accident changed everything. Yes, of course, something terrible must have happened to him. He would have never stood her up. Ben was never late for anything.

"Oh my God, is he dead?" Kaitlyn screamed into the car. *That was a little over the top,* she thought. She didn't need the officer thinking she was glad if he were.

"No, Mrs. Gordon, he's not dead, but he is unconscious at the moment."

"Oh," Kaitlyn replied, wishing she hadn't said the word. She didn't need the officer thinking that she was disappointed. Kaitlyn needed to clear the silence between them. "Please, tell me he's okay?" *Did she really care if he were? He'd been beating and controlling her for years and now the moment something happened to him, she cared?* she thought. No that wasn't it. She just wanted to know that she was okay. That she had nothing to worry about. That he wouldn't hurt her.

"He was taken to Edon Hospital just inside the state line in Ohio. I can give you the address if you wish."

"Yes, of course." Kaitlyn pulled onto the shoulder of the highway and quickly shifted into park with her hazards on. She dug inside her purse for a piece of paper and a pen. "Okay, I'm ready. What hospital?" Kaitlyn asked and wrote down the address and name of the hospital Officer Moore had given her. "I'll be there as soon as I can," Kaitlyn said as she typed the address into the navigation system in her car. She was about to hang up, then asked, "Is he all right? How bad are his injuries?"

"I'm not sure, ma'am. I was the one who found him, but then the EMTs started working on him and took him straight to the hospital. I'm so sorry."

There were no tears streaming down Kaitlyn's face as she listened to Officer Moore apologize to her about the accident that Kaitlyn was sure Officer Moore hadn't caused.

"Mrs. Gordon are you still there?" Moore asked.

"Yes, I'm here. I'm on my way. According to the GPS, it will take me three hours to get there." With the frame of mind she was in, she really shouldn't be driving at all, but she didn't care. She needed to get to the hospital.

"I can be at the hospital when you get there," Officer Moore said, snapping Kaitlyn from her thoughts.

Kaitlyn nodded, forgetting that she was on the phone. "That would be nice of you. I should be there in a few hours. I'm coming from Illinois."

"Let me give you my cell number so you can call me when you get close. I can meet you at the hospital, Mrs. Gordon."

Kaitlyn grabbed the paper from the passenger seat and scribbled down Officer Moore's number. "Yes, yes, I'll do that. Thank you so much for calling."

"It's my duty, Ma'am," Officer Moore said, then ended the call.

A horn honked at Kaitlyn as she eased back onto the highway and quickly turned the wheel back toward the side of the road. This time she glanced in her mirror before continuing onto the highway. Kaitlyn took in a deep breath. She had a long drive ahead of her and she needed to keep her focus on the road, but her mind kept repeating the word Ohio. Adam lived in Ohio.

~ ~ ~

Three hours and ten minutes later, Kaitlyn parked her car in the parking lot of Edon Hospital. She grabbed her purse and opened the car door. The lights of the hospital were lit up like the fourth of July. She hadn't realized during her drive how quickly the day had turned into night.

She started toward the entrance of the hospital when she was approached by a black woman wearing a t-shirt with Edon Police embroidered onto the left breast area and blue jeans. "Mrs. Gordon?" Officer Moore asked.

Kaitlyn had called Officer Moore when she crossed the state line, telling her what she'd be wearing. "Yes," Kaitlyn nodded. She imagined the officer being younger by the tone of her voice through the car speakers and was surprised by how much older she was in person and that she'd chosen to be a police officer. She didn't look like someone that could rough up some bad guys.

Officer Moore held out her hand, but Kaitlyn didn't take it, so she let it drop to her side. "I was just inside talking to the receptionist." She stopped talking and held out her other hand. "I found this at the scene." Moore held out the wallet she'd found at the wreckage. "I thought you'd want to have it."

Kaitlyn took the wallet. It was a gift she'd given Ben four Christmases ago. She had it engraved on the lower corner on the outside. *To my loving Husband, Love Kaitlyn. Wasn't that a crock of shit,* the voice said in her head. She flipped the wallet over and over in her hand before rubbing her thumb over the words. "I need to see him," she said, choking back on her words. No matter what he'd done to her, she needed to see him. She needed to see with her own eyes that he was suffering as much as she had been all these years from his hands hitting her.

"I can go with you if you want?" Moore suggested.

Kaitlyn nodded.

They walked into the hospital and toward the receptionist's desk. "I'm here to see my husband, Ben Gordon. He was in an accident earlier today."

"Can I see your driver's license?" The woman behind the counter asked.

Kaitlyn handed her the ID and the woman typed in Ben's name and gave Kaitlyn his room number. "Just take the elevator to the fourth floor and make a right. The door will be on your left."

"Okay," Kaitlyn whispered. Her body began to shake, and her legs felt as if they were about to buckle beneath her. Officer Moore must have seen that she was about to fall to the ground and placed an arm around Kaitlyn.

"Are you okay?" Moore asked sympathetically.

Kaitlyn nodded. The officer was kind enough to help guide Kaitlyn to the elevator and rode up with her to the fourth floor. Once at the nurse's counter, Officer Moore spoke to a nurse.

"Thank you so much for all you've done," Kaitlyn said before the nurse took Kaitlyn to where Ben was.

"It was no problem. I'll check in with you tomorrow and see how he's doing. I'll need to ask him some questions—if he's awake, that is," Moore replied before she turned and walked out the glass sliders and to the elevator.

Kaitlyn walked to the side of the bed, looking down at Ben. His right leg was in a cast and raised up in a sling to help with swelling. The top of his head and face were wrapped in a white bandage. She grabbed hold of his hand and squeezed. No tears came as she stood beside the bed. She wondered if she should make it look like she cared and was devastated by his appearance. Just in case Officer Moore was still watching.

Something shifted inside her. She wasn't afraid to lose him, was she? Even after everything he did to her, could she be scared that he would die? She had lost someone she loved once before, and it tore her world apart. Ben couldn't hurt her here, not while he was unconscious lying in this hospital bed.

A thought came to her. If he woke and was a different man, would she stay with him? But she couldn't stay. Didn't want to stay. Ben had hurt her. Betrayed her. He had taken Adam away from her.

10

The Day after the Accident

Nurse Leah walked across the room. “You know, I don’t mind coming in here and taking care of you,” she said to the man lying in the hospital bed. The man with no name, no identity. The same man from the crash who was pronounced brain-dead. She still couldn’t believe that the doctor had found a tumor in the man’s brain. Hadn’t the man known that there was something wrong and gone to see a doctor? Didn’t he suffer from headaches or nausea? Maybe even dizziness because of the tumor’s location?

“I’m sorry that we haven’t contacted your family and let them know that you’re here,” Leah said sympathetically. “You had no identification on you when you were brought to the hospital. So far I haven’t heard of anyone finding your wallet.” She liked talking to her patients even if they didn’t answer back—or couldn’t, for that matter. She also knew that they could hear her; all coma patients could, they just couldn’t speak or respond.

Leah had made sure that she was on the roster to help take care of him. No matter what Dr. Amal said, she couldn’t help but care for this man lying here. There was just something about him. She didn't want to give up hope that this man wouldn't come out of this. A flash of a memory came back to her and she squeezed her eyes shut. This wasn't the time to think about the past and what she had done to her dad. She couldn't change the past or bring him back after what she'd done to him.

When she arrived home after her shift ended last night she had done some research. As exhausted as she was from working extra hours all week, she searched through all her textbooks and the web to find out everything about brain-dead patients. There had been some cases, though extremely rare, where patients had come back. It had happened and that was the kind of faith and hope Leah held in her heart.

She wasn't one to give up on the people she tended to every day. They were like her family. A part of her. Granted, she knew better and was also told not to get too close to the patients that came into the hospital. She honestly tried, but her heart was full of love. Her adopted mom taught her to be kind and to help everyone that needed help and couldn't take care of themselves.

Leah rolled down the blanket placed on the man's tanned, sculpted body. Every hour, a new heated blanket needed to be placed on the body. Without the brain working, there was no way for the body to heat itself.

She wished that she could see all of his face, as half of it was covered in gauze due to third-degree burns on his face and the side of his head. She knew that his eyes were a shade of blue because she stood next to the doctor when he shined a light in his eyes. It wasn't much to go on, but it was better than nothing.

She had overheard Dr. Amal saying to the head nurse earlier that three to seven days is given to keep any patient that is brain-dead on life support unless a judge has given a motion for them not to be taken off. If family is contacted the hospital is to wait for them to say goodbye to their loved one. This meant that she needed to find out who this man was and to help find his family before Dr. Amal let him die. Granted, he was already dead.

~ ~ ~

After Leah's shift was over, she drove to the Franklin Police Department, hoping that someone there could help her. Leah had lived in Franklin her whole life after she was adopted at birth. Though they weren't her biological parents, she loved them like they were.

Leah turned into the parking lot of the Franklin Police Department, parked her car, and went inside. The station wasn't as busy as she thought it would be after the accident on the Turnpike. Although she had never been in a police station before, TV somehow made it look like a constant circus of angry men and women. Leah wasn't sure why her mind thought of a police station as a zoo of criminals running around. The place was dead. Not dead, as in everyone was lying on the ground dead, but dead as in there weren't any cops hauling anyone away. No men cuffed and shouting that they get to make a phone call. She only saw police officers sitting at their desks doing paperwork and talking on the phones.

Leah straightened her posture and walked up to the counter, "Excuse me, but is there someone I can talk to about the accident yesterday on the Ohio Turnpike?"

"Give me just a moment and I'll get the officer in charge to speak to you." The blond uniformed officer behind the desk picked up the phone and dialed a number. She spoke in a hushed voice, then hung up. "Someone will be right out," the woman officer said, smiling.

Leah nodded.

"You can wait over there." The officer pointed to a set of chairs along the wall.

Leah turned and walked to the chairs along the cream-colored wall and sat down. She scanned around as if looking for a magazine to read and wondered if that was something police stations even carried. She didn't think so because it wasn't like being at a doctor's office.

A few minutes later, a shadow appeared in front of her. Leah looked up to see a tall, muscular, yet slender man standing in front of her. From what she could tell, he wasn't one of those bulging muscle men. He seemed to be built just right. She shook her head. What the heck was she thinking of his body for? *Get hold of yourself, Leah,* she thought to herself.

"Are you the one who asked about the accident yesterday?"

Leah swallowed, shaking the pornographic images from her head. She began to feel intimidated by the man in front of her. Was it because he was in law enforcement or because of his tanned muscular build? There she went again, thinking about what his body looked like under his clothes. She wasn't sure why his appearance had gotten to her, and it didn't really matter. She was here to find out what she could about the man lying brain-dead in the hospital.

"Um, yes," she said as she stood. "My name is Leah James. I work at Franklin Hospital and a man was brought in yesterday from the crash with no identification on him. As of right now, we can't contact anyone to let them know where he is and how he's doing," she stated. "I was hoping that you might be of some help."

"Come to my office and I'll see what I can do," Sergeant Miles replied.

Leah felt all eyes watching her as she walked in step behind Sergeant Miles. They entered a room at the end of the hall. She scanned the walls and saw framed diplomas and awards arranged in a diamond shape with one photo of the officer's graduating class in the middle, she assumed. She wasn't here to find out about the officer in front of her. She was here only to find the family of the man in the hospital.

Sergeant Miles cleared his throat, bringing Leah out of the zone she seemed to be in. She sat down in the chair by the desk as the officer took a seat directly in front of her.

"Is there anything you can tell me about the man you're wanting information on?" Sergeant Miles asked.

"Well, I can only give you a description of the man. He's brain-dead so he can't tell me who he is. He can't talk."

"I'm aware of what brain-dead means, ma'am. I hate to waste your time on this, but without any kind of name, I'm not sure what I can do for you."

"Is there anything from the scene that I could go through and maybe find a picture of him? Something that I can use to contact his wife?"

"What do you mean his wife? How do you know that he's married if he doesn't have an ID?"

"Well, he has a ring with his belongings. One would assume that it's a wedding band. Not many men wear rings," she said matter-of-factly.

"I see," Miles said, rubbing his chin with his thumb and forefinger. His skin looked smooth and soft, as if he had just shaved before he came into work this morning. "Well, I could try and get a print or some DNA from the ring. Run the samples in our database and see if he's in the system. But that would only be if he's done something illegal or ever been in the military."

Leah nodded. It was the only choice she had. "How long would it take to get the results back?"

"One, maybe two weeks."

"No!" she shrieked, startling the officer. "I need to know as soon as possible. They'll withdraw care for him in less than a week. I need to know by tomorrow, or two days at the most," Leah said, her heart beating fast beneath her blouse. She didn't mean to sound rude. She just wanted to find the man's family before it was too late—if he even had a family, but she was sure that he did. The ring was evidence that he had been or was currently married. "I can let the doctor know that you are searching for his family, and they'll have to wait for your report," Leah said, hoping that she was right.

"If you can provide me with his belongings, I can see what I can do. Since this is a life and death situation, I can make it a priority."

Leah had already thought of this and reached down in the huge bag she'd brought with her and pulled out a plastic bag holding the patient's belongings. "Here, this is everything I could find on him," Leah said, handing the plastic bag across the table.

The officer looked flabbergasted as he took the bag and placed it on the desk. "Leave me your contact information, and I will call you as soon as I get the results back, if there is any,"

Sergeant Miles said. "Just so you know, we do have other cases to work on. I'll do the best that I can, but I can't make you a promise that I'll find anything."

Leah nodded and scribbled down her name and number and left the room. She had less than six days to find the family of this man before it was too late.

11

Officer Adanya Moore was plagued by the notion that something wasn't right, but she didn't know what that was. She thought back on the past week, her mind shuffling over each day and its events but mostly her mind went to the ten-car pile-up on the Ohio Turnpike from yesterday. She had watched with attentive eyes as the firefighters and paramedics hurriedly and cautiously rescued the people from their vehicles. As quickly as one ambulance arrived another two were leaving and heading to hospitals around the area.

She replayed the moment when she found the guy trapped under the truck and wondered how his wallet had gotten from the truck to the place where she was standing. He hadn't been anywhere near that spot. It was after they had taken him away that she'd found the wallet. Sure, it was possible that it had flown from the vehicle he was in. Some men didn't keep their wallet in their back pocket when they were driving. Doctors had reported that sitting on your wallet was bad for your back, especially if it were thick and bulky.

She shook her head. Why was she even thinking about this? She'd met the man's wife and she, Kaitlyn, hadn't said anything different, although she hadn't spoken to the lady since last night. She hadn't asked her any questions, not like the ones swimming around in her head now. Moore noted that Kaitlyn hadn't called her about him not being her husband so why was this bothering her so much? She decided that later, after work, she would stop by Edon Hospital and pay Kaitlyn and her husband a visit.

Officer Moore folded and tossed the newspaper she had been reading aside. She wasn't sure which was worse, reading about the God-awful accident or standing there seeing it with her own two eyes. She'd have to go with the second one. Because she had been there, and it was the worst accident she'd seen in her entire career as a police officer. Officer Moore shook her head, not in disgust at what had happened, but in sorrow for those who had been hurt or died in the accident.

Moore stood and walked into the kitchen and refilled her coffee cup. She had to get ready for work soon, no matter how much pain she felt these past two days. She wasn't pregnant. She knew what pregnancy felt like from twenty-eight years ago. It had been her decision alone to give up her baby, for her child to have a better life than she could've given her. She was getting past the age to have children now and a part of her regretted what she did all those years ago, but it was for the best. She also made sure that the files were locked so she didn't know where her child was just in case she changed her mind. Of course, she hated herself for doing what she did, but once it was done there was nothing she could do. Besides, it wouldn't be fair to the people who adopted her child and raised her for Moore to come in and take back her baby girl. But that didn't mean she never thought about her daughter. Where she lived and what she did with her life. No matter what, Moore would always love her daughter.

She was sure her nausea had to do with the wreckage yesterday, but still she thought it would be best to see the doctor just in case it was a bug of some sorts. Didn't need to go spreading any infections or diseases around the office, but it could be that her body was terribly worn down.

Officer Moore sipped her coffee and trudged off into the bedroom. She came walking out fifteen minutes later, closing the door to her three-bedroom house that her father had left her when he passed away two years ago. She had always wanted a big family, but she knew that time had sailed right by her. She would die in this house, probably all by her lonesome. No sounds of kids running around, and no husband to kiss goodbye when she left for work. Maybe she'd think of getting a cat to keep her company, but she was allergic to cats. And a dog was out of the question. She was gone all day long and wouldn't be able to let him outside. She wasn't one of those people who chained their dog outside all day either.

Moore couldn't deny that she was lonely. She had been lonely ever since her father died. It wasn't like she hadn't tried to find a man, because she had. Each time she went out with a guy, all he wanted was to get her in bed. She wanted a relationship first, then came the sex. She couldn't deny that when she woke the following morning she didn't regret taking her date up on his offer. She wasn't easy. Had never been easy, even when she had become pregnant at eighteen. She didn't want to come off as a slut, sleeping with every guy she went out with. Wasn't that what these young teens called it these days?

At the office, she'd listen in on some of the gossip the guys talked about. Some of them had teenagers in high school and would repeat conversations that they heard their kids talking about, mostly about girls at school sleeping around with guys they barely knew as if they had some contest to win. Going behind their parents back and getting birth control at Planned Parenthood or wherever they could get them. So yeah, she didn't want to be like *those* girls, even if she was much, much older than them.

She climbed into her SUV and started the engine. She needed to stop this *poor me* attitude and start living her life. *Yep!* That's what she needed to do but saying and doing were two different things. She'd have to start with not working so many hours, which wouldn't happen since they'd made some cutbacks in the department. Working all the time wasn't going to get her any dates. There she was feeling sorry for herself again.

Moore turned on the radio and listened to her favorite songs from the eighties as she drove through town. Sometimes it seemed like a ghost town when she drove to work at eight in the morning. Nothing seemed to be open early anymore. Most places had to let some of their people go or even close their doors for business because there was never enough money coming in. This place was going to hell in a handbag if you asked her. Maybe she should just sell the house and move some place better, maybe even warmer, like Florida or North Carolina. Besides her job, there wasn't really anything keeping her here in Edon. Her mother had passed away when Moore was three years old and her father from heart failure a couple of years ago. She had been an only child so there was no one else but her.

Ten minutes later, she walked through the doors of Edon Police Department. She knew by the stillness around the office that her day was going to be a long one. "Thank God," she mumbled, mostly to herself. She didn't want to see another accident like yesterday. It was as dead as a mouse stuck to a sticky trap, but maybe that was a good thing. She could be living in Cleveland or Chicago and dealing with shootings every day, but it also made for a very long day with nothing to do.

She made her way to her desk and sat down. She had a couple of files to scan through and needed to return a phone call. For just a split second she thought about taking that early retirement. She'd been a police officer for over twenty years so why shouldn't she just retire and live it up? She laughed to herself. *Live it up?* She lived in a town where nothing ever happened. What exactly would she do with all her free time? Besides, she had another ten years to go before she could really retire if she wanted the full benefits.

"Hey Moore," Officer Trevon Woods said as he motioned her over to where he was standing but spoke before she even got out of her seat. "Want to go out for lunch later?"

Officer Woods was a black, handsome forty-four-year-old man who stood six feet two inches tall with bulging muscles, as if he worked out several times a week, which she was sure he did. Woods had been begging Moore for months to go out with him. She'd told him that she didn't want to date anyone she worked with because if it didn't work out they'd have to see each other every day. Woods said in return that he didn't care and just wanted to hang with her outside of work.

She stood, trying to keep her eyes from devouring his body like most women did when they saw him. She focused on the picture beside him of the Colorado mountains, wishing she were there right now instead of the awkward situation she was about to walk into. She walked over to where he was standing. "I told you I'm not interested in dating you. I'm not trying to be mean, but it's just not a good idea," she whispered as she took him by the arm and moved them toward the far wall, out of earshot of the other officers.

"It's just lunch," Woods replied. "I swear, I won't push you on the issue of dating. Just an officer to an officer, having lunch together as coworkers," he said, smiling his killer smile at her.

That smile always made her knees wobble, and she was afraid she might fall over where she stood. God, he was so handsome, she could consume him in one serving. "You know people will talk around here even if there's nothing going on between us," Officer Moore said. "There's not enough action going on in this town to get people to mind their own business. I honestly think they like meddling in other people's lives."

"Look, I know you don't want any kind of relationship. I just want to be friends. That's all," Woods replied, smiling again.

Moore nodded, feeling disappointed suddenly. She wasn't sure what he saw in her; she wasn't a beauty queen—well, not in her eyes. She did get the occasional look from other guys, but she always looked straight ahead, not making eye contact, and yet she wondered why she was still single. She shook her head. She had to think of work first. Maybe he was being sincere, and she was just making something out of nothing. She seemed to be doing that a lot lately. "Okay, yeah, fine. I'll have lunch with you, but I must warn you, I haven't been feeling too good the past two days." She wasn't sure why she had just told him that, but it was out there now.

"Have you seen a doctor yet?" Woods asked, concerned, resting his large dark-skinned hand on her upper arm and rubbing it up and down.

She smiled inside. She wanted to grab him, ravish and kiss him. “No, I’ll call and make an appointment after my work here is done,” she replied. She had to walk away from him because she knew she wouldn’t be able to handle the feelings she felt flowing through her body. She could feel his warm, large hand still on her arm. She didn’t trust herself and quickly walked away and sat down at her desk. She had to get ahold of herself, but she could still feel the weight of his hand on her arm. The motion of him moving it up and down. She could imagine her lips on his mouth. It’d been awhile since any man had touched her, even if it were only a friendly gesture.

~ ~ ~

By one, she finished her paperwork and headed out the door with Officer Woods behind her. They drove in separate vehicles because Moore wanted to stop at the hospital after they ate lunch.

They settled in a booth and Moore ordered her usual, Turkey and Swiss on wheat with a side of fruit, hoping that she’d be able to eat it.

She was always on the latest diet, not that she stayed on it long. Food was her enemy. She loved food, but food seemed to make a home in her body like an unwanted cockroach that never left.

“Been to see any movies lately?” Woods asked.

“No, I have Netflix at home.”

"Oh, well, maybe you'd like to go see one for change. You know, get out of the house, hit the town."

"Hit the town?" Moore questioned. "What town are you talking about? Have you seen where we live?" she chuckled.

"I meant we'd go into Franklin and see a movie. They have some new ones coming out this weekend. Have you ever been there?" Woods asked.

"Long time ago."

"Then you haven't seen what they did to the place. They have leather lounge chairs instead of the old theater seats," Woods said. "And you have to pick your own seats when you get your tickets."

"Sounds complicated."

"What's so complicated about picking your own seats?"

"Well, for one, I like to be able to go to the movies and just sit wherever I want to. I can't stand sitting too close to the screen; it hurts my eyes. What if we go and those are the only seats left to sit in?"

Woods scrunched his eyebrows together before replying. "Guess you got a point there. If it helps and you're interested in going, I have the app on my phone and I can preorder the tickets and pick our seats before anyone else."

"An app?"

"Yeah, it's the latest thing. Don't you have apps on your cell phone?"

"No, I only use mine for calling and occasionally texting someone. Isn't that what they're for?"

Woods chuckled and smiled. "You make me laugh, Moore. Still stuck in the past, before cell phones took over the world, I see," Woods said in his deep voice before taking a bite of his hot roast beef sandwich. He chewed, swallowed and then spoke. "I guess that's what I love most about you."

Moore didn't look up after Woods said the word *love*. She was afraid to. He said love? But how could he love her when they hadn't spent any time together? Though she had said the words to herself, she never uttered them aloud. Never around people. Because she did love him too. She had fallen in love with him the moment she'd met him, but she couldn't tell him that.

She took a drink of water. "Fine, I'll go see a movie with you, but it isn't a date. Are we clear?" But she knew it was. She not only liked Woods's smile, she loved the way he laughed. It brightened her day when she was with him, so what the hell was her problem? She had this great looking—no, HOT looking—man wanting to be with her, and she kept shooting him down. She was being stupid and afraid. She looked down and then over at him again before eating her sandwich.

12

One Week before the Accident

Ben sat inside his Chevy Malibu, looking at the rundown two-bedroom ranch. The place was a piece of shit! But he wasn't the one living there so it didn't matter to him how crappy it was. Besides he didn't expect her to have anything nice, nor did he want to see her after everything she did to him and wished that he hadn't come to the house at all.

So why was he here? Wasn't that always the question he asked himself when he came to Iowa on a business trip? Sure, he had a job to do, but part of him felt obligated to come and sit across the street from the house he grew up in. He knew when he drove to the house he once lived in before he was shipped off to foster care, it would bring back memories of his abuse.

He looked out the window of the driver's seat when he heard the door open. She was letting a cat out and that's when he saw her. He hadn't expected to see his mother still living in the piece of shit. She hadn't changed, just older and skinnier. She looked like shit! Her hair looked dirty and straw-like, as if she hadn't showered in weeks, maybe even months. Once he saw her, part of him wanted to meet her face to face and talk about what she did to him all those years ago when he was just a child and couldn't protect himself, but he couldn't get out of the car. He didn't want to get out of the car.

As he sat there, his thoughts wandered back to when he was growing up under his mother's care, before child services took him out of the house. If he had known that he would be just like her when he got older, he would have killed himself. He knew he still could, but why? He had a great life with a beautiful wife he was sure loved him back. He just had to make sure she understood the rules. The same rules he had to learn. His mother, on a daily basis, beat the shit out of him for every tiny thing he did or didn't do. He had to make sure that his room was pristine. If it wasn't he would get a beating that would keep him from attending school for a week if she hit him on his face or in places that would be seen by others.

If he mowed the lawn and there was a single line not straight, he got a beating. His mother didn't always use a belt. No, she would grab whatever she could find around her. Anything she could grasp and knock him upside the head with or use on his body, breaking his bones.

He didn't have a father or at least not one he knew about. Men came to the house, but they weren't his real father, just some disgusting shithead that wanted a quick roll in the hay and then they'd leave. Sometimes they came back, sometimes they didn't, but he didn't care. He stayed hidden in his room as often as he could.

He'd seen enough doctors in his time growing up and wondered why they hadn't noticed how often he was there. Granted, his mother did take him to different hospitals in the area. This went on until he was twelve years old. When the school found out about the abuse, they had him removed and put into foster care. This was when Ben began to change and be like his mother. Anyone that was mean to him in his new school, he beat up. Eight foster homes and eight schools later, Ben finally learned to manage his anger and show it only when it was necessary. He left Iowa and moved to Illinois the first chance he got. A place where no one knew him. He couldn't very well start a new life and be someone else in the same crappy town he was raised in.

~ ~ ~

Ben drove away from his childhood house and was back on the road and heading home to Kaitlyn. Although he loved driving, he wasn't sure how much longer he could keep this traveling to different states. He'd never thought about the time away as being an issue, until today. He could hear it in Kaitlyn's voice on the phone. The sadness of his absence from her was tearing her in two. At first it had only been one day a week, but then one turned into two and then maybe even a whole week. It'd be different if he wanted to be away from her, but he didn't. He would have to talk to his boss. The traveling needed to stop once he arrived back at work on Monday.

Kaitlyn was the one he loved the most. She was beautiful, smart, and the kindest person he had ever met. When he saw her for the first time on that fall day in November of his first year in college, he had to know more about her. He had followed her around for a year before talking to her. He had never told her about watching her. He didn't want to scare her and think that he was some kind of freak, a stalker who watched her every move. Come to think of it, it did sound creepy as he played it out in his head. Just the way he liked it. He knew he'd get her to fall in love with him and then he'd teach her The Gordon Way. The first rule was to **never talk back**. That rule didn't take as long as he thought it would. She talked, he hit. No, he liked punching the best. Punching made her understand that he was the one in control of their relationship, not her. He tried to keep it below her neck, so it didn't show when she was out of the house. Couldn't have people asking questions, especially since she worked at a school and did the grocery shopping.

Ben didn't care that she was working at the school several miles from their house as long as she was home when he got there. Dinner was to be hot and ready, and the house was to be clean. That's all he asked of her.

Rule two, **everything must be in its place**. Not one piece of clothing wrinkled. Not one speck of dirt was to be found, and he checked with a white glove, too, sometimes. He may have been raised in a filthy house; it didn't mean as an adult he had to live in filth.

Not one can of food turned slightly to the left or the right. It had to be exactly centered, all of them. Words facing the front. He checked them too. There was to be no dirty laundry in the hamper for more than two days. And all clothes must be ironed with a precise fold down the front of every pair of slacks he owned.

He'd made her afraid of him and that was a good thing. Although things had changed when she got in that car accident, and the tracker he had placed under the car had been damaged. Now, he couldn't watch her every move. He'd have to buy another tracker for when she got the car back from the collision center.

He stopped at a Mobile gas station a few miles down the road and filled up the car before getting onto Interstate 80 and heading toward Illinois. If he made good time, he would stop at work first before heading home to Kaitlyn. He put in a CD of his favorite music, zoning out his thoughts for the drive home. He didn't want to think about his life at this moment. Escaping into the music of Mozart and Beethoven helped him through many of his days. It kept the stress from eating at him and helped his head not to hurt as much.

Two hours later, Ben pulled into the rest stop. After using the restroom, he sat in his car, not because he needed to rest, but because of the pain he had been having in his head for the past couple of months. He shrugged it off, thinking it was just from stress at home and from all the driving, but the pain had gotten worse, along with some dizziness, which caused blurred vision. He had gone to see a doctor before he went out of town. The doctor had done some tests like MRI, EEG, and bloodwork. Ben had been more stressed since the appointment a week ago as he waited for the results, which came back as the worst news he ever received in his life. Worse than being taken away from his mother and living in a foster home.

Ben backed out of his spot and got back on the highway. He'd forget about work until Monday and enjoy the weekend with his wife Kaitlyn. He needed her and only her. She was what got him through his days. He decided at that moment he would try to be a better person. A better husband to her. The husband that swore he would love her until their dying days. Through the good times and the bad times. He wouldn't be this man he had been since he was a child. He would be home more and that was a promise he would have to keep. The hitting, well, he'd try and control his anger as long as Kaitlyn did what she was told and didn't provoke him.

13

Kaitlyn had spent the last three days since she'd found out about the pregnancy hugging the toilet. She couldn't ever remember being this sick before in her life. She spit into the toilet one last time and stood. She filled a cup with water from the bathroom sink, swishing it in her mouth then spitting it out into the sink. She wiped her mouth and left the bathroom.

God, she felt like shit! And the worst thing was, Ben was coming home. He'd been in Iowa the day before she had found out about the pregnancy, and then he had called that night to tell her he had to stay a couple more days to help train. She had pretended to be sad and upset about him having to stay, but the truth was, she was thrilled that he wasn't coming home. God, she couldn't let him find out about the baby. She couldn't let him kill this one too.

The memories of that day still seemed fresh in her mind. She had made a special dinner for him and then once they were finished eating, she had him sit down in the living room and told him she was pregnant. At first, he seemed to be okay with the news. Maybe even thrilled. She thought she'd seen him smile. He stood, taking her hand in his as if helping her to stand. She *assumed* they were going to hug and celebrate this precious moment. When she was on her feet, he swung back and drove his fist into her lower abdomen. Once, twice, three times. After the third hit, he let go of her hand and she doubled over in extreme pain. She gasped for air as if it had been knocked out of her. The next day she'd lost the baby. He let her grieve for two days then told her to get up and go back to work.

"There will be no more *poor me,*" he screamed at her, then added, "I don't want children, ever! So you better figure out a way to *not* get pregnant." But that was the thing: he didn't allow her to use birth control pills. He had said that they would make her gain weight. Make her body change in ways he didn't want.

Kaitlyn shook the memory away, her mind going back to the conversation they'd had on the phone. Ben had sounded tired when she talked to him this morning, but he said that he was fine and had stayed up late going over things with the new people at the bank. It wasn't ten minutes after she'd hung up the phone that she was in the bathroom puking her guts out and had been in there for the past twenty minutes.

Kaitlyn padded in her bare feet to the bedroom and crawled back under the covers that were once warm from her body, but now had turned icy cold. She was thankful that she had taken the last two days off work. She hoped by Monday, she'd feel better and could go back to teaching her students. Kaitlyn had heard of women being sick all through their pregnancy and prayed that she wasn't one of them. She couldn't see herself lying around in bed for nine months. But if that was the case, then she'd have to leave Ben soon and move as far away as she possibly could and pray to God he wouldn't find her.

Maybe it was a good thing she'd been in the car accident, otherwise she wouldn't have found the tracking device on her car. She couldn't believe Ben would do that, but then again, why was she surprised? And how long had he been tracking her? This she didn't know—probably from the beginning of their marriage, she was sure of it. He'd been extremely controlling right after they'd been married and then a different side of him came out that she'd never seen before. But what surprised her the most was that he hadn't hit her for wrecking the car. He was upset, but he didn't punish her, which to her was a good thing.

As a wave of nausea came over her, she leaped out of bed and ran to the bathroom, lifting the toilet seat just in the nick of time. Once she felt better, she decided to go in search of a bucket to keep beside the bed. Then it occurred to her that she should call the doctor and let her know about her symptoms. Maybe the doctor could prescribe her something for the nausea. She couldn't let Ben see her this way; he'd know that it wasn't the flu.

She went into the garage and found a bucket sitting high up on a shelf. She figured Ben had placed it up there because she couldn't even reach it with the tips of her fingers. She looked around the room and spotted the step ladder. Ben liked everything in a certain spot and knew when something was moved, even a millimeter. She hadn't realized how anal he was.

She grabbed the bucket before climbing down the ladder. She then placed the ladder back in the exact spot she'd taken it from, which was right next to a huge box. A box she didn't remember seeing a few days ago. She stepped back and read the side of the box. Generator? What did Ben need a generator for? She didn't recall them ever losing power when they had a storm. She decided she wasn't in the right frame of mind to be thinking about this at the moment. Ben did what Ben wanted to do. "If he wanted a generator then so be it," she said aloud as she walked back inside the house.

She stopped in the kitchen and poured a glass of Sprite to help her stomach. Physicians said to drink Ginger Ale for an upset stomach, but she didn't care for the taste and Sprite seemed to help. While standing in the kitchen, waiting for the fizz of the soda to settle, she thought of where she would live. Maybe California, even Arizona sounded good—no more winter days, but then Ohio slipped into her mind. Her lost love was from Ohio, but she didn't know if he were even alive, if he'd come back from the war after ending their relationship almost nine years ago.

Kaitlyn felt not only mentally drained but physically exhausted as well from the morning and needed to go lie down. She needed to clear her mind and figure out a way to leave Ben. She needed to think of the baby, but at the same time she needed to think about herself. If she could just make it through the mornings in the first trimester, then she would be fine. But she knew she didn't have control over her body. She would also have to tell the school and see if the principal could have someone in the class with her until the morning sickness passed, but eventually she would begin to show, and that meant Kaitlyn needed to run.

~ ~ ~

She sat up and swung her legs over the edge of the bed. No dizziness, so that was a good sign. She planted her feet on the cool wood floor and stood. The clock next to the bed read 11:33 a. m. She still had a whole day ahead of her.

She used the bathroom and made her way to the kitchen to make a cup of coffee. Just thinking about it made her mouth water. That was also a good sign. She placed a K-cup in the slot and pushed the button. Coffee instantly brewed into her cup and the aroma filled the room.

While she waited, she turned on the television in the kitchen. She thumbed through the channels but didn't find anything that caught her interest. She was usually at work around this time, so she wasn't even sure what was on TV. After several more clicks, she turned it off and decided that she'd grade the papers from Wednesday's class before Ben arrived home. She wasn't allowed to be working on school papers when he was home.

An hour later, she was finished with the school papers and made another cup of coffee. She had to watch how much caffeine she drank now that she was carrying. Most mothers would give up the coffee, but her doctor said that two a day wouldn't hurt the baby or its development.

Kaitlyn needed to get a couple of red pens from the office that they had in the house. She stood and walked to the den. Ben had bought an elegant cherry desk that sat in the center of the room. She sometimes worked in the office, and it was where they kept the office supplies that they used. Ben had bookcases built along the wall for Kaitlyn to place all her favorite novels that she loved to read. Some she had read several times by authors like Liane Moriarty, Heather Gudenkauf, Nicholas Sparks, and Kristin Hannah. She was even able to get a couple of them signed by the authors themselves when they came to town on their book tours.

She walked over to the desk and went to open the bottom drawer, and nearly fell on her ass. The drawer was locked. They had never locked this drawer before. She tried again, thinking that it was just probably stuck, but it was for sure locked and she was confused as to why Ben would have locked the drawer because she hadn't done it. Of course, she hadn't gone into the desk in… Well, she couldn't remember the last time she needed some supplies for work.

There would only be one reason the drawer was locked. Ben was hiding something from her, but why was he allowed to keep things from her, when she couldn't keep anything from him? Well, of course, she did keep secrets from him, but that was only because he punished her for doing things he didn't approve of. Things that were stupid and no one should get abused for. She began to get angry. "Damn him," she mumbled into the room. "Why did he have to be like this with me?" She had once loved Ben and was thrilled to have married him, but not now. Now, she wished for any guy but him. She wanted Adam back in her life. He knew her. He loved her. He treated her with more kindness than anyone ever had. And he never, ever hit her!

She pulled out the chair and sat down, searching the desk with her eyes, but saw nothing out of the ordinary. She opened the drawer in the center of the desk, hunting for the key to unlock it. There wasn't one. She had sworn that a set of keys had come with the desk. She looked down at the drawer to her left. It had a key lock on the front of the drawer, so she wasn't mistaken about there being keys.

She started opening the drawers on the right side of the desk. She started with the top drawer that held their joint checkbook first. She moved it aside and rummaged toward the back of the drawer, finding nothing helpful.

She moved to the second drawer that was used for filing their bills. Nothing looked different to her. She thumbed through the files, reading the name of each one. They were mostly folders for utility bills. She moved each one forward and checked between them. There was nothing hidden, but why was her mind thinking that there would be? Why would she think that Ben would be hiding something from her at all? Ben never kept secrets from her, did he? For one measly second, she almost believed that Ben would never keep secrets from her, and she laughed at herself for even thinking such a thing.

She closed the drawer and swiveled the chair to the other side and opened the top drawer. Nothing seemed to be out of place or missing. She tried the bottom drawer again, but it still didn't budge. Had he taken the key with him just in case she would need to go into the drawer? But there still remained the question as to why the drawer was locked to begin with.

Kaitlyn marched into the kitchen and opened the drawer that held a few tools and grabbed a flat head screwdriver. She inserted the screwdriver into the key hole as gently as possible without damaging or breaking the lock. She knew Ben would know and he would hurt her. She turned it slowly to the right. She heard something click and withdrew the screwdriver. Adrenaline coursed through her veins, making her heart beat fast and hard. She couldn't think straight. Her only response was to react because she was afraid of what she might find in the locked drawer. Every scenario played over and over in her mind. Why was it that when we are in a situation that it had to be something horrifyingly bad?

She grabbed the knob and pulled, the drawer rolled open. Inside were several plastic containers that Kaitlyn used to organize her supplies, or did Ben make her do it? He had always been picky with things being precise. She took the containers out and placed them on top of the desk until there was only a thick manila envelope remaining at the bottom of the drawer.

She felt warmer suddenly as the temperature in her body rose, making her feel hot and dizzy at the same time. She took the envelope out and plopped down in the chair. To her it looked like any other manila envelope, but this one had the words Adam Tucker written on it. Knots twisted in her stomach with fear and confusion. She searched her mind, thinking of what could be inside. Adam? Why would there be an envelope with her ex-lover's name on it from nine years ago? She swallowed down the bile rising in her throat as she lifted the flap.

14

Two Days after the Accident

Leah reached over and shut off the alarm blaring beside her. She had worked late last night and was scheduled to return to work at 8 a.m. this morning. The hospital was short on nurses due to vacations and a couple of women on maternity leave, but she didn't mind the extra hours.

She sat up, turned, placing her badly needed half-painted toes on the cold wood floor of her bedroom. She sat stretching her arms above her head and bending her back. God, it felt good to stimulate the muscles before starting her day.

She straightened and stood, trudging to the bathroom and then went into the kitchen for her morning coffee. The first taste of coffee was always the best. It felt as if it awakened every part of the body, making it feel new again—something she needed these days from working so many hours. Her mind was wrapped around her one patient that didn't even have a chance to live life again—might never get to drink his favorite beverage or eat his favorite meal. She wanted desperately to find his family because she refused to believe he didn't have someone out there wondering where he was and if he were okay.

She walked over to the sliding glass door and opened it wide. Sunshine poured onto her brown sugar skin, making her feel warm all over. The vitamin D soaking into her face made her feel alive. This was the thing she enjoyed the most every morning besides her coffee: waking up and feeling the warm sun against her skin, although she knew winter was right around the corner, and there wouldn't be as much sun for days or weeks at a time.

She stepped out onto the patio of her apartment and rested against the railing. Her dark brown eyes traced over the lake that surrounded the building she lived in. The ducks were already splashing in the water, dunking their heads down into the water and back up again. What she would give to have that kind of life. No worries of going to work and paying bills every month. Just float around on the water and have fun with the other ducks. She laughed at herself for thinking of such a silly thing as being a duck. But she on occasion wondered about things like that—life between animals and humans.

She finished her first cup of coffee, went back inside for a refill, and then got ready for work. She was looking forward to seeing her patient today, hoping that by some miracle he opened his eyes and was awake. She tried to remember the doctor's warning about not getting too close to any of the patients, especially those that will not recover, but she couldn't help herself. There was just something about him that intrigued her. Maybe it was her loneliness for a man in her life? She laughed out loud to herself. She was saying this after thinking of thebrain-dead patient? "You do need to get out and get a life," she said as she looked at herself in the bathroom mirror. "You're starting to lose your mind, girl." She laughed again.

Although it sounded strange, she needed—no, she wanted—to find out more about him. She wanted his family to at least say goodbye to him. She ached to know his name. To know if he had any children that he was leaving behind. Was he married or divorced? Some people still wore their wedding ring even though they weren't together with their spouse, not wanting to let go of the past or the love they felt for someone. Divorce wasn't always something both people wanted. She knew that from her best friend who had just recently split from her husband. They'd been together almost seven years and then one night he said that he didn't love her anymore and left. Leah had to console her friend for weeks before she accepted her husband leaving her. Maybe that's why she didn't date much. Love these days, just didn't last like it used to.

Leah headed back into the kitchen, washed out her coffee cup and placed it in the strainer to dry. She grabbed her things and went out the door, closing it behind her. She took the stairs not because there wasn't an elevator—there was—but because she enjoyed the exercise. Granted, she was on her feet all day long, but being active was who she was. It kept her feeling young, not that she was old. Twenty-seven was young. She still had time to settle down and have children, one day. *At least,* she thought to herself like she did when it came to families. *I won't do what my real mom did. If I get pregnant, I'd keep the baby, with or without a man to help.* Leah didn't know why her biological mother had given her up; she just assumed she didn't want her.

Twenty minutes later, she arrived at the hospital and parked her car. When she exited the elevator on the fifth floor, she walked to the nurse's station and clocked in on the computer. She went to the cabinet that held all the patients' charts but didn't see her patient's chart anywhere. She walked back to the nurse's station and looked there, but still she couldn't find it. Dread washed over her as she thought of the worst. Had they decided to withdraw care for him, and didn't bother to tell her? Not that they had to call her and ask for her permission. How could they do that to her when she was his nurse? She hadn't had the chance to say goodbye, just like when her father died. She hadn't had any time to find John Doe's family. Anger swept over her as she thought of Dr. Amal. He had done this, she was sure of it, and she'd let him know what she thought of him the next time she saw him.

Maybe she was overreacting, and her patient was still in his room. She should have checked there before assuming there was something wrong. Was the doctor in with the patient? She quickly walked to the room he was in yesterday, but when she got there, someone else was in his bed. She looked at the whiteboard and saw the name *William Browne.* She walked closer to the bed. Nope, it definitely wasn't her brain-dead patient. She left the room in search of the head nurse. She poked her head into every room, but it wasn't until she got to the last room on the left that she saw her.

"Excuse me, Melissa," she whispered. "Do you know what happened to my patient in room four?"

"Oh, he was moved to the second floor. We needed the room for, you know." She put her hand to the side of her mouth and whispered, "People that will get better and need us." She gave a half-smile and then went back to whatever she was doing.

Leah stepped out of the room and rested against the wall in the hall. "The second floor?" Leah mumbled to herself. She'd never see him again now that they had moved him. She would have to find time to go see him on her breaks. "This is unbelievable! My patient deserves this room more than any other sick or critical person in here," she stammered.

She'd just have to keep busy. That's what she had to do. She glanced at her watch. She had two and a half hours before her first break. She slowly walked back to the nurse's station to find her schedule for today and who she would be taking care of.

At ten-thirty, Leah quickly made her way to the elevator and rode down to the second floor. She had looked on the computer to find the room number that he was in. No, he wasn't her patient anymore, but she couldn't stop thinking that way. He was still her patient and she'd visit with him until... Well, until she found his family. Hopefully by then Sergeant Miles would have found out who he was, and she could contact his family.

She arrived at his door that was left partly open and went inside. She took several steps and saw him lying there still unresponsive. The breathing tube was still attached and the ventilator moving up and down.

She let out a breath, relieving the stress of this morning's fatigue. She moved closer and stood next to his bed. She could hear the hospital sounds drifting in through the open door. She felt nervous that someone would find her here and tell her to leave, but no one came, and she was thankful for that.

She placed her hand on his and squeezed, praying that he would open his eyes and ask her where she'd been and that he was waiting for her. She laughed at herself for thinking such a thing. He was brain-dead and for him to wake up would be an absolute miracle.

She spent the next five minutes talking to him as if he were there with her and they had been friends forever. She talked about her mom and a little about work, but mostly, she just stared at him, wishing and hoping that he'd open his eyes, but he didn't. She left the room, but not before she told him that she'd be back on her lunch break to see him again.

The moment Leah exited the elevator on the fifth floor her cell phone buzzed. She stopped and looked at the number. She didn't know who it belonged to, but then remembered that she'd given the police officer her number. She stepped over to the wall, away from doctors and nurses walking past her and answered the call.

"Hello?"

"Hi, this is Sergeant Miles. You came to talk to me yesterday about the man with no identification?"

"Yes," Leah replied, waiting for him to continue.

"I'm afraid I haven't been able to get anything from the ring or off the partial shirt you brought in," he said.

"I see. Is there anything else you can do? Anything I can get for you?" Leah wanted to stay hopeful that there was something, anything Sergeant Miles could do to find the man's family.

"Well," he paused. "I can send someone over to do a dental or get fingerprints. But again, if his DNA isn't in the system then there's no way to get you the information you need. I'm sorry."

Leah's shoulders drooped. "I understand," she replied. "With the breathing tube, I don't think a dental can be done. What do I need to do? I mean, is there anything, something I can get you?"

"I can start with the fingerprints, but I can't make any promises that it'll work. I'm assuming your hospital doesn't have the Biometric Identification System that most hospitals have?"

Leah had heard about the new identification for patients, but Sergeant Miles was correct. Franklin Hospital was a fairly large facility, but after it had been built, the hospital didn't have any more money to buy that kind of equipment. "No," she replied. She knew that if they had such a thing, she wouldn't have gone to the police station for help. "Thank you for all that you've done. I will see if there's something else we can do," she said and ended the call. She didn't want to give up on her patient but felt both hopeless and defeated.

15

Kaitlyn woke with a start, her neck kinked from the awkward position she'd fallen asleep in. On and off throughout the night she had slept either in the lobby or at the side of the bed in the chair beside Ben.

She rubbed the back of her neck and looked over at Ben, who was still unconscious. All she wanted was for him to wake up. She needed to know if he was the same Ben from yesterday. Some would question why she stayed. They didn't have any children together. Well, scratch that. With all that had been going on in the past week, it had slipped her mind just now that she was indeed pregnant with his child. She wasn't sure why she stayed. Could she actually love him? No, that she knew wasn't why. Maybe at one time. Yes, of course, when they had dated and the first few months of their marriage, but now? No, there wasn't an ounce of love inside her for him. Counselors and therapists would say that she stayed because she was accustomed to the abuse. She was a battered wife, controlled by his threats and anger. A familiarity that became part of her everyday life. She couldn't deny that at times she did wish him dead. She couldn't lie and say it hadn't crossed her mind.

She scanned the room, something she hadn't done the night before because she was more concerned with the well-being of this man she called her husband. This man who was supposed to love her and protect her, not abuse her.

She wondered if it was still night? She stood, stretching her back and legs, then walked over to the window. She turned the long white stick hanging down; light instantly poured in through the open slots.

It was definitely not night. She'd slept on and off through the night, exhausted by everything that had happened in just one day. She turned back around and viewed the room. Plain white walls surrounded her, with a whiteboard listing patient information, the name of the nurse on call, and tests that were done and still needed to be completed.

She looked out through the narrow window on the door of the room and saw a bathroom in the far corner of the ICU and walked in that direction. She would freshen up and then find the cafeteria to get some much-needed caffeine in her system.

After using the restroom, she came back into the room and grabbed her purse from the back of the chair. She asked the nurse behind the counter where the cafeteria was located and gave her cell number just in case Ben should wake up.

She climbed into the elevator and rode to the ground floor, where she spotted the cafeteria the moment the doors opened. She wasn't hungry until she smelled the scent of eggs and bacon, surprised that she hadn't felt sick this morning. Just two weeks ago she'd found out that she was carrying a baby and was hugging the toilet.

She took small steps as she slid her tray along the metal bars, looking at the hot plates of food. She grabbed one and placed it on her tray and stopped when she reached the coffee machine. After paying, she glanced around the room for an empty seat and saw one against the wall. Most everyone in the room was either a doctor or nurse; a few were visitors here to see their loved ones, though it was early in the morning and people were probably at home just waking up.

Kaitlyn sat and added a couple of Splendas to her coffee and stirred. She placed the cup to her lips and blew away the steam before taking a sip. Once the hot liquid made its way down her throat, she felt almost human again. Her thoughts were still on her husband lying upstairs. She wondered when they would move him to a different room, out of the ICU. Maybe when he woke they would, then she could stay with him in the room all night.

She hadn't asked Officer Moore what happened, nor did Officer Moore volunteer any information about the accident. She went back to her thoughts. Who was she kidding? She didn't have to play the loving wife game when no one was around. Her mind could think all it wanted about marriage and love and that she should stay with him, but she had already made the decision. She wasn't planning on staying now that she was pregnant, but she couldn't leave him while he was unable to take care of himself, could she? No, she'd wait until he was back on his feet again. God kept him alive for some reason or another. *Maybe this will change him? Make him a better man?* She almost laughed out loud at the thought.

Did she really want to know about the accident and who was at fault for her husband lying upstairs unconscious? Yes and no. Maybe she was afraid to know what happened. Maybe she already knew and once the truth was out she'd know that he had caused it. Now she was speculating without even knowing the facts. The accident must have happened right after they'd gotten off the phone. She knew this because Ben had said he just entered Ohio, and Officer Moore said it was early yesterday morning. Which meant as anal and controlling as Ben could be, he was driving while talking on the phone. Which meant he probably wasn't paying attention to the road. She didn't know, but the next time she saw Officer Moore, she'd make it a point to ask her.

She set her cup down and started picking at her food. Her belly growled and gurgled when the food entered her stomach. *The baby is hungry*, she thought, but knew she or he was too small yet to want food. She smiled and rubbed her belly under the table where no one could see her.

When she finished, she threw away her garbage and placed the tray on the cabinet with the rest. She got back in the elevator with her coffee and exited on the fourth floor. Her eyes were drawn immediately to the police officer talking to one of the nurses at the counter. It wasn't the same one from last night because this one was a white man, not a black woman.

She stepped over to the wall and pressed her back against it. Was she having a panic attack? Her breath was caught in her throat. She swallowed and closed her eyes, taking in another slow breath. Her shoulders fell back, her body relaxing with every breath going in and out of her lungs. She opened her eyes, looking in the direction of the officer, and her body began to tremble again. Why did she feel that they were looking for her? They could be here for anyone. Besides, she hadn't done anything wrong. They wouldn't know about Ben abusing her, but what if they knew he caused the accident and were going to charge him? Why was she even assuming that he had caused the accident? Maybe it was someone else. Her mind was spinning out of control. Why was she thinking these things? She didn't care what happened to him.

She stayed near the wall as she picked up her pace, keeping her eyes to the ground. Once she went through the sliding glass door, she focused her gaze at the door of Ben's room, hoping that she looked invisible. Once she slipped into the room, she closed the door behind her and pressed her back against the cold metal.

She relaxed and looked straight ahead at Ben. Had this been all his fault? Part of her wanted to know, but the other half, not so much. Besides, he was the only one in the accident so why would he get into any trouble? Again, why was her mind thinking all these things? It was just an accident, period!

She walked to the bed, setting her coffee cup down on the night table next to the bed. It was Saturday, but she still needed to let her boss know that she might not—no, would not—be in school next week if Ben still didn't wake up.

She pulled out her phone and searched her contacts for Scott Flannigan, the principal of Lakeport High, and clicked on his phone number. She placed the phone to her ear and waited. When he didn't answer, she left a brief message about what had happened, where she was, and her cell number where she could be reached.

After ending the call, she looked at the battery life on her cell. Twenty-five percent wasn't going to get her far if she stayed here all weekend. She dug in her purse for a charger, which she had with her because she would sometimes forget to charge her phone at night and would need to charge it when she was in her classroom.

She dumped out her purse onto the end of the bed and found the charger. As she placed the items back in her purse she saw the manila envelope that she'd placed in her bag a week ago. The one she had found inside the locked drawer in the office. The one with Adam's name written on it. She had put the envelope in her purse after she had gone through the contents because she wanted to show them to Ben at dinner yesterday and simply forgot about it, until now.

She couldn't believe when she opened the envelope that it was filled with letters from Adam when he was in the Army. Letters she had never received from him. Letters that were sent after she had received the Dear John letter from him. She had no idea how Ben had these. Had he confiscated her mail at the school? Had he been following her way before they had met on that rainy day eight years ago? Had he been stalking her the whole time? She felt nauseous just thinking about it. He had to have because she knew she had never seen these before. They were all dated after the Dear John letter and they were open, which meant Ben had read them.

She spent several hours sitting on the floor in the office reading through each and every one of them with tears running down her face. He had said he loved and missed her and wondered why she hadn't written him back. She retrieved the letters she had hidden away so Ben wouldn't find them. The letters Adam had written her before the Dear John letter was sent and placed the letters side by side. That's when she realized that the handwriting was different. Had Ben written the Dear John letter and not Adam? Adam probably thought that she didn't want to be with him anymore because she hadn't written him back. But wouldn't he have received her last three letters pleading him not to do this, that she loved him? Or did Ben take them too? If he did, they weren't in with the rest of the letters because she had gone through all of them. She had rummaged through the desk and found some papers with his writing on them, and they did match the Dear John letter. This, she knew, was the last straw. She needed to confront him about the letters or just take her shit and get out. She had thought that Adam didn't want her anymore but from reading the letters that wasn't the case. Adam had wanted her more than anything.

She looked down at Ben, who was lying comfortably in the bed. She was done after this. Once he was better, she was leaving him. She wasn't going to sit back and wait for the day he wasn't going to hit her again because she knew that day would never come. He had four years to stop, but each time was worse than the next. Each time made her hate him even more and she wanted nothing more than to kill him in his sleep, but she never did. She was too afraid to be sent to prison, but sometimes she thought if she could handle him beating her then what difference would it be if the women in the prison beat her too? Maybe she'd beat them up instead, letting all her anger out on them from all the years of abuse. Then finding the letters? She had lost the love of her life because of him. To be honest, she wasn't sure why she was here now; maybe she wanted to let him know she knew about the letters before she left him.

She placed everything back inside her purse and set it on the floor next to the chair and looked for a plug-in that she could use that wouldn't affect any of Ben's machines. A conniving thought came to her that she should just unplug them all and let him die, but she wasn't as cruel as he was. She couldn't be liable for his death, could she?

After finishing, she sat down in the chair and was startled when she heard a rapid beeping sound fill the room. She automatically looked up and over at her husband and saw that he was looking at her. Her hand flew to her mouth. "You're awake," she whispered. She thought about sitting there and doing nothing but decided that she should pretend that she cared and would play his game for just a little while longer. Long enough to know if he was the same Ben she had been married to all these years.

She smiled at him and jumped out of her chair, nearly pushing it over with the back of her leg. *Too much enthusiasm,* she thought. She stood, leaned in and kissed him. "How are you feeling? Should I go get the doctor? Yes, of course, I should." She laughed at herself, something she always did when she got anxious. She rambled on, answering her own questions. She stood and looked at him. "I'll go get the doctor," she said and left the past.

16

When he first saw her sitting there in the chair in front of him, she looked like an angel with the florescent lights beaming down around her body. There was something about her, but he wasn't quite sure yet what it was. Had he seen her before? Was she someone close to him?

He knew that he was in a hospital because he saw all the equipment around the room, and he was lying in a bed. He could feel the IV needle in his right hand when he tried to move it.

After the woman made a phone call, she stood and went through her purse, looking for something. When he thought that she was going to look at him, he closed his eyes, not wanting her to know that he was awake—at least, not yet. He wanted to know more about her and why she was here. Was she someone special that he couldn't remember? A girlfriend maybe? Or a sister or an aunt? He didn't see a ring on his finger, so she couldn't be his wife. His thoughts were hazy, clouded with uncertain segments of his life. He squeezed his eyes closed, forcing himself to recall something, anything that put him here in this bed. This hospital.

Nothing.

He couldn't recollect anything from his life. He wasn't even sure where he came from, what town he lived in, who he was. The stress of his thinking made the machine next to the bed beep rapidly, and the woman sitting in front of him looked up and into his bright blue eyes. When she smiled, her eyes lit up like nothing he had never seen before, or had he?

"You're awake," she whispered.

He wasn't sure if she was sad or excited that he'd opened his eyes. But she did seem pleased to see him, didn't she? He wasn't sure and felt as if he were getting mixed signals from her. She leaned in and kissed him on the lips. Her lips felt warm on his, and he didn't want her to stop. It was a longing deep inside of him. Part of him remembered this feeling he was having. Something he had felt before, but he couldn't recall when and with whom.

"I'll go get the doctor," she said, then she was gone from the room.

He tried to sit up, but his head felt fuzzy, so he lay back down against the softness of the pillow. His left hand touched the right side of his head and felt the bandage covering some of his face. His eyes fell on his leg that was in a sling, hanging from a pulley. He had broken his leg, but he wasn't sure how. What happened to put him in the hospital? The days and months before seemed like a blur. Everything before these last few minutes seemed to not exist. The more he tried to think, the more his head began to hurt. He looked up at the ceiling;

the brightness of the lights made him blink several times before he looked away and at the door of his room. The woman reappeared in front of him. She was the most beautiful thing he had ever seen. This he was sure of.

"The doctor will be here soon," she said, sitting in the chair next to him.

She gave him a faint smile, almost as if she was forcing herself. She reached for his hand and he felt her trembling. Her hand was shaking. Was she scared?

Then a warm, tingly feeling coursed through his body, a sensation that made his heart beat faster. He didn't want to look away from her. There was just something about her that made him feel alive. Something he was sure he had never felt before and if he had, when?

"How are you feeling?" a nurse said when she came into the room holding a chart in her hands.

For the first time since he woke, he opened his mouth to speak. "I feel fine." His voice sounded scratchy and dry from the lack of saliva in his mouth and throat. He looked over at the beautiful angel next to him.

"When will the doctor be here to see him?" Kaitlyn asked the nurse.

The nurse looked at her watch on her right arm. "He's making his rounds, but he should be here shortly," the nurse replied. "If you ask me, doctors seem to show up for work whenever they feel like it, but don't go telling the doctor I said that." The nurse let out a sardonic snort.

He listened to the conversation between the two women, especially the soft and gentle voice of the angel-like woman beside him. But it was the words the nurse said that caught his attention.

"I'll make sure that the doctor comes in as soon as I see him. You visit with your wife, and I'll be right back," the nurse said before exiting the room.

My wife, he repeated in his head. He was married to this beautiful woman beside him. He wanted so much to know her name. He wanted to know everything about her. Then it hit him: he didn't even know his own name. His brain was foggy. The more he thought the more his brain started to hurt. It was worse than having a headache. Much, much worse. The machine beside him started to accelerate, the numbers rising two digits at a time.

"Are you okay?" Kaitlyn asked. "Do I need to get the nurse again?"

He shook his head and closed his eyes. He took in slow, deep breaths, and the machine began to drop in numbers. Once he felt calm and could talk, he did. "What is my name?" he asked the lady beside him.

She looked up and into his eyes. Her face stiffened. Her eyes looked at his in a rapid motion.

He couldn't tell if she were saddened by what he'd asked.

She replied, “Ben. Your name is Ben Gordon.” She sat looking at him. Her eyes gave him a cold stare.

“I’m sorry,” he said. Before he could ask any more questions, the door to the room opened and in came a man wearing a white doctor’s coat.

“Well, I see that our patient is finally awake. How are you feeling? Having any difficulties swallowing? Any headaches, dizziness?” The doctor spoke quickly, throwing out question after question.

“Dizziness. No headaches, but my head does hurt if I try to remember what happened to me,” he replied quickly before the doctor could speak again.

“Doctor?” Kaitlyn questioned. “Before you came into the room he asked me what his name was. What does that mean? Is there something wrong with his memory?”

The doctor looked up from the chart in his hand. “He was in a terrible car accident, and there was some damage to his head. Most likely he has some form of memory loss due to the accident, but I’ll order a CT scan just to be sure that there’s no swelling in the brain that may have developed since yesterday,” the doctor said. “We did have to remove a small metal fragment that was located near the side of his brain. Could’ve been from the accident.”

“Could’ve been?” Kaitlyn questioned.

"Yes, I didn't see any opening in the area, and it looked like scar tissue had formed around the metal object, so I would say it's been there for a while."

Kaitlyn gave Ben a quizzical look.

"But it's not uncommon after the kind of accident he was involved in not to remember certain things. It might take him some time before things come back to him. But it'll be helpful if you're here to fill in the blanks."

Kaitlyn nodded. "Yes, of course." Keeping her eyes on her husband, she smiled.

"He's awake and looks to be doing fine. I'll put in the order for the CT scan, and we'll go from there." The doctor wrote down some notes. "If the tests are normal, I'll have him moved to a different room," he said and then left the room.

He had been looking at Kaitlyn the whole time the doctor was in the room. This beautiful person beside him was his wife. Someone he knew nothing about but felt like he'd known her forever.

17

Officer Moore smiled for the first time in a long time as she drove to the hospital. Officer Woods had gotten her to laugh and it felt good to let it out, something she hadn't done much of lately. She hadn't had time yesterday to go to the hospital, so she decided that she'd drive there first thing this morning.

She parked the SUV and entered through the revolving glass doors of Edon Hospital. She didn't bother to stop at the receptionist's desk in the lobby because she already knew what room Ben Gordon was in.

She stepped onto the elevator and rode up to the fourth floor. Once outside the ICU, Officer Moore felt a heaviness in her heart. She had stood just outside these doors a couple of years ago when her father had a triple bypass and had to be in the ICU ward. He had spent two nights in the ICU, and they had allowed her to stay with him, not because she was in law enforcement, but more because they all had known and loved her father just as she had. He had passed away three days later.

She inhaled a deep breath before walking toward the sliding glass doors of the ICU. The doors swooshed open and she stepped inside. The smell of disinfectant seemed to overpower her nose and she sneezed several times into the crease of her elbow. When she looked up, a couple of the nurses turned her way. They must have thought she was sick, but it was just the smell triggering her allergies.

"I'm fine," she said. "I'm not sick, just the smells tickling my nose." She waved a hand in the air. All heads turned back to what they were doing before she walked farther into the room.

Moore walked up to the counter, but there was no one sitting on the other side. She looked around the room. Most of the nurses were busy attending to patients in the rooms. That's when her eyes saw a woman, maybe Ben Gordon's wife, sitting inside the same room her father was in. It didn't mean that Ben was going to die. That would be absurd to think that. It was just a room, besides her father was in his mid-seventies and his heart was getting old. He had heart disease, and the doctors said that it would happen eventually. There was nothing anyone could do to save him when he developed a staph infection after the surgery. She knew who he was in a better place, but it didn't make her miss him any less.

She placed both hands on the duty belt around her waist as if she were about to have a shoot off and walked toward the room. The lady sitting beside the bed turned, but it wasn't the same woman from the other night.

"Pardon me," Moore said. "I thought you were someone else."

"No problem," the dark-haired woman replied, looking startled.

Moore had that effect on some people when they saw her coming. A black woman in a police uniform. Like women, white or colored, couldn't be police officers, or was it the fact she was black? Both, she was sure. She hated when people thought women couldn't have the same jobs as men could. *Horse puckey,* she thought before turning and walking away.

When Officer Moore turned around she ran right into one of the nurses she knew. "I'm so sorry," Moore said, holding out her hands to stop them both from falling. "I was looking for the male patient from the accident, on the Ohio Turnpike. I thought he was in that room, but he's not," Moore said before taking a step back and away from the nurse.

"Oh, yes, Ben Gordon. He was moved to the third floor this morning. Doctor didn't see any concerns to have him in here any longer. Besides, we needed the room for someone else," the nurse replied. "You know how it can be sometimes when you need to make room in a space that's too small?"

Officer Moore nodded. "Do you know if he's conscious?"

"Yes, actually he is. Woke up this morning. The doctor sent him for a CT scan and then moved him down to the third floor."

Moore nodded again. "Okay, thank you. Have a good day!"

"You too, Moore," the nurse said as she walked away and into another room.

Moore left the ICU and climbed back into the elevator. After the doors closed, she pushed the button and the metal box jerked and then started to descend in a slow rickety movement. She thought of her life passing her by and how not only did she live alone but she would die alone too. She never took life by the reins and took chances. No, she sat back and was literally watching everything and everyone pass her by. Occasionally, she'd wave at them while sitting on her front porch sipping sweet tea, but maybe it was time to come out of her shell and get out there and live a little. Go watch a movie with a friend or have a dinner other than in her own kitchen. She was thinking of Trevon Woods.

The metal box came to an abrupt halt and the doors opened. She quickly stepped off just in case the cables snapped, and the elevator shot down to the garage, ending her magnificent life. She gathered her composure and walked down the hall and into the closest restroom. She shoved open the first stall door and vomited into the white porcelain toilet.

She knew she hadn't been feeling very well lately. She wiped her face clean as she stood in front of the sink. Part of her felt humiliated for being such a wuss. She was a police officer, for God's sake, someone who put her life on the line every day, and one little shake of an elevator and she was scared out of her mind and throwing up. What kind of person did that? And why was she acting like this? She stood up straight, looked into the mirror and tossed the paper towel in the garbage. She turned and left the restroom in search of the nurse's station. Once she found it, she asked for Ben Gordon's room. Moore followed the directions down the hall and to the third door on her left, room 315.

The door was ajar, so she pressed it open and stepped inside. The rubber on the bottom of her boot caught on the newly polished floor, making her fall forward, her night stick smacking into the door. She nearly fell into the room on her face but caught herself before making a total ass of herself. This sure as hell wasn't her day.

Kaitlyn sprang from her chair. "Are you okay?" she said as she tried to catch Officer Moore.

"Yes, I'm fine. Just tripped is all." Moore straightened herself and walked farther into the room her, eyes catching sight of Ben. "I heard that you were awake," Moore said as she gathered her composure.

"Yes, he woke up early this morning."

"Do you think he's up for any questions about the accident? It's always best to ask them when they first wake so that they don't forget." Officer Moore walked over to the end of the bed, pulling out her notepad from the pocket of her shirt.

"Well," Kaitlyn replied. "I'm afraid he won't remember anything that happened."

"Why do you say that?"

Kaitlyn stood and motioned for Moore to follow her outside the room. Once outside in the hall, Kaitlyn closed the door behind them. “Since he woke this morning, he hasn’t been able to remember anything…” she paused. “He doesn’t remember me or that I’m his wife.”

Officer Moore studied Kaitlyn’s face as if waiting for her to say she was joking, but she could tell that she clearly wasn’t. Before Moore could say anything, Kaitlyn spoke again.

“The doctor says he is suffering from head trauma, and he may or may not recall the events of the crash or parts of his life,” Kaitlyn said. “The doctor can’t tell me if this will be a permanent thing. He may in time start remembering, but we won’t know for sure.” Kaitlyn looked down at the floor. “He didn’t know his name—or mine, for that matter.”

“This is terrible. I’m so sorry to hear that.”

Kaitlyn nodded.

“This must be very hard on you.”

Kaitlyn nodded again; her body started to tremble.

Moore reached out her hand and squeezed Kaitlyn’s arm. “Is there anything I can do? Maybe if I ask him some questions he’ll remember something? Do you care if I ask him? I’m sure you’d like to know what happened? What caused the accident?” Moore asked, hoping not to sound like she was pressuring the woman. “There were ten cars involved in the accident, and we would like to find the underlying cause of this. Two were killed and more than ten injured.” Moore said this hoping to get some kind of reaction from the woman.

Maybe she was dismayed and needed time to process the information.

"Oh my God!" Kaitlyn's hand flew to her mouth in dismay. "No, please go ahead. I know you have a job to do. Also, you should know that the doctor is releasing him tomorrow to go back home."

"Oh?" Moore replied. She was caught off guard by this piece of information. "Well, he isn't under arrest, and I do have your cell number to call you if I have any farther questions." She didn't want them to leave the state, but what else could she do? Ben Gordon wasn't under arrest. She couldn't keep him here against his will. Not unless she found something on him first, but it wasn't like it was a murder investigation or anything.

"Of course, call me anytime," Kaitlyn replied.

They both went back inside the room. Kaitlyn sat back down in the chair beside the bed, and Moore took her spot at the end of the bed, so she could look at Ben while she asked him questions.

"Hi Ben. My name is Officer Moore. I'm the one who found you in the wreckage. You were trapped under a truck. Do you remember any of that?"

He shook his head.

"Do you recall anything earlier that morning? Where you came from? Where you were headed?"

Again, he shook his head.

"I'm going to name some stuff, and you let me know if you recall anything or if it means something to you," Moore said.

He nodded.

"Do you normally keep your wallet in your back pocket? Or do you place it in the center console where the cup holders are?" She watched as he looked past her, as if thinking hard about what she asked. "Take your time."

He blinked and said, "I'm not sure. Maybe the console."

"That's okay. Kaitlyn, do you have his wallet on you?"

"Yes, of course," she replied, digging inside her purse for it. She pulled it out and handed it to Moore.

"Thank you. Ben, does this wallet look familiar to you? Do you want to hold it, maybe look it over?"

"I don't understand your questions," Kaitlyn asked.

"I'm just trying to trigger his memory. Sometimes if a person holds an object it will help jolt something loose."

Kaitlyn nodded.

Officer Moore handed him the wallet, watching as he turned it over and read the inscription and looked over at Kaitlyn. He then opened the wallet and looked at the things inside. A couple of credit cards, his driver's license, nothing else. He had no pictures, which Officer Moore had found odd, but not uncommon. "Anything coming to you?"

He didn't answer right away, as if he needed to find the words within himself, then said, "A man hitting a semi-truck."

18

Later that day after Officer Moore had left, Kaitlyn felt Ben's eyes on her. She watched him look at the necklace around her neck. She touched it, smoothing her fingers over the cut of the diamonds. Her thoughts automatically went back to the day he had given her the heart-shaped blue diamond necklace. When Ben had returned home that night from being out of town, he presented her with the necklace. All the gifts that he gave her were breathtaking and beautiful. The necklace looked expensive, which didn't surprise her. He always seemed to buy the most expensive jewelry for her. She was sure that it was another gift from him to make up for the fight that they had before he left when he tried to strangle her.

She wanted to confront him about the envelope that she had found in the locked drawer but thought better of it, even though what he had done made her furious. She knew he would change it all around and get upset and then he'd hit her for starting a fight after he'd given her something nice and he had just returned home. Then the thought of the baby came into her mind, and she shut her mouth and threw away the thoughts to protect her unborn child. She couldn't risk him hitting her in the stomach.

She could visualize the scene playing out as if it had happened because the truth was, the fights always ended the same. She would get punched and end up cleaning up after he'd wrecked the house. She knew he'd be upset with her at first, but then his behavior would change, and he would act different, almost protective. "Why were you snooping around in the office?" he would question her. As much as she would want to say something and argue with him, she knew better. She knew it wouldn't end well. He would change back to the Ben she knew all too well. Yelling and screaming at her to mind her own stupid business and keep out of his things. Then he would hit her and walk away from her, leaving her bleeding on the floor. Not only would she have to clean herself up, but she'd have to make sure not one speck of blood was left of the floor or furniture.

Besides, if you were wanting to keep something from someone, whether a gift or even papers, you'd hide it where they wouldn't look or find them. A locked drawer in a desk that was used by another person wouldn't be the smartest place to hide something. Her thoughts were driving her insane. She didn't even have feelings for this man lying in the bed in front of her. If anything, this game of trying to let everyone see that she cared and loved this man was sickening. She didn't care about him. She actually wished he had died in the accident instead of forgetting who he was. It would make life so much better, wouldn't it?

She heard his voice through the haze of her thoughts and blinked several times before seeing his face come into view. She smiled over at him lying in the bed, fragile and helpless. This made her fill up with delight inside, like a child getting a toy that they've been wanting for a long time. The roles were changed, and she was now the caretaker. She smiled.

"Hi," he whispered.

"Hi," she said back. "Do you need anything? Water? Soda?" she asked. *Maybe some morphine to put you to sleep?*

He slowly shook his head, wincing at the pain.

She saw his expression and smiled inside but didn't say anything. "Are you warm enough?" Kaitlyn asked. Why was she being so finicky with him? Ben didn't like to be babied. He usually was the one taking care of her. Not that she needed to be taken care of.

"Yes, I'm fine," he replied.

"So…" she stressed. "Is there anything you'd like to know about me? About us?" Her eyes fell from his face to the sheet over his body. She knew she should keep eye contact with him. Ben hated it when she didn't look him in the eyes.

"How long have we been together? Been married?" he asked.

She looked up and into his eyes when he spoke. She couldn't remember his eyes being as blue as they were at this moment. Was it the lighting in the room? She wasn't sure. She swallowed before answering. "We met in our second year of college at Lewis University. We ran into each other and one thing led to another. We've been together ever since," she said, as hate filled her heart. Those were the days when he didn't hit her. He had showed her nothing but love and respect. She knew now that it was his plan all along. To reel her in and then show her who he really was.

"What are you thinking about?" he asked.

"The day we met."

"Can you tell me about it?" he asked.

She smiled and took a sip of water and spoke. "It was Junior year. I was running late to my first class, and out of nowhere I bumped into you. My books went flying everywhere. You were so kind to help me gather them in the pouring rain." She laughed. "By the time we were done, we were soaked to the bone. I skipped my first class and we went and got hot chocolate in the cafeteria. Luckily my next class wasn't until ten. So we sat in the corner of the room, talking and drinking our hot chocolates." She sipped her water again before placing the glass down by her lap.

She looked up and saw him watching her again, his blue eyes looking into hers. Her heart swelled as if wanting to love him as if it were the first time they had met. She would never forget the past four years. She would never forgive him for all that he had done to her. Did he honestly think she would forget? Feel sorry for him? Then another thought came to her—was he playing a game? Did he really not remember? Or was this a trick to get her to stay? To care for him?

19

Nine Years Earlier

Adam noticed that none of the seats on the plane were occupied, maybe because the airline officials let military board first, but then again, he always seemed to be the first at everything. Maybe that's why his Sergeant choose him when it came to certain tactics.

Adam made his way down the aisle and took his seat by the window. He was glad he got a window seat because that way he could look out as they were taking off. He could watch from the sky how the ground below seemed to get smaller and farther away from him and almost disappear.

He'd only been on a plane one other time and that was when he'd flown from Ohio to Florida for boot camp. When he had landed in Deland, Florida, he had almost missed the transportation bus that was to take him to the Army base. He hadn't known where to go after the plane had landed and all the passengers got off. He had never been inside an airport before. It didn't occur to him that he should follow the other military officials who had taken a shuttle train from one part of the airport to the other where the parking and baggage claim area was. He had made it to the bus one minute before it was about to leave the airport bound for the Deland Army base.

His parents weren't much into traveling—well, except for his father, who seemed to pick up after Adam graduated a month ago from high school and moved to the Carolinas with his new wife. He had thought that his father would never leave Ohio, but apparently, he didn't know him all that well. His parents never went out of the state of Ohio for a vacation because his mother said that there wasn't anything out there to see. Everything Adam needed was right there in their hometown in Edon, Ohio. Maybe that's why he had decided to join the Army, so he could see the world.

Once the passengers were on the plane, they were off to Chicago, Illinois. He had eight months of training there and then he'd be shipped overseas for God knows how long. It all depended on the amount of time it took to find the refugees and what his Sergeant ordered them to do in Afghanistan.

He was glad that basic training was over because most nights he didn't get more than two hours of sleep. The drill sergeant loved to wake them up and have them running ten to twenty miles at night and then another twenty more miles in the hot, smoldering sun.

In Adam's free time, not that he had a lot of that in the Army, he liked to work out and run even more miles. He even made time to write home to his mother, who he knew was probably lonely since he'd left home. If he'd known that his father was going to pick up and leave them, he wouldn't have joined the military half way through his senior year.

After the plane landed in Chicago and all the passengers exited the plane, he followed them off and toward the baggage claim. He wouldn't get lost again, although all the airports seemed to be different. Chicago, O'Hare, appeared larger because there was no shuttle like in Deland. He walked from the terminal to the baggage claim, which took him under the road where the planes drove and then back up to solid ground.

After he gathered his surplus duffel bag, he headed outside and took a taxi to the U.S Army Department of Defense, where he'd be working for the next eight months. He checked in with his Commanding Officer and was then escorted to the room where he'd be staying.

There was no one else in the room so Adam unpacked, stowing his things away in their proper places. He made sure that his bed was pristine. He had always been neat and tidy before he joined the Army, maybe that's why he seemed to fit in so well. Besides, he didn't want his new Commanding Officer to find anything wrong after he'd just arrived. He changed into his running clothes and headed outside. He loved to run; it helped him to cope with life and relieve any stress he may have, which he didn't. The first day was a free-day to do whatever he wanted. Adam would make his way around the base and memorize where everything was.

That evening, Adam and some of the other recruits went off base. One of the guys in his squad had heard about a party at some college nearby. He wasn't a partier like some of the guys he'd met, but he did enjoy the scenery and having a couple of beers to relax.

The music was loud, not that it was uncommon at a party, but he also hadn't been to one since he finished high school. The guys went in their own direction, leaving Adam standing alone. He walked around outside and found where the kegs were set up and grabbed a plastic cup.

"Hey," a guy said from across the table. "Haven't seen you around here before."

"No," Adam replied as he filled his cup.

"Are you from around here?"

"Nope."

"Not much for words, are you?"

"Didn't know I had to introduce myself to you," Adam replied. He wasn't usually rude or even a hard ass when he was around other people. He just hated when people, especially guys, acted tough and needed to know everything. Adam hadn't done anything wrong except for coming to a party with the guys from his barracks. He just wanted to relax and watch people get drunk and let loose.

"I'm assuming that you're from the Army base."

Adam nodded.

"Yeah, the haircut gave it away."

Adam automatically ran a hand over his head, feeling the soft hairs against his hand. Yes, it was probably a dead giveaway that he was in the military. "What year are you in?"

Adam asked, changing the subject. He decided to just be social. He was a guest at someone's party.

"Junior," the guy said, taking a drink from his cup. "You got a name?"

"Adam. You?"

"Bryan."

Adam held out his hand for Bryan to shake. "It's nice to meet you, Bryan."

"Same," Bryan replied.

The two of them talked for several minutes before Adam saw a beautiful girl walking toward them, most likely getting herself a drink. She was with a couple of other girls. They were giggling at something one of the girls said. He stepped back away from the keg so that they could get themselves some beer.

He watched as the girl with brunette hair laughed, but in a shy way. He could tell that she was a person who didn't get out much and probably kept to herself. Her friends had most likely dragged her out too, like the guys in his squad had done. He listened as they talked about nothing in particular.

"Amanda are you going to dance?" asked one of the girls.

"Yeah, sure, maybe after I get a couple of drinks in me," Amanda replied. "How about you, Kaitlyn?" Amanda asked.

Her name was Kaitlyn, and she was the prettiest girl he'd ever set his eyes on. Just as he looked over at her, she smiled back at him. He wanted to talk to her, to get to know her, but then he remembered that he was only here for a short time and that getting involved with someone wasn't something he should be doing. Long distance relationships didn't work out when you were in the military. He'd seen it more times than he could count. But what if he just talked to her, just for the night? It would be a nice feeling and a memory he could carry around with him in his time in the Army.

"Sure, I'll dance with you," Kaitlyn replied.

The girls squealed and laughed as if dancing was something funny and they had never done before.

Kaitlyn took the full cup of beer that her friend handed her and stepped away, so she could take a sip without spilling it. Adam kept his eyes on her when she wasn't looking and then quickly looked away when she looked over at him. This went on until the girls walked away, but not before Kaitlyn smiled over at him and joined her friends. She kept looking back over her shoulder as if she wanted him to follow her. He was shy when it came to girls. He had dated a little in high school but focused more on sports and working odd jobs to make money to buy his first car. He had always thought that relationships could wait until he got older and he was more mature.

He finished his beer and refilled his cup before walking around and seeing what was happening elsewhere at the party. He saw a couple of the guys from the base talking to other people and having a good time. He waved and made his way around, heading to where the music was getting louder. Adam went inside the house and stood near a wall at the back of the room. He looked out onto the dance floor that's when he saw her. Kaitlyn was dancing with the same girls that he had seen when they arrived. He stepped closer to get a better look. She must have seen him too because they locked eyes once again. He smiled at her and gave her a little nod, his way of saying hello. She smiled back. And before he knew it, she was walking toward him. His heart beat faster with each step she took toward him. Perspiration formed under his shirt, and he was glad that he wore extra deodorant and threw on some cologne before coming here, unaware that he was about to meet the girl of his dreams.

"Hi, my name's Kaitlyn," she said, smiling up at him.

He swallowed. "Hi, I'm Adam," he replied as the smell of her perfume entered his nose. His legs felt weak. He stepped back and pressed himself against the wall for support.

"Well, Adam, would you care to dance with me?"

"Oh, ah, I don't dance," Adam replied. Which was true. He had never gone to any dances at school, except Prom, but that was different.

"Sure, you do; everyone dances after they've had a few drinks," she giggled.

He could tell that she was already feeling tipsy. He drank down the rest of his beer and placed the cup on the table beside him. She took his hand and dragged him onto the dance floor.

The music changed to a slow song and she wrapped her hands around his neck, looking into his eyes.

"You're not from around here, are you?"

"No, I'm from Ohio."

"What military are you in?"

"How did you know?"

"One, I haven't seen you before. Two, the haircut. Not too many guys around here get a buzz cut just for the hell of it," she laughed.

He nodded. "You from around here?"

"Yeah, I've lived here my whole life. I go to Lewis University, south of here."

"What are you studying?"

"I'm going to be a High School English teacher."

He smiled, thinking about when he's finished with the Army in another three and half years that he was going to go to school to be a teacher. Coincidentally, an English teacher.

"What are you thinking about?" Kaitlyn asked.

"It's just that," he paused, "I plan on being a teacher once I'm done serving my four years in the Army."

"Oh, yeah?" she smiled. "What do you want to teach?"

"English Literature," he yelled over the music that had changed from slow to fast and very loud.

She smiled at him and kissed him hard on the lips.

He kissed her back, pulling her into him, surprised at how good it felt to be kissing her. He had never felt this way with anyone before. His head was spinning with emotions he'd never experienced in his life. The adrenaline raced through his body. The room seemed to get hotter the longer they stood there kissing. He knew if she let go of him that he would fall over from dizziness. They both slowly pulled away from one another, looking into each other's eyes.

"Do you want to go outside and talk?" Adam asked.

She nodded.

He took her hand and left the dance floor. They ventured outside and found a gazebo where they could talk without having to yell. He talked about his childhood and family, mostly his mom, and why he joined the military. "I wanted to go to college but couldn't afford it," he said to her.

"What do you do in the Army?"

"Special Forces."

"Wow, really?"

"Yes. Does that scare you?"

"No, I'm trying to picture you as an English teacher after you've been working with weapons. Almost like a bad-ass teacher," she laughed. "Macho man teacher. Sounds hot," she giggled.

He laughed along with her and then leaned in and kissed her again. She took his every breath away, making him feel like he was floating, and she was the angel carrying him.

From that day on, Kaitlyn and Adam spent almost every day together. On warm days, they spent time at the beach and took walks in Grant Park. They even strolled around Lincoln Park Zoo looking at all the animals. In the eight months that Adam was stationed in Chicago, he had spent all his free time with Kaitlyn. They went to parties together. He even took her to the movies and bought her expensive dinners, although she had protested that he didn't have to take her to those kinds of places. She was fine with inexpensive meals. And most of all, he didn't need to impress her. She loved him for who he was, not for what he could give her, she told him, and it deepened his love for her.

Since the night of the party, he had fallen in love with her. He knew he was leaving soon, but he couldn't help loving her with everything that he had. She was everything he'd always wanted in a woman. He hadn't expected to find her so soon, but he also wasn't ready to lose her. He had extended his stay to ten months. He knew it would only last so long, and he would have to leave her behind. They exchanged rings as a token of their love for one another.

He knew there was no way he could be with her and be in another country at the same time, but he didn't want to lose her. He knew of others at the base who had used Skype and Facetime to see their loved ones, but he couldn't, could he? He had never felt this way and it scared him to death. What if he turned out to be like his dad and after twenty years, left without thinking twice? No, he knew he wasn't anything like his father. Love like this only came around once in a lifetime.

He didn't want to lose her and would do everything to keep her.

Two days before he was to leave, Adam sat on his cot lacing his boots. It was breaking his heart to say goodbye, for how long, he didn't know. She had her life here in Chicago, and he had three more years to serve in the Army. In just two days he was being sent out of the country not knowing *when* or *if* he'd return to the states because it had occurred to him that he could get killed over there and Kaitlyn would never know. He knew in his heart that he'd never forget about her. She would always have a place in his heart because she had all of his heart.

20

Seven Years Earlier

Ben sat at the base of an oak tree watching her laugh with her friends. Her name was Kaitlyn and he had been watching her for the past year. Well, in all truth, since he had seen her with that Adam guy at the party when Freshman year started. He knew he had to get them away from each other, but Adam had made it easy when he was deployed to Afghanistan.

Ben had followed Kaitlyn and retrieved her mail once she dropped it off at the office in the school building. Every day for several months, Ben took Adam's letters, only to replace them with one Dear John letter to Kaitlyn. He had kept one of the envelopes and unsealed it and replaced the letter inside, so she could see that it had been shipped from overseas. He watched her fall apart after reading the letter outside on the lawn under the shade of a tree. She was devastated. He wanted to console her, but it wasn't the right time. He had to make sure it was the right time to run into her. He needed her heart to be ready for him, not filled with the love she felt for Adam.

He knew all her classes by eavesdropping as Kaitlyn and her friends walked through the halls going to their next class. He knew where she liked to go after school. Most of the time, she studied by herself in the library three days a week. He sat several tables away, pretending to read as he watched her. The way her eyes moved when she read and the one dimple on her cheek when she smiled—there was just something about her that intrigued him, and he knew he had to have her. He needed to come up with a plan to run into her. Make it seem like she wasn't watching where she was going. He gathered his things and left the building. Tomorrow he would meet her, and she would be his girlfriend and one day his wife.

He wasn't a psychopath who stalked women; no, he loved the control he had with women. He knew it had to do with the way he was raised and not receiving the attention he so desperately needed and wanted when he was a child. The hardest part was letting go when a woman didn't want anything to do with him, but he would do whatever it took to get Kaitlyn to fall in love with him.

His parents weren't together, never married as far as he knew. He didn't even know where his father was and if he were still alive. Ben was not hugged or pampered in any way. He was treated with discipline. He would show the woman he fell in love with that ever-lasting love does exist. The woman he loved would get everything she desired. He would make her love him back, and she would forever do as she was told. His mother had taught him the rules of life and what was needed in a relationship, and he would follow those rules and teach them to the one who stoled his heart.

~ ~ ~

It was an early fall morning as Ben stood beside a tree, rain sprinkling down around him. There wasn't a blue sky in sight, just a layer of gray, which made the atmosphere around him seem depressing. His planned intervention with Kaitlyn wouldn't have been as dramatic if it were sunny.

He spotted Kaitlyn running out of her dorm in a hurry like most mornings, racing to get to her first class. He'd have to change that part of her. Being late was not something he liked. Ben stepped out from behind the tree just as the light rain began to pour and walked toward the sidewalk and into Kaitlyn's path. Her books sailed out of her hands, flying and landing on the wet sidewalk. "I'm so sorry," Ben said. "I'm such a klutz."

Kaitlyn had glanced up and into his blueish-gray eyes. She looked frozen in time, as if she'd seen a ghost, then looked away, gathering her books that were being soaked in the rain. "It's my fault. I was in a hurry and wasn't watching where I was going," she said apologetically. "Shit, I'm already late, and Mr. Herman is going to be pissed."

"Then why don't you just skip class, and we'll go get a hot chocolate and dry off," Ben suggested, smiling. He was good with getting women to do what he wanted.

Kaitlyn gathered the rest of her things and stood, looking at her watch. Rain drizzled down her face; her hair matted on the top of her head. She sighed. "Yeah, I guess. I'm already fifteen minutes late, and my teacher gets upset if you walk into his class after it has started."

"Then it's settled. We'll go to the cafeteria and get ourselves a nice hot cup of cocoa," he replied with his movie star smile.

They walked together and sat in the back of the cafeteria, away from others who were eating their breakfast before they had to go to class. Ben watched as Kaitlyn squeezed the remaining water from her hair and flung it over her shoulder. It didn't matter if her hair was wet or dry or if she didn't have on any makeup, she was captivating and beautiful. She was everything he had hoped, and he would do whatever it took get her to be his. He would mold her into the woman he so desired.

She seemed to hesitate whenever she looked over at him. It almost seemed as if she knew him but couldn't remember from where. Ben knew she'd never seen him before; and why he was here with her now. "So, what is your name?"

"Ben," he replied. He could tell that she was disappointed by his name. Was she hoping that he was Adam? They did look somewhat alike. Their eyes were the same color.

"Ben what? Do you have a last name, Ben?"

"Ben Gordon, and yours is?"

"Kaitlyn Costa. What classes are you taking?"

"Business classes," he replied. "And I'm taking Accounting classes as well. I love numbers and figuring out all the different ways to use them. My mother always said I should be a scientist or something, but science isn't my specialty. Too much involved in science than just numbers. What about yourself?" Ben asked even though he already knew. He piled lies on top of lies as he spoke. His mother had never praised him for anything. To her, he had never done anything good enough and she told him so. He was a disappointment to her.

"I'm studying to be a teacher. An English Literature teacher. I love words and what they portray when you read and write them. I love writing quotes and would like to write my own book someday," she said, smiling before sipping from her cup. "I also want to inspire kids to read and write. Literature is so much more than people think. The words if written correctly can take you to places you've never been before. Worlds that don't exist, like Harry Potter, but in our minds, that world does exist and it's fascinating," Kaitlyn said, playing with the ring on the necklace around her neck.

"I bet you'll be a great teacher," Ben replied. He could see that when she talked about the things she loved most, her eyes lit up. It made her more beautiful than she already was. It made him fall more in love with her than he had ever imagined he'd fall in love with any one person.

"It's something I've always wanted to do since I was a little girl. My parents got me into reading at a very young age. We didn't have a television in the house, so I just read."

Ben laughed, “No television? How could you not have a television?”

“My parents didn’t believe in corrupting one’s mind when there was so much to learn in books.”

Ben nodded although he didn’t agree. He loved television, especially cop shows. “What year are you in?”

“Junior.”

“Same here.”

She looked down at her watch, signifying to him that she was getting ready to leave and head to her next class.

“It was nice meeting you today,” Kaitlyn said as she sat up and began scooting out of the booth they were in. “Sorry that I ran into you again.”

“No, it was my fault. I should’ve been watching where I was going,” he replied. “I hope I didn’t ruin any of your books or homework.”

“Nah, the books will be fine. They’re used books anyway,” she said as she stood, fixing her clothes and then putting her coat on. “Thanks for the hot chocolate. It really was nice of you to buy it for me.”

“It was my pleasure. Will I see you again? Maybe I could take you out for dinner or we could catch a movie sometime?” Ben asked, giving her his killer smile and praying she didn’t say no.

“That would be nice. I’d like that. Finals are coming up, so how about after that? Like during our winter break?”

"I'll give you a call."

"But you don't have my number."

"I was hoping that you'd give it to me," he smiled.

She smiled back. "Maybe I was waiting for you to give me your number," she said.

He grabbed a napkin from the dispenser on the table and wrote down his number and handed it to her. "I'll be waiting," he said.

She smiled back at him as she took the napkin with his phone number on it and walked away.

Ben couldn't stop smiling. She was everything he had always wanted. Not only was she beautiful and smart, but she wanted to see him again. His plan was working after all. He was so afraid that he would scare her off, not that he did or said anything to her that would. He was sure if she ever found out about him watching her, or that he had switched the letters between her and Adam, she would hate him forever. He couldn't have that happen. He wouldn't lose her after just getting her. No, this one was the woman for him, and he would do whatever was necessary to keep her.

21

Three Days after the Accident

Leah finished her rounds and went down to the second floor to spend some time with the unknown man before heading out for lunch. Without help from Sergeant Miles, she was at a dead end and would have to start her own search. An idea formed inside her head: she should find out more about the accident. Maybe there were things she didn't know. Would Sergeant Miles tell her what she wanted to know? Would he let her see the file, so she could see if there was something that could help her? She didn't know these answers and would have to find out for herself.

She climbed out of the elevator and walked toward the unknown man's room. She turned the knob and pushed the door open. As she walked into the room, she felt that something was wrong. When the bed came into view she noticed that there was no one in the bed. In fact, the bed was freshly made. The room looked as if no one had even been in it at all. She turned, rushed back out the door and toward the nurse's station.

"Excuse me," Leah asked. "Where did the man go that was in room 219? He was just here earlier.".

"Dr. Amal is ordering the withdrawal of care," the nurse replied. "I'm not sure if it's been done already, but you'd have to talk to the doctor."

Leah screeched in horror. "What! He had no right to make that call with my patient."

"Actually," the redheaded nurse with freckles that covered her entire face said, "he wasn't your patient. I understand that you've been visiting with him and wanted to find his family, but sometimes you just can't play God."

"I wasn't playing God! That man deserved to say goodbye to his loved ones," Leah shot back.

"And how would he be able to do that when he's brain-dead?"

Leah huffed, feeling defeated. "I meant that… that his family would want to say goodbye to him and now they can't." Leah held back the tears forming behind her eyes. She couldn't allow herself to fall apart in front of this person she didn't know.

"I'm so sorry. I know how hard you've been working to locate them, but there's nothing you could've done," the nurse said sympathetically as she placed her hand on Leah's.

Leah nodded, but said nothing. She inhaled, turned and walked away. She could still find his family, right? Would she be considered foolish if she continued to look for them? Maybe, maybe not, but she couldn't give up like she did with her real mom. No, she would start talking to people from the scene. They could help her find the truth, but she wasn't a police officer; she was a nurse with no training on how to find the people that were in the accident.

Leah grabbed her things from her locker and headed out the door to her car. There were other police stations in the area. If they couldn't help her then she'd go to Edon for answers. Someone there would have to have the answers, right? She knew that there were other hospitals that had taken people from the accident; someone had to know something.

As she made her way to her car she stopped short, noticing Dr. Amal getting out of his fancy, expensive car. She knew better than to say anything to him; besides, she was still fuming about what he did or was about to do. Speaking to him now would only make things worse between them and she could lose her job. She should just pretend that she hadn't noticed him and get in her car and drive away, but she couldn't. She had to say something to him. She wanted to say something to him. Yet, she didn't want to lose her job over something like this. If she let the words out of her mouth that he was a complete asshole who didn't give two shits about any of his patients and that he was a heartless doctor who shouldn't be a doctor if he didn't care about saving them...yeah, she couldn't say that to him, even if it were the truth.

She squeezed her eyes closed and opened them, looking in the direction she saw Dr. Amal. He was gone. She twirled around, looking frantically for him, but didn't see him anywhere. Had she imagined it was him? That he was there? She didn't know for sure, but out of nowhere a thought came to her. She turned back toward the hospital and went inside, taking the elevator down to the basement where the morgue was located.

She had to be sure thebrain-dead man wasn't down here. Where else would he be? If Dr. Amal had requested the withdrawal of care then he'd have to be down here until he was taken to wherever he was going to be buried, right? Yes, she was sure of it. Besides, she'd been through this when her father died. Granted, it was a different case. He wasn't brain-dead like this guy was, but still she knew that once they died, they were taken to the basement to prepare them for burial—or was that the funeral home's job? She wasn't sure.

She stood outside the door, her hand raised and ready to knock, or maybe she should ring the bell that was on the wall. Changing her mind, she rang the bell and stood back, waiting for someone to let her in.

A tall middle-aged man with bony shoulders, long black hair, and thick glasses opened the door. "Yes?" he asked.

Leah swallowed, holding up her nurse's badge. "Yes, hi, I'm sorry to bother you, but I'm looking for a man that was brought down here sometime today or even last night."

"Lady, I got five guys down here and three women. If you want to take a look and see if one of these is your guy, be my guest," he said as he stepped back to let her in.

She nodded and stepped into the room. She was thankful that she was a nurse because the stench down here could knock you on your ass or have you running to the sink.

The door closed behind the tall man as he motioned around her and walked to where two of the men were lying on the table waiting to be cut open. He didn't ask her, nor did he hesitate before pulling the sheet back for her to see if it was the man she was looking for.

She shook her head.

He moved to the other body and did the same thing.

Not her patient either.

The man walked over to the wall and pulled on the handle and the drawer opened. Leah stood on the other side as he pulled back the sheet.

22

Ben turned but didn't see Kaitlyn anywhere. His leg was no longer in the harness that hung from the ceiling, but now propped up on two pillows to keep the swelling down as much as possible. The doctor had said that he would be released tomorrow, that he could go home with his wife, Kaitlyn.

Just the thought of it made him smile. He couldn't get her out of his mind since he opened his eyes and saw her. There was just something about her, a longing of some sort that he couldn't figure out. It was like he'd known her forever but couldn't remember all the details. It was a stupid thought, really, because if he was married to her, of course he would and should feel something for her. Something that he could recognize or picture. They had been married for...well, he couldn't remember how long she said they were married. The door to the room opened and Kaitlyn came walking in. He smiled the moment he saw her, and she gave him a soft smile back.

"You're awake," she said.

He nodded. He felt almost shy around her, but at the same time he didn't. Would he ever be comfortable the moment she walked into a room? Maybe it was because she was so beautiful and how her eyes sparkled when she smiled at people.

She walked toward the bed, placing her cup of hot coffee down on the nightstand. She then leaned over and kissed him on his lips as if she'd done it a million times before. Wouldn't he remember those lips touching his? God, this having no recollection of his past was torture.

Kaitlyn sat down in the chair beside him, holding his hand. He didn't want her to let go. He wanted to hold onto her forever. Did she feel the same since he was in an accident and nearly died? He couldn't tell. He didn't know how to read her. He could tell she wasn't herself, that something was bothering her.

"I have something that I need to tell you," she said.

For a second, he felt scared. Had the doctor said something to her? Something bad? Was he never going to get better? Never remember his life with her? He didn't want to ask, but his mouth opened, and he spoke. "What is it?"

She squeezed his hand a little before speaking. "I'm afraid you may never remember our life together," she said.

He grabbed his head, squeezing his eyes closed. The pain at times was excruciating. Was there something wrong with him and she didn't want to tell him that he was dying?

"Ben, are you okay? Should I get a nurse?" Kaitlyn said, sounding panicked. She stood from her chair, leaning over him. She touched his head, her smooth hands against his cheek.

"No, I'm fine, really, I am." No, he wasn't, but he didn't want her to leave his side. He needed her but didn't know why. He felt absent without her near him. The pain slowly disappeared. Was it caused by his sudden thoughts of never remembering her? This he didn't know but would try and remember to ask the doctor.

She nodded. "Okay, would you like some water?"

"Yes, please. Thank you."

She looked at him with a puzzled stare for several seconds before she grabbed the pitcher sitting next to her. She poured him a glass of water and handed it to him. He watched her as he drank from the glass. He could tell something about her had changed. Had he said something wrong? It had to be about his head hurting. Yes, of course. Women were fragile. They get upset about the smallest things, especially when someone they love is hurt. He searched his brain on what he was doing days, even months ago. Nothing. He drew a blank. God, it was making his head hurt worse thinking about everything going on around him.

"It's fine," she said. "Things will come back to you in time. Just like the doctor said. It's too soon, and you shouldn't try so hard. You shouldn't force yourself to remember," she smiled slightly.

He could tell she was hurt by what he'd said, and he wanted to make it better. He wanted to remember their life together and what it was like to love her. Hopefully, when he returned to their home wherever that was, everything would come flooding back inside him and he would be the man she had married. But that was the thing—he didn't know what kind of man he was with her. Did they make love every night or a few times a week? Did they have friends that they hung out with? Go for walks or just stay inside and enjoy each other's company? He didn't know any of this. He didn't know anything about her, and it made his head ache.

He wanted to remember what it felt like to touch her body. To kiss her lips. To love her the way she deserved to be loved. He wondered about their life together. If they argued or enjoyed every minute with one another. Nothing came to him, and it felt like his brain was being tortured in a vise.

"Was I a good husband?" he asked, but the shocked expression on her face told him all he needed to know.

23

After leaving Edon Hospital yesterday, Officer Moore couldn't get what Ben said out of her mind. She had decided that she would sleep on the information for the night and see what the next morning would bring her.

Sitting at the kitchen table, she was able to put together what he was trying to tell her. She left the house and drove straight to the station on a quest to find the truth. She knew exactly what Ben Gordon meant when he said *man hitting semi-truck*. She couldn't get him to answer any more questions after that or about what he had said and possibly saw. He had closed like a turtle in a shell.

The minute she arrived at the station she saw Woods sitting at his desk. "Hey, Woods, have you seen the file on the man that hit the semi-truck on the turnpike?" Moore asked as she walked to her desk and started scanning through the files piled on top. She had just cleared her desk the other night; where did all these files come from? She didn't know or even have the time right now to figure it out, but she was sure that the other guys in the office probably placed them there, so they didn't have to work on them.

"Uh, yeah. I think Weaver has it. Why?"

"I might have a breakthrough in the accident." *Or it might be nothing*, her mind spat at her. *Don't go getting your hopes up and then fall on your ass.* Her mind was always trying to make her think that she wasn't good enough around these guys that she worked with. No one knew how hard it was to work with men who acted like chauvinistic pigs, thinking they were better—well, all but Officer Woods. He respected Moore and how hard she worked. Maybe that's why she liked him the way she did.

"What'd you find?" Woods asked as he stood beside her.

She could feel the warmth of his body next to her. The smell of his Gucci cologne entered her nostrils, making her feel light on her feet. She swallowed before speaking. "Well, I was at Edon Hospital yesterday checking in on the man from the accident, Ben Gordon." She needed to step away from him because she wasn't sure if she could control herself at that moment; besides she had work to do and needed to focus on the case. Woods standing there looking so sizzling hot and smelling so delicious she could eat him up wasn't helping her find what she was looking for.

Woods nodded.

Moore continued, "He said that he recalls a man hitting a semi-truck but said nothing more. I couldn't get him to tell me if he knew the guy or if he just saw it happen," she frowned and continued looking for the file on her desk but didn't find it and moved to the desk behind her.

"That's Weaver's desk," Woods said.

"Yeah and?" Moore said as she continued her search. "Found it!" she cheered as if she won a prize, holding the file in the air. She turned back around and sat down in the chair at her desk. She opened the file and saw a photo of the man. It was an older photo because she knew from the scene that his face was no longer recognizable. She read over his identification card. His name was Scott Wards. He lived on Kansas Street in Franklin. He was twenty-eight years old. "What a shame," Moore mumbled.

"What?" Woods questioned.

"The kid was only twenty-eight years old."

"That's not a kid."

"Well, to me he was. He died too young if you ask me." Moore scanned through the file but didn't find anything else that could help her. He had no alcohol in his blood, nor were there drugs in his system. He died of natural causes. "Guess I'll need to take a drive over to his house and see if I can talk to his family. Maybe one of them knows something."

"Maybe they'll know this Ben Gordon guy," Woods noted.

"Doubtful," Moore replied.

"Why's that?"

"Ben Gordon is from Illinois. He was just passing through, and you know how it ended."

Woods nodded. "Do you want some company? There's nothing going on here at the station. Could sure use some fresh air."

Officer Moore looked up and into Woods' eyes. It did sound like a good idea and she loved his company. "Let's go then," she said as she stood, closing the file, but also taking it and the one she had on Ben Gordon with her.

They both piled into the SUV and headed in the direction of Scott Wards' house. The sun that was out when she left home was replaced by dark gray clouds releasing a light drizzle. Moore hadn't listened to the news this morning, so she had no idea what the weather was going to be like. She had too much on her mind right now to think about what was happening outside in the town of Edon.

Moore made a right and then turned left two streets down. She knew her roads, mostly because she'd lived here her whole life. Edon wasn't huge by any stretch of the imagination, but it was big enough for six thousand or more residents to live in. In some areas, the houses were close together and in others, like her neighborhood, they were farther apart.

One block later, she crossed over into the town of Franklin and parked across the street from Scott's house. There was a car in the driveway, but that didn't mean anything. The car could've belonged to Scott since he'd most likely been on a motorcycle. The records hadn't said anything about him being married or anything, but that didn't mean he didn't have a girlfriend or parents that lived with him.

"You okay, Moore?" Woods asked.

Moore nodded, "Yes, I'm fine, just nervous is all." This was a big deal to her. There had never been a huge investigation case in Edon before. She didn't want to go messing things up and have the other guys at the station laughing at her.

"What do you have to be nervous about? You didn't do anything wrong."

"I know that," Moore said as she gave Woods a look of foolishness. He quickly looked away. "Hey," she said, touching his large brown hand that was lying on the seat next to her. "I didn't mean anything by that." She wanted to smack herself in the head for her actions. She really liked Woods and now she was screwing everything up because she didn't think before she spoke. She really needed to watch how she portrayed herself around others, especially Woods, if she wanted any kind of relationship with him. Days ago, she didn't want to think about having a boyfriend-girlfriend relationship with Woods, but she had let her guard down and allowed her feelings to surface. Not that it was a bad thing. Woods was a terrific guy, but that was the problem. She knew he was too good for her and wondered why and what he saw in her. He was outgoing and handsome. He was funny and always had things to talk about. She loved the way he laughed and made her feel. She was funny too, wasn't she?

"Sometimes you can be a real ass, Moore." Woods opened his door, climbed out and walked to the front of the vehicle.

Moore sat watching him through the windshield, knowing that she had hurt his feelings and hadn't realized how self-conscious he seemed to be. He was a big old muscular teddy bear to her. She laughed inside. *I'm an ass?* She blew out a breath. She'd have to fix this between them before she lost him for good. This was why she didn't date men at work. She pushed open the heavy door, climbed out, and slammed it shut. "Let's do this," Moore said.

Moore took the lead and crossed the street. They walked up the sidewalk to the front door of the house. Moore looked around the porch. The furniture was fairly new, no signs of mold on the cushioned chairs. There were planters filled with vibrant flowers and hanging baskets overflowing with philodendron cordatum vines along the roof of the porch. Moore touched the soil, revealing what she already knew. The flowers had been watered recently. Besides the day of the accident, there had been no rain until the rain drops that had fallen minutes ago, but there was no way the rain had watered these pots with the overhang of the roof. She turned and observed the house. The paint looked fresh, maybe within the last year or two. There were no piled-up newspapers or mail overflowing in the mailbox next to the door. She saw all the signs of someone living here after the accident.

She turned and scoped out the neighborhood and saw nothing out of the ordinary. Nothing but a well-kept community. Moore turned back around and rang the doorbell. She could hear the chime of the bell throughout the house.

"Maybe no one's home," Woods suggested.

"Let's give it a minute," Officer Moore replied without sounding, once again, too demanding. "They could be coming from upstairs or from the shower." After another minute or two, Moore rang the bell and knocked on the door at the same time. The sound echoed loud around them. After a few seconds, she heard someone call out.

"Just a minute. I'm coming, I'm coming," the female voice said.

The deadbolt turned, and the door creaked open. In the doorway stood an elderly woman, probably nearing her eighties. "Can I help you?" she asked in a shaky voice. Her hair was untidy as if she'd just woken up.

Moore could tell the woman looked afraid. How often did two black people show up on a white person's porch? Not often, she was sure. Moore nodded and cleared her throat. "Good morning, ma'am, sorry to have bothered you. My name is Officer Moore." She flashed her badge for the woman to see. "I'm with the Edon Police Department and this here is my partner Officer Woods," Moore said as she tilted her head toward Woods. She could see a slight smile surface. The corners of Woods' lips turned upward.

"What can I help you with?" the woman asked, looking more relaxed.

"Has anyone been here to talk to you recently, say in the past day or two?"

The woman shook her head. "What's this about?"

"Are you related to Scott Wards?"

"Well, yes. He's my grandson."

"I'm sorry, but is it possible we could come in and speak to you for a few minutes?" Moore asked.

"Sure, is everything all right? Has anything happened to him?" The old woman stepped back to let them in.

Both Moore and Woods looked at each other before they stepped inside, waiting as the woman closed the door behind them. The old woman took the lead, wrapping the ties of her robe around her thin waist, and slowly walking into the living room to sit down on the sofa.

"Please have a seat," the elderly woman offered. "Would you like something to drink or eat?"

"Thank you so much for your kindness, but we're fine," Moore said. She'd never had to tell anyone that their child or grandchild had died.

Woods sat first, then Moore beside him. Moore opened the file and took out the photo of Scott. "Is this your grandson?"

The old lady took the photo and stared at it for a few seconds then nodded. “Is everything all right?” she asked again. “He hasn’t gotten himself into any trouble, has he? I keep telling him to be careful, but you know how kids don’t want to listen to what you say. Ever since he was a teenager he was always getting into some kind of trouble. Thank the good Lord he joined the Army and made something of himself,” the woman said. “They don’t want to listen about when you were a kid and how things used to be,” the old woman rambled on, then shook her head, handing back the photo. “What has he done?”

Moore swallowed. “Has anyone been here to talk to you at all in the past couple of days?”

“Um, I’m not sure. Maybe if I think hard enough I can recall,” the elderly lady said. She looked away and then back at Moore and Woods sitting in front of her. “Oh, I’m so rude. Could I offer you anything to drink or eat?”

Moore and Woods looked at each other and then back at the elderly lady. “No, thank you, we’re fine,” Moore replied then asked the lady again about anyone coming to talk to her.

“Come talk to me? Why would someone come see me?”

Moore took in a breath and then spoke. “Ma’am, I’m afraid there’s been an accident. Did anyone stop by from the police department?”

"Police? Let me think…oh, yeah, I think he said his name was Officer Cleaver, but I'm not certain. I can't recall much these days, you know. Getting older has its downfalls."

"It sure does," Moore replied as she looked from the woman to Officer Woods, who was sitting skin to skin next to her. Moore cleared her throat. "Do you mean Officer Weaver?"

"Oh, yes, Weaver," the woman corrected herself as she nodded her head.

"Did this Officer Weaver say anything to you? Like why he came to see you?"

"I'm not sure," the elder woman answered, looking confused. "What's this about?"

"Well, the reason we're here is because… Well, I'm afraid your grandson Scott was in an accident."

"Oh, no." The woman's hand flew to her mouth.

"I'm afraid he didn't make it. I'm so sorry," Officer Moore said. "Is there anyone I can call for you? Do you need someone to stay with you?"

"There isn't anyone else. He's my only grandson. My only family."

"His parents?" Woods asked.

The old lady shook her head. "They both died in the plane crash on 9/11. Sad really, both dying the way they did. Scott was staying with me when it happened. Poor boy was only eleven when they died." The woman frowned. "I think that's why he joined the military. Did you know he was in the Army?"

Moore nodded. She had read the file before they came here. "Any friends who hung out with Scott?" Moore asked.

The woman started to shake her head, then stopped. "Yes," she said, placing her hand to her face again, then pointing a finger at Moore. "He has a friend he knew from the Army he still hangs out with and goes riding with. I think, oh, what was his name again. Adam. I think his name is Adam. Yeah, that sounds about right."

"Does this Adam friend have a last name?" Moore knew of an Adam, but what were the chances that it was the same Adam Moore knew from Edon? There had to be several Adams around with that name, right?

The woman shook her head. "Don't recall his last name. Was Scott on a bike?"

"Bike?" Officer Moore questioned. "Like motorcycle?"

"Yes. Adam and Scott were always riding their motorcycles wherever they went. I told them both that they should wear helmets, you know. Just in case they're ever in an accident."

Moore knew that no helmet would have saved Scott.

"He may have been riding with him. Did you talk to him? He'd be able to tell you more about Scott since they hang out all the time."

"Do you mean Adam?"

"Yes."

"Do you happen to have a photo of Adam?" Moore asked.

"No, I was never one to take pictures of Scott and his friends."

"No yearbook? Anything?"

"No, we couldn't afford those things. Did you know they wanted sixty dollars for one of those books? For what? To sit on your shelf and never open," the woman spat. "I love memories, but I ain't spending sixty bucks on one," the woman said in disgust.

"Okay, well, if there's anything else you can think of," Moore said, handing the woman one of her cards, "just give me a call." Moore knew the woman was probably lonely, but she couldn't sit here talking about things that weren't connected to the case.

"Do you know what hospital he went to?" the woman asked. "My grandson, Scott. I'll need to make arrangements for the funeral," the lady stated.

"He was taken to Edon Hospital. You can call them, and they'll get you in touch with the right person."

"Oh, thank you. I greatly appreciate you coming to my house," the woman said. "You're so kind."

"It's our job, ma'am," Woods replied, nodding his head toward the woman.

They all stood at the same time and headed toward the door. Officer Woods reached out and pulled open the door, sunlight pouring in at their feet. The dark clouds had sailed away, bringing out the warm sun. Officer Moore followed Woods out onto the front porch. Moore turned, asking two more questions. "For my records, what is your full name? And did you or Scott know anyone by the name of a Ben Gordon?"

The woman replied, "My name is Gilda Wards. I'm afraid I don't know anyone by that name. I haven't heard Scott mention anyone by the name of Ben Gordon."

"Okay, well, thank you for your time, and again, I'm so sorry for your loss," Moore said and went down the stairs and walked toward her vehicle where Woods was waiting for her. She climbed into the truck and sat, staring out the windshield. She recalled the moment she arrived at the scene that there were two motorcycles. So where and who was this Adam?

"Are you okay, Moore?"

She cleared her throat and turned toward Woods. "Yes, sorry, I'm fine. Just sad to know that she doesn't have anyone else now that her grandson has died." Once the words were out, she instantly thought of herself and how lonely she had been since her father passed away a couple of years ago.

"I'm sure she'll be fine. She seemed okay when you told her."

"I know, but some people are good at holding it in until they're alone, and it scares me that she has these absentminded moments." She knew that the lady was most likely suffering from an early onset of Alzheimer's and that being alone now—well, that seemed frightening to Moore. What if something happened to her?

Moore decided at that moment she'd check in on her from time to time and make sure she was all right. She hoped that one day she didn't end up like this woman, living all alone with no family or man to keep her company. She knew all too well because she was that kind of person. At work, she had to look and be tough around the other guys, but at home it was just her and no one around to see her cry.

Moore started the truck and drove around the block, heading back in the direction of the station. She'd see if she could find out any information on this Adam guy and what hospital he was at, if any.

24

After Leah looked at the last remaining bodies in the morgue she was confused. None of the bodies were her brain-dead patient. “If he isn’t here, then where did Dr. Amal send the body?” she whispered to herself as she headed toward the elevator. When the doors opened to the lobby, sunlight shone through the skylights, lighting up the enormous room. The drizzling rain from this morning had departed, leaving nothing but sunshine.

Her eyes crept along the wall of the lobby and fell upon the clock. It was past her lunch break now and she would need to get back to work. Before the doors to the elevator closed, four more people climbed inside. The doors shut, and she hit the number five.

By the time she reached the fifth floor, there was no one left inside the elevator. She was alone to think about the brain-dead patient and where he could be. She had no idea and knew that the nurse wouldn’t have lied about Dr. Amal, would she? She couldn’t think of any other scenario. If he didn’t release the body, then where was it? If he did, where was the body? Both questions led back to the same answer. Leah had no idea where he was and if he were gone from this world. Maybe she should leave well enough alone.

The elevator stopped, and the doors opened. Leah stepped out and walked toward the counter. She placed her purse inside the cabinet and grabbed a chart from the rack. Leah would have to keep herself busy until her shift was over and then make a stop at Edon Police Department after work. There had to be someone there who could help her find the man from the car accident, right? She could only hope so. Otherwise, she would just have to let this go and move on with her life. She wondered if she should have put this much effort into finding her real mother. After this, maybe she would start looking for her again. What was the worst thing that could happen?

~ ~ ~

Leah parked her car in the lot at the Edon Police Department. She sat behind the wheel and looked at the building. She didn't want to sound like a crazy person walking into the police department talking about a missing brain-dead patient. She had to get her story straight before going inside.

She turned to the sound of a door slamming to the right of her. Leah had never noticed too many black women as police officers, especially in small towns like this one. Edon wasn't small, but it wasn't big either. Franklin, on the other hand, had more than twenty thousand residents, but no black female officers that she recalled.

Sometimes, when she sat at places and saw a colored woman like herself, she would search their faces to see if they looked anything like her, but Leah was sure that her bio-mom was no police officer. Tough women like that don't go giving up their babies. For all she knew, her real mother was dead.

"Hey Moore, are you heading out?" Leah could hear the tall, handsome colored man yell from the inside of her closed car window. He was dressed in uniform like the other officer sitting in her truck. Leah could tell that the man liked the woman by the way he presented himself when he talked to her.

"Yeah, I have an appointment to be at," Moore replied.

Leah couldn't see the woman's face, but that was okay. She wasn't here to look for her real mother. She was here to find anything she could from the accident three days ago. She was determined to get answers. Leah shut off her car and climbed out. She walked up the ten steps to the front door of the old brick building.

"I'll get that for you," Officer Woods said as he reached his hand out and pulled open the door.

"Thank you," Leah replied as she turned and smiled at Officer Woods before walking through the door. Leah didn't see the look on Woods's face after she smiled at him or that he took a step backwards, letting the door slip from his hand and then regaining his composure before almost falling backwards off the steps.

Leah walked to the counter. “Hi, is there someone I can talk to about the accident on the Ohio Turnpike a few days ago?”

The man behind the counter closed the file he was reading. “Exactly what is this pertaining to? Did you see something happen? Film the accident?”

“Officer Dean why are you interrogating this lady the way you are?” Woods said from behind Leah.

“I just thought… I mean, maybe she saw something,” the officer behind the desk recoiled from Woods’s deep voice.

“Well, you don’t go throwing out questions when people walk in off the street, especially when they are asking you questions. I’m so sorry, Miss. Is there something I can help you with?” Woods asked.

Leah turned and smiled again. “Yes, I would like to talk to someone about a man who was in the accident.”

“Sure, follow me; I’ll help you the best I can,” Woods said as he led the way to a room, so they could have privacy.

They walked down a corridor and stopped in front of a small room with a table and three chairs. Woods motioned for her to go inside. “Have a seat,” he said as he closed the door behind them.

Leah pulled out the chair, the metal legs scraping against the floor. She flinched then took a seat. She watched as Officer Woods sat down in front of her, grabbing a note pad and pencil.

"Could I have your name and a phone number before we begin?"

Leah rattled off her name and cell number.

"So, what can I help you with, Miss Leah James?"

Leah took in a shallow breath before telling him the story of the brain-dead man and finding his family. "I'm not sure where he is now, but he's missing," Leah said, feeling stupid about being here at all.

"I see," Woods replied.

"No one that I know of from Franklin or here has come to see the man, besides Sergeant Miles, but that's only because I went and saw him first. He even said that there was nothing that he could do without having any kind of identification on the victim."

Officer Woods nodded.

"Do you think that you can help me?" Leah asked. Woods sat across from her, looking mesmerized. Leah's eyes looked toward the closed door as if looking to escape. Well, for one this officer was staring at her instead of talking. Second, it made her feel very uncomfortable. "I should go," Leah said as she scooted back her chair.

The noise startled Officer Woods as he jumped up from his seat, dropping the pencil in his hand. "I'm so sorry," he said. "You just look like someone I know. I'm sorry for staring. As for the man in the accident, unless there's a body I'm afraid there's nothing I can do."

"Oh, I see. What about his belongings?"

"I thought you said that Sergeant Miles from Franklin had them checked?"

Leah swallowed. The officer was right. What was she thinking, that he could find something that the other police officer couldn't? She was a fool for coming here. "I'm sorry for bothering you. I'm not sure what I was thinking or how you could help me," Leah said as she made her way toward the door.

"Wait!" Officer Woods said loudly. His hand reached out to touch her but dropped to his side.

Leah opened the door and bulleted down the hall before he could stop her. She walked quickly out the doors of the police station and to her car. She pressed the button, locking the door once she was inside the comfort of her car. What the hell was wrong with her? No, it wasn't her, but the way Officer Woods was looking at her. It was as if he knew her or was undressing her. Whatever it was, it creeped her out.

Leah looked out the windshield and saw the same officer standing at the door watching her. She started the car and quickly drove away. She would have to figure out what her next move would be. She could do this on her own. She didn't need their help. She shivered as if shaking off the disgusting feeling she had experienced as she drove toward home. She knew for certain she'd never step foot in the Edon police station again.

25

Four Days after the Accident

Kaitlyn pulled the car up along the curve where Ben was waiting in a wheelchair with one of the nurses. She climbed out and quickly walked around the car to open the door. Once Ben was securely fastened into the passenger seat, she drove away from the hospital. She wanted to get Ben home and, on his feet, again. But she didn't want him to remember the way he used to be. She didn't want him to be the man she married. The man that swore to protect her, but in the end, only hurt her.

Three hours later, Kaitlyn took the exit and drove toward their home. Ben had fallen asleep on the drive, which gave her more time to herself to think about the past few weeks. Would she want Ben to remember? No, of course not, but what difference did it make? She was leaving him as soon as he could take care of himself.

She loved Ben once a long time ago and that's the way she wanted to keep things. She gave him her heart after losing the love of her life. She was afraid to love again when they had met on that rainy day, wondering if it would end the same way it had with Adam. She'd been cautious when it came to Ben in college, but after months of him persuading her, she reluctantly went out with him on a date and they'd been together ever since. She could see now that he had controlled her from the start, and she was naïve to allow him. Had she been vulnerable, and Ben had taken advantage of her? Her heart still fresh and broken from losing Adam?

She'd sat for hours on end after years of marriage and put the pieces together. He'd never been physically abusive until after their marriage. He was a total gentleman who opened car doors and brought home flowers, not someone who tortured her in ways no one could imagine a husband doing to his wife. There were times she wanted to suffocate him with her pillow after he had fallen asleep but was scared if she didn't succeed, he'd kill her for sure.

Kaitlyn turned the corner. Their house appeared in the distance. She crept down the street until their driveway appeared and pulled in. God, it was so good to see her house again. Although she hadn't been gone long, it seemed like forever in her mind. She would miss this house she called home, but she knew that she needed to leave for her baby.

She turned off the car and looked over at Ben, who was staring at her. She jumped in her seat. She seemed to do that whenever he looked at her that way, afraid he would hit her, even touch her. She swallowed then spoke. "We're home." She felt sick to her stomach. She was about to take him into their home and was scared to death. Paranoid. Ben always waited until they were behind closed doors before he punished her.

Ben turned from her and looked at the house. "So this is our home?"

"Yes. Do you remember it?" She placed her hand on the door, readying herself to run. But from what? His leg was in a cast; he couldn't chase her.

"No. But maybe once I'm inside something will come to me," Ben said as he opened the passenger door.

Kaitlyn got out and opened the back door, grabbing the crutches for Ben.

He slowly took hesitant steps toward the house. "I don't think I'll ever get used to these things," he chuckled. "I haven't used them since the war."

"War?" Kaitlyn questioned.

Ben didn't seem to hear her question as he made his way toward the house.

Kaitlyn hadn't known that Ben fought in any war. He had never told her about being in the military, nor had she known about any broken bones. Ben hadn't shared his past with her. Her mind raced back, trying to remember if there were scars on his body. Most of their love-making, especially after they were married, was him forcing himself on her. Yes, she had seen scars on his body, but he wouldn't tell her where they had come from.

She stopped and stared at the ground, her mind shuffling through their life together, but came up with no recollection of him ever telling her about fighting in a war. When would he have been in the military? They had met in college so there was no way he could have unless he lied about his age, about everything he ever told her. She'd have to sit and search her mind later and find the missing pieces he had to have told her. Was she so obsessed with thoughts of Adam that she didn't remember Ben telling her? Yes, that was definitely what had happened because she had thought about Adam a lot after he had left for Afghanistan and when she started dating Ben.

She looked up and over at Ben, then at the house. She forgot about the ten steps leading up to the front door. "Maybe it would be best if we use the garage. There're only two steps to get into the house in there."

"Sure, that'll be fine."

Kaitlyn walked toward the garage door and tapped in the four-digit code. The garage door rose, clanking and rattling as the chain pulled the door up.

"I'll have to fix that when I'm able to walk without these things," he said. "Sounds like it's in need of some grease."

Kaitlyn stood in her tracks and stared at him. "You've never fixed a thing in your life. Do you even know how to grease the gara—?" She stopped talking, waiting for Ben to look at her in a way that told her she would pay for speaking to him in that manner, but he didn't look at her. He didn't even sound upset.

"It's no different than a chain on a bike," he said, making his way inside the garage.

After he cautiously took the two steps inside the house, Kaitlyn walked ahead to make sure that there wasn't anything in his way. Not that there would be. Ben hated having furniture on every wall. He liked space, and everything needed to be in a particular spot.

"Do you want to lie down in bed or on the sofa?"

"Bed sounds fine."

Kaitlyn nodded. "Follow me." She took the lead and flicked on the switch in their bedroom. The bed sat in front of her in the middle of the room. It was neatly made of course, and she was grateful for that. She slept on the right, closest to the bathroom. She walked to the left side of the bed where Ben slept and started removing the decorative pillows and placing them on the floor. Then she peeled the blankets back for him.

"I always sleep on this side," he said as he pointed the crutch to the right side of the bed, then carefully made his way to the bed.

Since when? You've always slept on the left. Are you sure you're all right? I mean since we have gotten home you've been, I don't know, different. You've never told me about being in the war and now you say you've always sleep on the right side of the bed, which I know you haven't in all the years we've been together, Kaitlyn stood thinking all of this but knew better than to say it. She didn't need to start a fight. Not when they just arrived home.

He sat down on the edge of the bed and positioned the crutches against the nightstand where they could be reached when he needed to get up. Ben pressed his palm against the side of his head.

Kaitlyn went over to him. "Are you all right?" She had to listen to what the doctor had told her before leaving the hospital with Ben and not push for his memories to come back to him. "It will only cause him stress if forced. You must let them come back on their own," the doctor had said.

"Just a headache is all. Could you please get me some Tylenol or Advil?"

Kaitlyn didn't speak the words she was thinking. Ben had never so much as taken a baby aspirin in the eight years she'd known him. "How about I get the pain meds that the doctor prescribed," she said as she left the room, returning with the bottle and a glass of water.

After Ben took the meds, Kaitlyn helped him into bed, pulling the covers up to his chest. "You get some rest, and I'll check in on you in an hour or so."

"Okay," he replied and closed his eyes without any hesitation.

Kaitlyn stood looking down at him. Granted, she knew that it most likely was from the accident, but even the little things he would have remembered, right? And the war? She definitely didn't recall him talking about ever being in a war, in the military. It was like she hadn't know him at all. What if the accident changed who he was? That was unlikely, wasn't it? Could a head injury change who a person is? She'd have to call their doctor and set up an appointment. Did Ben even have a doctor of his own? She hadn't recalled him saying anything about him going to one. He almost always never got sick. Ben would need to be checked out, and his bandage on his face would need to be removed and cared for, though that was something she could do at home.

She left the room, closing the door behind her. She needed answers but didn't know where to start or who to talk to. Maybe she would start by making an appointment with her doctor and go from there. This way, they could work together to try and remember the past. The past Kaitlyn didn't seem to know anything about.

After making the call, she went into the office and logged onto the computer. She typed in traumatic brain injury and clicked on memory loss. She read until she got to retrograde amnesia. It said that as people get better with their head injury, long-term memories start to return. Some may return like a jigsaw puzzle in random order. The site didn't say how to get the brain to remember things, but she assumed that would come in time. Ben would recall his life in bits and pieces.

As she read farther down the page, she came to a paragraph about a Specialist in memory loss. She hit print. She'd show this to the doctor. The paragraph also said to write things down every time the person remembers something. Kaitlyn opened the drawer next to her and took out a pad of paper. She'd keep track of Ben's memories as he remembered them. She wrote down war, aspirin and bed.

She clicked off the computer and walked into the kitchen. Ben stood in the family room staring at a photo of them. She hadn't heard him get up, but the office was on the other side of the kitchen. She walked and stood behind him. "That was taken a year ago," she said. "We had just come back from a cruise in the Bahamas."

He shook his head. "I don't remember that trip."

She nodded. "Would you like to look at other pictures of us? Maybe one of them will trigger your memory."

"Sure."

Kaitlyn walked over to a cabinet near the far side of the room and grabbed a photo album from the shelf. There were only two, one from their wedding and the other from trips they had taken, not that they went on vacation much with Ben always being on the road.

When she turned around, he was standing right behind her. She was frozen where she stood, nowhere to go. Panic ran through her body. He was going to hurt her? Had he been pretending to not remember anything until they were home?

She looked into his eyes. There was something different about them. Something she hadn't seen in a long time, but that couldn't be. This was her husband Ben, not Adam. Though they hadn't seen each other in nine years…and yes, they had some features that resembled one another, but she would know them apart, wouldn't she? She didn't know this. She hadn't seen Adam since he left and the photo she had of him was from nine years ago; surely, he didn't look the same. She had never seen him with hair, just a buzz cut.

Her mind spun back to the past. She remembered that day like it was yesterday, running into Ben on that rainy morning and looking at his face, in his eyes. The same color blue that Adam had. She almost for one split second thought Adam had come back for her. Wouldn't that be something? She still wished to this day he'd never left and went off to Afghanistan. She didn't even know if he were alive or dead. He left her here and then never returned. She was the one that received the Dear John letter, not him, because she would have never left him.

He gently touched her face, and she flinched. She could tell from his reaction that he'd seen her pull away. She waited to see if he would do anything. He didn't. He just stood there looking at her, and she was wishing with all her heart that it was Adam and not Ben standing in front of her. The past she had with Adam came flooding back to her. She had to leave Ben and find Adam.

26

Four Years Earlier

After thirteen months in Afghanistan fighting the endless war twelve years after 9/11, Adam was stationed at Fort Bliss in El Paso, Texas, where he served the remaining two years of his enlistment. When he was off duty, he took classes at the local college near the base. He wanted to fill his time with as many classes as he could to get his degree toward becoming a teacher once he was out of the military. Sometimes he thought about staying in the Army for his full twenty years, but he didn't want to give up his dream of becoming an English teacher, not that he couldn't be one after he retired from the Army.

Adam wasn't alone in the Army. He had many friends in his barrack that he hung out with when he wasn't studying or doing his daily duties. Adam met Scott Wards and became best friends. While out in the field, Adam had found out that Scott was from Franklin, Ohio, the next town over from Edon, which was ironic to them both. Not only were they neighbors separated by two towns, but they had also enlisted in the Army at the same time and were stationed together all four years. They not only were assigned to the same barracks together but were teamed together as Operational Detachment Alpha.

Special Forces Soldiers consisted of twelve members, each with their own specialty. Scott served as a Special Forces Communication Sergeant who operated every kind of communications gear, while Adam, a Special Forces Weapons Sergeant, operated and maintained a wide variety of weapons.

As busy as Adam's life seemed, there was never a moment while in the military that he didn't think of Kaitlyn and wished he could be with her. He hated seeing his buddies with their significant others, holding hands and kissing. It made him miss Kaitlyn even more. There were many times he picked up the phone to call her. He had gone as far as to dial her phone number but stopped on the last digit and hung up, his heart beating fast as the blood pulsated through his veins and the tears threatened his eyes. He shielded his face away from anyone who could see. He should have never given her up so easily after receiving her last letter saying she didn't want to hear from him again. She was the love of his life and always would be, and now he had to live with the decision she'd made, even though it destroyed him.

All he wanted was to hear her voice and know that she was doing okay. To know if she was missing him as much as he missed her. That she had made a mistake breaking up with him. Kaitlyn, he knew, wasn't someone who would move around from place to place. When they spent those ten months together in Illinois, he could tell that in her heart she was to live in Chicago the rest of her life. She was raised there. Her home was there. He respected that and would never ask her to leave her home. Had he even asked her if she wanted to go with him once he came back to the States? No, because he didn't want to hear her say no.

He had seen many things fighting the war. His fellow soldiers getting killed or hurt from bombs exploding as they drove through the towns of Afghanistan. Many had lost body parts or their lives. Adam thought that he might not survive himself. One day it had happened. He and his Unit were driving through a town of Banaq, scouting out possible shooters, when a bomb exploded, and pieces of debris penetrated Adam's face. He had many facial surgeries to help reconstruct the damage that was done. He still looked like himself, but there were areas on his face that were different than before. Scars lined the side of his face where the doctors had to pull the skin, but only he saw the difference. He himself had feared putting Kaitlyn through the *not knowing* if he would make it back to her, but he didn't want to let her go. He knew in his heart that he'd never forget her or stop loving her. He had to respect her wishes of not contacting her again. It killed him inside to know that someone else would one day get to love her and spend the rest of their life with her.

When his enlistment ended, Adam went back to his hometown in Edon, Ohio, and finished the remaining courses he needed to become a teacher. After he finished college, Adam applied as an English teacher at Edon High School, where he had graduated years before. He lived with his mother until he was able to buy his own house near Lake Erie. He had never dated nor wanted to date anyone; he was content living alone in his house for the rest of his life. Although he wanted to have a wife and several children running around, he just couldn't make himself be with anyone other than Kaitlyn.

In his mind, it was Kaitlyn who helped him make it through the war. He carried the only thing he had left of her, a picture of the two of them at Navy Pier two weeks before he was deployed and the promise rings they had exchanged before he left. There was never a time he didn't look at the picture of them together in all his years in the Army. Of course, the picture was beginning to fade from the wear and tear from carrying it, but he kept the photo and had it framed and placed next to his bed where he could look at Kaitlyn every morning and every night.

He wasn't sure what they called people who only had their heart set on one person. His mother was the same way. After his father left them, to his knowledge, his mother never dated anyone. When he was gone for those four years, he had come home to visit on occasion, and his mother hadn't introduced him to any man. Adam had decided that he'd make his job and the students he taught his life and that's just what he did. They became his children although they were fourteen years old.

Scott left the Army at the same time as Adam, both heading back to their lives before they joined the Army. Scott found work as a dispatcher for 9-1-1. Since he served as a Special Forces Communication Sergeant it was the perfect job for him. They hung out as much as they could when they weren't working, buying their first motorcycles and taking long rides on the highway or on some country road in Indiana, which was only a few miles outside of Ohio.

Scott was known to be a daredevil when it came to fast things like motorcycles. He at times drove faster than the legal limit, Adam following behind him. Neither wore helmets when they rode. Adam's mother wasn't a fan of motorcycles and protested when he talked about buying one. She was furious when he showed up with a brand-new motorcycle and no helmet. He eventually talked her down and promised that he'd be careful when he was out riding.

Once Adam was home and working as a teacher, he became curious as his emotions regarding Kaitlyn began to reignite. Now that he was three hours away from her and no longer on the battlefield where he could get shot and killed, he wanted to find her and did an Internet search. He'd found out where she was living and on a warm, sunny summer day, Adam climbed on his crotch rocket and drove to Illinois.

He drove slowly through the semi-empty streets, cautious of children playing near the road. He came to a stop sign across from a small church. There were cars parked along the street and in the parking lot next to the church. It wasn't Sunday, so he knew that there had to be a wedding at the church. People appeared and began to stand along the sides of the walkway outside the church. He nodded to himself when he saw to his left a limo decorated with a *Just Married* sign on the back and two strings of cans and paper-mâché streaming from the bumper. Before he shifted to drive away the doors to the church sprang open and out came the bride and groom. They walked down the steps as family and friends threw what he assumed was birdseed at them as they made their way to the parked limo. The bride was laughing as she dashed down the sidewalk, her hand intertwined with the groom's.

Adam wasn't sure if it was all the noise around him including the motor from his bike, but the laugh sounded familiar. He looked in his mirror and was glad that no one was waiting behind him. He maneuvered and parked the motorcycle along the side of the street and watched as the newlyweds made their way to the open door of the limo where a man stood, holding the rear door open. The woman laughed again, but it was her face that made his heart stop. It was his Kaitlyn, he was sure of it.

Her smile.

Her laugh.

Her beautiful brown wavy hair.

His heart broke all over again. He watched as they kissed before getting inside the limo. He shifted gears and without looking, drove through the intersection. A car horn honked at him as they almost collided with one another. He sped off down the road, tears watering his eyes under his sunglasses. The love of his life had gone on with her life as if he had never existed.

A couple of miles down the road he pulled into a parking lot of a park. He shut off the engine and looked around. There were no other cars in the lot. He placed his face in his hands and wept. He'd lost her forever. She looked so happy, so beautiful in her wedding dress. That could have been him next to her. He was a damn fool to let her go, and now he would have to live the rest of his life without her. He should have fought for her and made her reconsider. He should have told her that he wouldn't be in the military forever.

He dried his eyes with his shirt and started his bike. He would go back home now. There was nothing more he could do. He had loved deeply and lost the one thing that meant everything to him, knowing she would forever stay in his heart.

27

Kaitlyn had waited years for Adam to come back to her. Even though she loved Ben, her heart would always belong to Adam. It had been said that there was one soulmate for every one person in this world. Kaitlyn's was Adam. She was sure of it. He made her laugh in ways she'd never laughed before. He was the first man she'd ever slept with and gave her whole heart to. He made her complete. His touch ignited her, even when he didn't touch her. She could feel it when he was near. He made her feel good about herself, like she could do anything she wanted to. He never held her back; if anything, he pushed her forward toward whatever she had her heart set on.

They wrote to each other every week and called as often as they could. Several months after Adam left and was deployed in Afghanistan, Kaitlyn received a letter saying that she should let him go and that he didn't love her anymore. She cried for days, weeks, and months. She stopped going out with her friends to parties, mostly because it reminded her of how they met. She didn't want to meet anyone else or love again. She was content living alone and being single. In her heart, she knew that he still loved her; she could feel it. Something must have happened to him, she was sure of it. He wouldn't write her back no matter how many letters she mailed to him.

As time went by she focused more on her studies and spent all her time in the library. If she didn't have exams to study for, then she read all sorts of books, hoping one day to write her own novel.

The only time she seemed to hang out with her friends was when they walked to class together. She laughed at their jokes and pretended that she was interested in what they were talking about, but all she thought about was Adam and how he was doing. If he were still alive. Wouldn't she feel it inside herself if he were dead or hurt? That's how much she loved him. She knew that people died from broken hearts because it happened to her grandparents. It wasn't six months after her grandma passed away that her grandfather died of a broken heart. She had sat with him the day before, and he told her how much he missed her. When she came back to the hospital early the following morning, she was told that he had passed away just moments before she arrived.

She'd spent several hours a week scrolling through the Internet and obituaries looking for any information on Adam, praying that she wouldn't find his name in any of the articles. Her life seemed to only be focused on him. She knew that it wasn't healthy, but she loved him and wanted nothing more than for him to show up at her dorm and say he was sorry and that he missed her and would never leave her again.

She would catch herself wondering if he was still fighting the war or if he were stationed somewhere else. Kaitlyn for a while would search the many faces of men who walked by her at school or that she saw at the coffee shop off campus, which also became a hangout of hers. She hoped that one day Adam would reappear and surprise her, but he never did. He was only in her dreams and would forever stay in her heart. Each passing day, he never showed, and she closed her heart to love. She had taken the ring off her finger and placed it on a chain around her neck.

After a year of studying and making the Dean's list, Kaitlyn slowly began to lose herself. She had on several occasions, been late to class because she forgot to set her alarm and slept in from studying all night. One day she raced out of the dorm into the pouring rain and ran right into another student. She looked at him and for one split second he looked almost like Adam, but it wasn't her Adam. Although the eyes were the same color, his face was shaped somewhat differently. The nice man helped her with her books that were getting drenched in the rain and suggested since she was already late to class that they should dry off over a cup of hot chocolate.

"So, what is your name?" Kaitlyn asked.

"Ben," he replied.

"Ben what?"

"Ben Gordon, and yours?"

“Kaitlyn Costa.” She found herself staring at Ben’s face. There were so many things that reminded her of Adam. His eyes were blue, depending on how the light hit them, and he had the same shade of brown hair that Adam had, or she assumed he had, since she’d never seen him with long hair, but he wasn’t her Adam. She’d have to come to realize that Adam wasn’t coming back. He ended their relationship, and she was to move on without him. She had gone through the withdrawals of their now-nonexistent relationship. Shock, denial, fear, loneliness, and then anger. Anger was the worst and her friends pointed it out to her more times than she could remember. “Quit being such a bitch, Kaitlyn,” her friend Lisa had said several times. So Kaitlyn started to distance herself from them more and more.

Ben and Kaitlyn talked about what classes they were taking for the jobs they would have after college and about their lives growing up. Nearly an hour later, Kaitlyn stood from her seat at the booth, gathering her things. “I need to get to my next class,” she said.

“Will I see you again?” Ben asked.

“That would be nice,” she replied, though part of her wasn’t sure she was ready to be in a relationship when she still constantly thought of Adam. Ben asked for her number, but she insisted that he give her his number and that she would call him when she was ready, whenever that would be. He wrote his phone number on a napkin and handed it to her and she walked away.

It was another month before she called Ben, wanting to wait until after exams were finished. They met for lunch at her favorite coffee house down the street. They started to spend time together. At first it was only a couple of hours, but then that led to days, then weeks. By the time the following summer came, they were inseparable. Kaitlyn hadn't replaced the love of her life but had tucked him away to the back of her heart where on occasion she would allow herself to think of him, remembering their time together and how happy she had once been.

She knew it wasn't fair that she still loved another man as deeply as she did. She kept his letters and the picture of them at Navy Pier before he left. She kept them hidden away inside a book that she knew Ben would never open or read. Ben was not the reading kind, and she was okay with that. There were other things that they had in common, like watching movies together and occasionally walking around the block, at least until after graduation.

The day graduation came, Ben had gotten down on one knee and asked her to marry him in front of the whole graduating class. Of course, she was embarrassed, but that was Ben, always seeking attention and wanting to be front and center. That was the difference between Adam and Ben. Adam, she knew, would have made the moment more romantic and private. Just the two of them, alone where they could make love afterwards. Adam didn't need all eyes on him like Ben, but she did love Ben—maybe not in the same way as she did Adam but she loved him nonetheless.

When the day came, and they were to be married in the church near Kaitlyn's hometown, she thought of Adam. Wrong she knew, but God, she couldn't let him go. He was an addiction she couldn't live without. She just wanted Adam to tell her to her face that he truly didn't love her anymore. That he wanted her to be happy with Ben and that he was the perfect guy for her. Or he could say that he was wrong, and that he loved her more than anything in this world, but of course that didn't happen. He never walked through the doors of the church and proclaimed his love for her as she hoped he would.

When the inner doors to the church opened and the music began to play, she began to walk down the aisle in her father's arm. She looked up and saw Ben waiting for her at the other end. Everything that she had thought about minutes ago was tucked away never to be thought about again.

The wedding lasted less than half an hour and then they walked arm and arm down the aisle as Mr. and Mrs. Ben Gordon. When the main doors opened, Kaitlyn and Ben were greeted with their family and friends waiting to throw the traditional birdseed at them as they walked down the stairs and toward the limo waiting for them.

Kaitlyn laughed, her head turned back toward the people behind her and smiled. She hadn't paid much attention to the man across the street sitting on his motorcycle, otherwise she might have stopped him before he rode off, nearly causing an accident. But she hadn't seen him. She hadn't known that Adam was there watching her.

28

Five Days after the Accident

Morning

Officer Moore sat at her kitchen table. Her thoughts were on the doctor's visit the day before. Dr. Meadde had recommended that an ultrasound be done to see what could be causing the discomfort, abdominal pain, and recent abnormal bleeding. She had always had irregular periods, but she knew it had to be something else causing this, along with the sharp pain that was surfacing more often and the sudden constipation, all within the past couple of weeks.

"What is it?" Moore whispered as she listened to the *whoosh whoosh* sound on the screen as the wand moved around on her lower abdomen.

The technician didn't speak, only moved the wand around in the gel placed on Moore's stomach. She stopped only to type something on the computer in front of her and then moved the wand again. "The doctor will come in and talk to you after I'm done, after she looks over the images," the technician said, her face showing no expression.

Moore was trying to keep calm and not let herself think that something was wrong. The doctor would look at the images and send Moore out the door with a clean bill of health.

Well, that's what she kept telling herself. Think positive, not negative her father used to tell her. It just puts more stress on the problem at hand.

When the technician finished, she wiped the gel off and placed the wand back in the cradle. "The doctor will be with you shortly." She left the room, leaving Moore to stew in her thoughts.

Moore couldn't bear to know if there was something tragically wrong with her. What if it was cancer? Her mother died of ovarian cancer. Moore still had many years of her life left to live. She knew the day would come that she'd die alone. But she swore at that moment that if she did have cancer and she beat it, she would tell Woods that she loved him and had loved him for years. She only stayed away because they worked together. "What a stupid rule," she mumbled into the empty room. She could've been living with the man and maybe been married. Now her thoughts were getting ahead of herself. What if he didn't feel the same about her? What if he just wanted to be friends now, after the way she treated him yesterday? She squeezed her eyes shut, forcing the thoughts away. She couldn't think about that right now. She had her health to worry about. She'd deal with the rest of her life after she talked to the doctor.

Moore had been here before, maybe not in this same room, but Dr. Meadde was her doctor since she was pregnant twenty-eight years ago. The same awful silence filled the room as she waited for the doctor to tell her the news. It was a day she'd never forget.

Ten minutes later, there was a knock on the door and in walked Dr. Ann Meadde, looking more distinguished with her short white hair. She had stood by Moore's side and helped her with the decision to give the baby up for adoption back then.

"Let's see what we've found here," Dr. Meadde said. The doctor grabbed the warm gel and applied some onto Moore's skin. She took a couple more measurements, then whipped the wand around near her ovaries, circling until she came to a stop.

"Well, don't keep me in suspense. What did you find?" Moore asked nervously, holding back the tears.

Dr. Meadde pointed to the screen. "I'd like to have this image confirmed by another doctor, but it looks like it may be a tumor."

Moore swallowed. "Is it cancer?" *God, please don't let it be cancer,* she thought.

"We'll have to do more tests to confirm. When's the last time you had labs done?"

"I'm not sure."

"It shows in your record that you haven't been here for your annual in two years. What's going on, Moore? You've always been on top of things. Your health, for one."

"Yeah, I know. With my dad dying and all, I just pushed it aside."

“I don’t think we would have found it two years ago. Sometimes these things just appear out of nowhere,” Dr. Meadde stated. “I’d like for you to fast tomorrow—no liquid or food after midnight or in the morning until after labs. I want bloodwork and a urine sample done. I’ll send these straight over to the other doctor and call you with the results within a day or two.

A day or two? “Okay,” Moore replied. How was she going to keep herself busy over the next two days?

Moore stood from the kitchen table and walked into the bathroom. After brushing her teeth, she grabbed her jacket and keys. “Let’s get this over with,” she mumbled. Once in the truck, she drove toward Franklin hospital where Dr. Meadde’s practice was. Moore didn’t like going to doctors where she lived. She didn’t want anyone knowing her business, especially when it came to her health.

Once labs were done, she drove straight to McDonald’s for a cup of coffee. “Oh, what the hell,” she whispered softly and ordered a sausage egg McMuffin with cheese to go with the coffee.

She parked in a semi-empty lot next door to the restaurant and ate. She seemed to eat more when she was stressed. She knew this was going to be a long and endless day ahead of her. She’d have to plunge herself in her work just to keep her mind off what the doctor may have found. “It may not be cancer so stop making yourself sick over this,” she said in the privacy of her truck. “Dr. Meadde will find nothing wrong.” She was trying to keep her mind on a positive note. It never paid to think negative about things.

Moore pulled into the parking lot in front of the police station. She sat for a few minutes, looking out the windshield. Her mind was whirling on the last few years of her life. Why had she held off living all these years? What was she afraid of? Since her father died, she wished she knew where her daughter was, not to intrude in her life, but to apologize to her for giving her up. She’d done it because she thought it would be better for her baby. There was nothing wrong with wanting her to have a better life. She knew she couldn’t have provided a good life for her. What if she had kept the baby and then went off to the police academy? Her father would have helped raise her, but she didn’t even give him the choice. She’d made the decision without her father because she thought she was doing the right thing, but now, not so much. She wanted to take it all back because she was going to die without ever knowing her daughter. Without telling her that she loved her and that she thought about her every day of her life. Of course, she wasn’t certain that she was dying, but the doctor hadn’t said otherwise.

Moore opened the door and climbed out. She walked up the walkway to the entrance of the station, which seemed like a million miles away. Each step felt heavy in her boots. She took a deep inhale and opened the door. She couldn’t handle it if someone asked her what was wrong. She'd fall apart, but she couldn't fall apart. She had to be strong.

Before she could sit in her comfy chair at her desk, Woods approached her. He touched her arm as if pulling her away from her desk. She looked over her shoulder at him. His face was—well, she wasn't sure what his face was telling her. Had something happened to him?

"What is it, Woods?"

"I need you to come with me. I need to talk to you alone, now."

Before Moore could argue, he practically dragged her down the hall and into an interrogation room.

"Have a seat," Woods demanded, but in a soft, caring voice.

"What's this about? What's wrong?"

Woods closed the door behind him and pulled the chair out from the table and sat down. He looked over at Moore, who seemed to be looking at him with heavy-lidded eyes. Without saying a word, he opened the folder lying on the table and pushed a photo of a woman into Moore's view.

29

Leah couldn't get the image of Officer Woods's face out of her head. The way he looked at her made her feel extremely uncomfortable. That's why she left the station in such a hurry, practically running to her car like the building was on fire. She didn't think that he'd hurt her, but there was just something about him that made her feel so uneasy. Why was he staring at her the way he was? She wasn't sure, but all she knew was that it creeped her out. Going there was a mistake and she wasn't going back and hoped that she didn't run into him again. It was a good thing she lived in Franklin and not Edon.

Leah grabbed her next patient file and walked into the room. The patient was an older lady, in her eighties. According to the chart, eighty-one to be exact. Leah watched as the woman's eyes followed her through the room. A tube had been placed down her throat to help her breathe.

"Ah, you're awake," Leah said. The woman tried to speak. "Don't try and talk right now." Leah looked over the chart again. "It seems that you were brought in yesterday evening due to a massive heart attack. If your vitals are strong, then we can remove the ventilator."

The lady nodded.

"So, your name is Gilda Wards?"

Gilda nodded.

"Well, Gilda, it's nice to meet you. My name is Leah, and I will be the nurse taking care of you today. Can I get you a warm blanket?"

Gilda nodded.

"Okay, I'll go get that now and then check your vitals." Leah left the room, returning with a heated blanket. After placing it over Gilda's body she scanned over the machines, writing down the numbers of Gilda's blood pressure. Leah jumped when she heard Dr. Amal speak behind her.

"So how's our patient doing?"

After gathering her composure, Leah spoke. "She seems to be coherent, and her vitals look good and stronger. We should be able to remove the tube today now that she's awake."

"I don't see why not. She seems to be alert like you said. Let's get some bloodwork done and remove that nasty thing from your throat. Do you agree, Mrs. Wards?"

Dr. Amal spoke to the patient with kindness, which puzzled Leah. Usually he was an ass and rude to everyone around him. "I'll get that done now," Leah replied. She wanted to ask him about the brain-dead patient, but was it a good time to ask? Would he jump down her throat like the last time? He'd probably reply that it wasn't any of her business, which it wasn't, was it? She didn't want to overstep her boundaries again with Dr. Amal, but damn it, she couldn't help herself.

"Dr. Amal, could I please speak to you out in the hall?" Leah asked.

Dr. Amal nodded and walked out of the room, Leah trailing behind.

"I know you'll say it's none of my business, but I need to know about the brain-dead patient," she said in a low voice. Her eyes sketched over his, waiting for him to start yelling at her.

"You are correct. He isn't any of your business, but if you need to know, he's been moved to the coma ward where I should have placed him in the first place. I'm waiting on the judge to give me permission to turn off the life support."

Leah's mouth gaped open, stunned by the words he'd just told her. "He's still here? I thought… I mean, I was told you stopped treating him."

"Yes, and it was for your own good. We have a job to do here, and I need you to focus on the people that are here now and need you. Not on some man that is already dead," Dr. Amal said. "I don't mean to sound harsh, but there's nothing we can do for him. He needs to be let go, as you people call it. Where I come from, we don't allow our people to suffer. It's always best to let them go in peace."

Leah nodded. "Yes, of course, you're right. I'm sorry for wasting your time," she replied, but all she could think about was that he was still here, and she would go see him after her shift was over.

"Have you found his family yet?"

Leah lowered her head. "No, not yet."

"This is a warning to you. Don't do something stupid and go losing your job over this patient," Dr. Amal said, then walked away.

Leah stood there as Dr. Amal walked away. Would he have her fired over this? She was only trying to help the brain-dead man, but losing her job because she wanted to find the man's family? She couldn't lose her job; she loved working here.

She gathered her composure and went back into the room to take Gilda's blood and remove the tube. Although nervous about what Dr. Amal might do, Leah couldn't hide her smile as she worked. She wanted to go see John Doe as soon as she was finished here, but should she? Even after what the doctor had said, she still wanted to find his family. She shouldn't even consider continuing the search, but she wanted to. She needed to. Besides if it were after her shift was over, he couldn't fire her for that, could he?

Half an hour later, Leah removed the breathing tube and helped Gilda to sit up.

"Thank you, dear," Gilda croaked. "You look so much like a woman I met yesterday. Same eyes, same smile."

Leah smiled. She knew that the woman was just being kind. "No need to thank me, it's my job."

"Rose?" Gilda muffled.

Leah looked from Gilda to the doorway of the room. “I’m sorry, but visiting hours aren’t for another hour, if you could please come back later.”

“Oh, well, can’t I see her since I’m here?” Rose Tucker asked.

Leah looked beyond the door to see if anyone else was watching. “Well, I guess so, but make it short. Gilda needs to get some rest.”

“Sure, of course,” Rose replied as she walked toward the bed. “I heard from your neighbor that you were taken to the hospital when I stopped by your place twenty minutes ago. Are you all right? What happened?” Rose asked, coming to stand beside the bed.

“Yes, I’m fine,” Gilda replied.

“You had a heart attack,” Leah interrupted. “I would say you’re one lucky woman. Thank God you had that alert necklace around your neck.”

“Oh, goodness,” replied Gilda. “I wasn’t aware that I was having a heart attack. Can’t remember much these days.”

“Well, I agree with the nurse. Thank God you were able to get help. Where was Scott?” Rose asked but could tell she said something wrong.

“The police came to my house yesterday and said that he was killed in an accident,” Gilda said.

“Oh my God! Killed? How?” Rose shrieked.

“I guess there was some kind of car accident. They didn’t say how it happened, just that he was killed on his motorcycle.”

“Oh, dear Jesus. That is terrible,” Rose replied. “I didn’t just come here to see how you were doing. I was wondering if you or Scott had seen Adam lately. I haven’t seen him since Labor Day,” Rose said. “That was a week ago. He never stays away that long. I hope he’s okay.”

“Well, maybe he has things to do. I’m sure he’ll call you,” Gilda said.

“Never mind my problems. How are you feeling?”

“I’m better now that this sweet nurse has taken the tube out of my throat. It was so uncomfortable. Hard to swallow.”

Rose nodded.

“How’s Adam?” Gilda asked. “The black police officer was asking about Adam.”

Leah looked over at Gilda. Her friend had just told her that she hadn’t seen him in a week. Black police officer? Leah instantly thought of Officer Woods.

“Is your mind still forgetting things?” Rose questioned. “And what black police officer?”

“What? I don’t know what you’re talking about. I don’t remember you telling me about Adam. Or about this black police officer you’re talking about,” Gilda protested as if angry.

"I mentioned that I haven't seen Adam in a week and that I'm worried. You're the one that was talking about a black police officer."

Leah's mind began to whirl. Gilda had just said her son Scott was killed and now Rose's son Adam was missing too. Her mind went straight to the accident on the turnpike. She wasn't sure if she should say anything, but what if he was in the accident too and Rose didn't know? Were there still other patients in the hospital here and at Edon? Her brain was curious as usual and with her kind heart she wanted to find out more about this Adam guy.

"Some policemen came to my house yesterday. They said Scott had been hurt. I can't remember if they said what happened. I should call him and find out."

"Gilda, you just said that Scott was in an accident," Rose said.

"Oh, was he? Maybe I should give him a call," Gilda replied.

"I can call him since he's your next of kin," Leah interrupted. She knew that Gilda was ill and didn't know what was really happening around her.

"That would be so kind of you. What's your name again, sweet girl?"

"Leah," she replied. She felt bad for Gilda and wondered how long her dementia had been going on.

Leah and Rose looked at one another. "I can give you Scott's number," Rose said.

Leah nodded.

"I'll be right back to visit with you, Gilda."

"No, problem. It seems that I'm not going anywhere."

Both Leah and Rose left the room. Leah wanted to find out more about Rose's son Adam but didn't want to do it in front of her patient. Leah would try calling Scott's number, but if he didn't answer, her next choice would be to call the police station and confirm if Scott was in the accident and killed like Gilda had just told them. She dialed Scott's number, but it went straight to voicemail. Which meant it had been turned off or destroyed in the wreck. "Does Scott usually have his phone off? I mean with his mom not remembering things," Leah asked.

"Mom? No, Gilda is Scott's grandmother. To answer your question, I'm not sure. Adam is the one to ask. They have been friends since they met in the Army nine years ago."

Leah nodded. "Have you tried calling your son? That was stupid, of course you have."

"Yes, I have, several times and it too goes straight to voicemail too."

Leah's mind was spiraling with questions. *Is it possible they were both in the accident?* She raked her brain going back to the day of the crash. Granted, there had been at least ten or, so people involved in the accident, and they had been split between the two hospitals. Then it hit her. John Doe could belong to either of them. She needed to know and if she was wrong, then at least Leah could narrow it down to who he was. Why didn't she think of this earlier? She should've visited everyone from the crash. She wasn't a detective, she was a nurse, and yes, she loved helping people. Detective work wasn't her field, but for some reason she needed to finish what she started. Her thoughts raced through her head.

"I hope this doesn't sound crazy, and I'm sure you have watched the news in the past few days."

"What's this about?"

"Do you recall hearing about the accident on the Ohio Turnpike last Friday?"

"Yes, it was such a horrible accident. All those people hurt. What does this have to do…" Rose stopped talking. "Do you think my Adam was in that accident?"

"I'm not sure, but if you happen to have a photo of Adam, I could find out if he's at this hospital and if not, I can check with Edon Hospital," Leah said. She could see Rose's eyes start to well up with tears.

"Yes, of course." Rose opened her purse and pulled out her wallet, handing Leah the most recent picture she had of her son.

Leah looked down at the photo in her hand and gasped. It was her John Doe.

30

The dream seemed real and maybe to him it was. He was standing on sand, then gun shots filled the air. The image changed to an accident. Cars were piled up on the road.

Ben jolted to a sitting position, his clothes clinging to his sweat-covered body. He could still see the images in his head. He replayed the scene but didn't know for sure if it was him or if he was watching someone else. It didn't make sense to him. He had no idea why he was standing in a desert with buildings all around him. Would Kaitlyn know about these dreams he was having?

He looked over his shoulder and down at the empty side of the bed. Kaitlyn wasn't there. He heard a sound coming from the next room and grabbed his crutches. He saw Kaitlyn in the kitchen cooking. She looked so beautiful standing there. How could he not remember this or her? She turned and saw him standing in the hallway. She jumped, almost dropping the frying pan she was holding.

"I'm sorry. I didn't mean to scare you." He stopped. Should he say anything to her? He knew it was a memory but wasn't sure if he should wait and see if more came to him before saying anything. He didn't want to get her hopes up that he was recalling things in his life, but he honestly didn't know what part of his life he was remembering.

"What is it?" she questioned.

"It's nothing."

"Okay, if you're sure. I made us some breakfast. I have two poached eggs and jelly for your toast, just the way you like it."

"Since when do I eat poached eggs?" he replied in disgust.

Kaitlyn stiffened and looked at him as she gripped the pan in her hand in terror. She swallowed. "You…you've always liked poached eggs," she stuttered. "I'm sorry, I'll make you anything you want," she said.

He could tell that she seemed frightened of him all of a sudden. Had he said something wrong? "Oh, I'm sorry but I really don't like them now. Could I have two eggs over easy instead?" he asked. He watched as she studied him for a minute before replying.

"Sure, I can do that for you," she said, grabbing the plate and tossing the poached eggs in the trash. "I guess you hit your head pretty hard in the accident if you can't remember what foods you used to like." She let out a soft laugh, as she looked over her shoulder at him.

He could tell she feared him, but he didn't know why. "I'm going to use the bathroom. I'll be right back," he said and left.

Kaitlyn stood without saying a word.

Ben went back into the bedroom and closed the door once he was inside the bathroom. He leaned against the counter, peering into the mirror. Who was he? Last night they had looked through the photo album, but nothing stirred inside him. He didn't remember a single thing. Not their wedding day or trips that they took. It was like he never existed.

After using the bathroom, he stripped off the shirt he was wearing and tossed it in the hamper. He went over to the walnut colored dresser against the wall. He needed to change into cleaner clothes, since the pajamas that he wore to bed were now wet with sweat. He opened the top drawer and found some lingerie. He couldn't help but smirk as he held up a thin red one-piece and imagined her, his wife, wearing it. The noise from the kitchen startled him and he dropped the lingerie on the floor. He quickly bent over and scooped it up when his eyes caught a glimpse of something taped to the bottom of the drawer. After placing the clothing back, he grabbed the envelope. He opened the unsealed flap and began to shuffle through the photos that were inside. His eyes grew wide as he looked at each picture. They were of Kaitlyn. Her body had bruises all over it. She must have stood in front of the mirror and took these, but how? Why did she have these? Was she in an accident? Should he take these to her and ask? No, he couldn't. She'd think that he was snooping in her things. It dawned on him that she must be hiding them, but from who? Him? Did he do this to her? Oh God, did he beat her, and she was keeping these as evidence? He choked back a cry as his body quivered with fear and disgust that he did this to his own wife. No wonder at times she seemed afraid of him.

"Ben, breakfast is ready," Kaitlyn hollered.

He turned, placed the photos back in the envelope and re-taped them to the bottom of the drawer. He closed the drawer and turned, looking for another dresser that had to have his things in them. He spotted another dresser against the wall by the closet and slowly with his crutches walked over to it. He opened the second drawer and saw men's boxers. He frowned. He didn't like boxers. He rooted through the drawer for some briefs but didn't find any. *What the hell is going on?* he thought. First, he had dreams that didn't seem familiar to him. Second, he hated poached eggs. Third, he found photos of his wife badly beaten. Fourth, he had never worn boxers in his life. It was like he was in someone else's body or brain. None of this seemed real to him. He had thought for sure that he would remember something once he arrived home, but nothing that pertained to their life together.

"Ben, breakfast," Kaitlyn said as she appeared in the doorway. Her eyes fell on his chest. She swallowed. "You don't want it to get cold, do you?"

He grabbed a pair of boxers from the top and held them up. "Was just going to change first," he replied.

"Okay, do you need any help?" she asked.

He shook his head. “I have to learn to do this on my own.” He could tell she was staring at something on his back and turned his body to face her.

She blinked then nodded. “Okay, are you sure? I mean with the cast and all, you might have trouble getting them on.” She pointed to the boxers in his hand.

“I’ll manage,” he said, hoping not to sound unpleasant. “I’ll call you if I need any help.” He waited until she left and went through the other drawers for pants and a shirt. He didn’t like half of the things he found in the drawers but grabbed what he needed and went back into the bathroom. He turned sideways to see if there was something that Kaitlyn saw on his back. Besides a birthmark poking out from the top of his boxers, he didn’t see anything out of the ordinary.

He changed as quickly as he could without falling and left the bathroom, his heart beating fast. He needed to calm down before he ended up hurting himself. Kaitlyn was placing the remaining plates on the table when he appeared.

She looked up at him. “That was fast.”

He pulled out the chair and sat, leaning his crutches beside him. “Looks great,” he said. “Smells great too.” He started eating. He looked up after taking the first bite and caught Kaitlyn staring at him. “Um, did I do something wrong?” he asked with his mouth full.

She looked at him quizzically, and then shook her head.

He could see that her eyes were wet, but why? He set his fork down on his plate and grabbed the glass of orange juice, swallowed and asked. "Is everything okay?"

"I just…I just have never heard you compliment me on my cooking before," she whispered.

"I didn't mean to make you cry," he said, wanting to get up and comfort her. What kind of man was he to her, to make her cry over something so minor as to praise her on her cooking? "Kaitlyn, I'm sorry."

"Please don't be. It's the nicest thing you've ever said to me," she whispered, wiping the tears away.

Inside, his heart broke and he wasn't sure why. He didn't remember the man he used to be, and yet, he hated himself for what he had done to her. How could he have inflicted that kind of pain on his own wife? The images in the photos flickered in his mind again and his stomach dropped, filling with disgust. He didn't deserve to be with her. She was better off without him, and he knew then that he must leave, but how would he drive with his leg in a cast? He'd have to wait until he was better. Five, maybe six weeks until the cast came off. As soon as he was better, then he'd go. Yes, that's what he'd do. She deserved so much more than an abusive husband. She deserved a man who would love her and was gentle and kind to her.

31

Twenty-Eight Years Earlier

Adanya Moore sat in the chair of the doctor's office, staring at the pale green walls around her. The color, not something she would have picked for any wall, resembled the way she was feeling. Like shit!

Her nerves were on edge as she waited to hear the results of her pregnancy test. She was only eighteen and would be graduating high school in two weeks.

Two weeks!

And she screwed up her life by getting pregnant. Well, she didn't know for sure if she was pregnant, that was why she was here, now, sitting in this God-awful green room. If the test came back positive and she were pregnant, it would ruin all her chances of being accepted into the police academy. She dreamed of becoming a policeman ever since she was little. Her father was a police officer, and her father's father was a police officer, so this was her dream too, and something she had to do. It's what she was born to do. She would be a damn good woman police officer.

Adanya sighed.

She couldn't be pregnant. Not now. She had years ahead of her to have a baby. Now was not a good time. Once it was confirmed, she'd have to tell Roland Hayes, her boyfriend of three years. He had big plans himself since he got a full scholarship and would be going off to college to one day play in the NBA.

Roland wanted her to go with him, but she had her own dreams to live. She hadn't told him yet that she wasn't going with him away to college. Of course, she knew that they would eventually go their separate ways because she wasn't leaving her dad and knew that Roland wasn't coming back once he left the town of Edon. There was nothing left here for him but her. His dad was a raging alcoholic and used to hit Roland, but once he grew into a man, his dad knew he didn't stand a chance against him.

Adanya had already been crying over the day she'd have to say goodbye to the man who stole her heart. She didn't want to lose Roland, but there was nothing she could do and had to accept what path God had given her. They were still together as a couple, but she had to toughen her heart because she didn't want to bawl her eyes out on the day Roland said goodbye and left her and Edon behind.

She couldn't tell him about the pregnancy and shatter his dreams. Besides, if she were going to have a baby, she wasn't going to keep it. There would be no way of raising a baby. She didn't have a job. No income to pay for the child. She'd seen how much her father struggled being a single parent raising her. She couldn't do that with this baby. She didn't want to ask her father for help. "God, he is going to be so disappointed in me," she mumbled, wiping away the tears sliding down her face. Her father was her world, her strength. "How could I mess up like this?" She'd been taking the pill after Roland and she started dating and became sexually active. Roland also used a condom for the *added protection*, he'd called it. "So much for that." So how did this happen?

Adanya sat up straight when she heard the faint sound of a knock on the door. Sweat rolled down the back of her neck, and her heart pounded fast beneath the t-shirt she was wearing. This was it. The moment she was waiting for. The answer that would stop her from living her life. From becoming a great police officer.

"Adanya?" Dr. Ann Meadde said as she closed the door behind her. "You're going to be a mom."

Adanya swallowed the lump in her throat. She began to feel dizzy. She was going to be a mom. No, no, no. This couldn't be happening. Everything that she'd worked so hard for was gone in an instant. She wouldn't be a police officer like her father, a man that she looked up to and adored since she first laid eyes on him.

"I can't be," Adanya whispered as she lifted her head, tears streaking down her face. "Maybe it's a false positive. Run another test!" she demanded.

Dr. Meadde said, “I’m so sorry, but you’re going to have a baby. There’s no chance that the test is wrong.”

“But I was taking the pill and Roland was using a condom. How did this happen?”

“I can’t answer that. There could be several different reasons. Maybe a broken condom or you didn’t use one once, and you don’t remember.” Dr. Meadde said. “Were you sick recently and on antibiotics? The pill doesn’t work when you’re using them.”

Adanya gasped. “I was sick with a cold two months ago and then I caught the flu.” Her eyes widened, and she shook her head. “It wasn’t the flu, was it? I was experiencing morning sickness. Oh God!” She cried harder, more tears rolling down her face. She was crying so hard that she began to dry heave. *This can’t be happening to me,* she thought.

“Breathe, Adanya. Take small, shallow breaths,” Dr. Meadde said as she sat beside her.

Adanya did what she was told until her body stopped shaking, but the tears still flowed down her cheeks.

“It’s most likely the case that you didn’t have the flu,” the doctor replied. “I want you to think about what you want to do.” The doctor held out a couple of pamphlets. “Read these over. One is about abortion and the other will help you if you’re looking to have someone adopt your baby. Unless you’re keeping it?”

"No! I can't keep it. I can't raise the baby on my own." Adanya placed her head in her hands as she cried harder. She couldn't keep the baby. What kind of life could she give him or her? What about the people in town? What would they say if they knew she was pregnant? If she weren't going to tell Roland, then she'd have to hide the pregnancy from the world. She'd never be able to leave her house.

"I'm here no matter what you decide. Take a few days and think about things before you make a decision on what to do."

Adanya nodded. "Thank you, Dr. Meadde. Can I have a few minutes to freshen up before I leave?"

"Yes, of course. If you want, you can go out the back. No one will see you there," Dr. Meadde replied sympathetically before standing and leaving the room.

"Thank you," Adanya replied.

Adanya sat in the small, pale green room. God, what was she going to do? She had to take the doctor's advice and think about everything before deciding. She didn't think she could kill the baby. An abortion was out of the question. If she wanted to keep the baby or give it up for adoption, that was what she needed to think about, and as for Roland, she wouldn't let him give up his dream. In two weeks, they were graduating from high school, and Roland was leaving shortly after that. He said that there wasn't any reason to stay after high school. He wanted out of his father's house as soon as possible. She was on her own, and it was best that he left before he found out that she was having his baby.

32

Seven months later, Adanya gave birth to a beautiful baby girl. She weighed seven pounds, three ounces and was nineteen inches long. The baby had taken after Roland, who was six feet eight inches. Her daughter would be tall like Roland or maybe short like Adanya, but she would never know because her mind was made up, and she was giving her daughter up for adoption. Adanya asked if she could hold her daughter and say goodbye before they took her away. In the past, this kind of request wasn't granted, just in case the mother reconsidered and wanted to keep the baby.

Adanya held her daughter in her arms. She watched the baby's eyes move as if she were trying to remember all the details of her mother before they parted. Adanya knew that this wasn't true. Babies didn't have that kind of memory until they were at least four or five years old. A nurse entered the room. "It's time to say goodbye, Adanya."

Adanya nodded, giving the baby a tiny squeeze into her chest and kissing her on the forehead. "Please forgive me for what I'm about to do, baby girl. I will love you always and forever," she whispered close to her daughter's ear. Then she was gone as the elderly nurse took the baby out of the room.

Adanya arrived home the following day from the hospital. She and her father had chosen to go to a hospital four towns away, just to make sure that no one knew about the pregnancy. For weeks, she stayed in bed, not wanting to do anything but cry for the loss of her daughter. It was as if she couldn't bear to live another day without her. She had made this choice before the baby was even born, but after holding her and looking into her beautiful brown eyes, she regretted her choice, but would now have to live with it. She knew that it was for the best, and that whoever had her would give her a better life—at least that's what she told herself. That's what she hoped.

At Adanya's request, her father made sure that the files were sealed, knowing that one day her daughter might come looking for her mother. Or was it that Adanya would go looking for her daughter? Either way, there was no trace of the adoption.

When she finally was able to get herself out of bed and stop mourning over giving up her daughter, she started exercising to get back in shape for the police academy. She would make this her goal, her life. She had nothing else.

She wasn't the only woman, but she was the only black woman who was enrolled. Men treated the women differently, making them feel as if they weren't good enough to be police officers, but all it did was make Adanya work harder. On her off-time, she was out in the training field running the course until she was able to get herself up the rope and over the wall. She became faster and was able to run through the course without falling or bent over from exhaustion. She made herself tough because she was all she had besides her father. She ran through the course faster than half the men in the academy.

Adanya graduated at the top of her class and was given two awards, one for her Academic Achievement and the other for being the Top Shooter in her class. Once the ceremony was over she started her career at Edon Police Station where her father worked.

There wasn't a day that went by that Adanya didn't think about her daughter. In fact, when she was out patrolling, she would look at all the babies. More so when the years went by and she knew that her daughter wouldn't be in a stroller, easier to see from the road. Though she was sure that her daughter was not living in the same town as her. The adoption service, she would have thought, wouldn't allow for the child to be near the parent that gave them up.

Another thing that occupied Adanya's time was searching the papers for Roland's name. He had left right after high school for college like he said he would. His dream was to one day play in the NBA. She'd followed his life for the first several years. After he finished college, Roland made headline news when he made the cut to play for the Chicago Bulls. She was so proud of him and had no regrets about not telling him of their daughter. *Look what he'd become,* she would say to herself. *You did good not telling him.*

Then two years after that, he was killed in a bus accident as the team drove to Wisconsin for a game. The bus had hit a sheet of ice, causing them to veer off the road and over a bridge. Tragically, there were only four survivors. Roland wasn't one of them.

She had kept all the paper clippings in a box hidden in her room. If she would have known what the future held, she would have told Roland about the baby because he was cheated out of a life and knowing his daughter.

If he had known, would he have stayed? Would he still be alive today? Adanya didn't know, but she couldn't change the decision she'd made or bring him back. Roland was dead, and her baby was somewhere in the world without her.

33

Five Days After the Accident

Afternoon

Leah took Rose by the arm. "Come with me. I need to show you something," she said as she walked quickly down the hall. Leah scanned her ID card. The doors zipped open and she slipped through the glass sliders, Rose two steps behind her. If she hadn't talked to Dr. Amal this morning about John Doe, then she wouldn't have known he was here. She wouldn't have given Rose back her son.

Ahead was the coma ward. Leah had only been in this section of the hospital once before, and it didn't look as if it had changed much. The walls were painted a plain eggshell color, no different from most of the walls in the hospital. There was several small rooms that fit two to three beds in each one. There wasn't a heavy census of coma patients, so finding him wouldn't be that hard. She went from room to room until she saw him lying there. She walked inside. He hadn't changed since the last time she'd seen him. When was that, two or three days ago? She couldn't remember. She walked to the side of the bed. Rose stood behind her.

"Why are we here?" Rose asked.

Leah turned around. “Because of him,” she said as she held out the photo of Adam that Rose had given her a few minutes ago. “He was in an accident and was brought here without any identification on him. He became a John Doe. I tried to find a relative, but there was no record in the database at the Franklin Police Department, so the doctor moved him here until we found someone,” she lied. She couldn’t very well tell her that they were taking him off life support. Not yet.

“I’m not sure what you’re blabbering on about. I just want to find my son, Adam,” Rose retorted.

Leah could tell that the woman was tired. Exhausted by the lack of sleep, she assumed, as she searched for her son, Adam. Leah handed the photo back to Rose. “That’s why I brought you here. I found your son.” Leah stepped back so that Rose could see the man in the bed.

Rose gasped, covering her hand over her mouth. “Adam? This is my Adam?” she questioned.

“Yes, I believe he is. The photo looks just like him.”

Rose stepped closer and bent over to touch his face that wasn’t covered by the ventilator. “I don’t know,” Rose said.

“Don’t know what?”

“He looks a little different.”

“Well, there is some swelling still to his face. He has some burns and deep cuts under the bandage, bruising even. He’s bound to look a little different,” Leah said, her gut twisting inside her. Was she wrong and this wasn’t the woman’s son?

"What's wrong with him?"

"I'm afraid that he's brain-dead."

"Brain-dead? As in dead?" Rose croaked.

Leah nodded. "I'm so sorry. I tried to find you," she whispered.

"May I see his lower back?" Rose asked.

Leah's forehead creased. "His back?" This was a strange request but maybe Rose had a reason.

"Yes, if it's my Adam," Rose said, "then he'll have a birthmark on his back near his right buttock."

"Yes, of course you can check his back. Which side?"

"Right side," Rose answered.

Leah walked around the bed and pulled the covers back. She cautiously slipped her hand under his back and rolled him gently to his side, moving the gown out of the way.

Rose came and stood next to Leah. There was no birthmark, but instead several scars. "Why would he have scars?" Rose asked as she leaned in to get a better look. "I'm not sure if I see the birthmark anymore."

Leah laid the man back down and covered him with the blankets, just as she'd found them. "I'm not sure, maybe he felt strange about the birthmark and wanted to have it removed? It happens sometimes." This she wasn't sure of but wanted to comfort the lady. "Is there anything thing else that you'd like to check?"

"Yes, actually there is. I'm still not convinced that he is my Adam. Sure, there may be some similar traits as in the photo, but I just… I just don't feel it in my heart that he is my son. Do you understand, my dear? I would know if something was wrong with him. I'd know if he were dead as you say he is."

Leah felt defeated once again. It had to be her Adam because who else could he be? There was no one else from the accident that hadn't been identified. He was the only one left, she told herself, though she didn't know for sure if there were anyone else. She hadn't asked or checked. "What would you like us to do?"

"I'd like to speak to the doctor first. Please get me the doctor," Rose said in a stern voice.

Leah went to the phone on the wall and paged Dr. Amal to come to the room they were in. Ten minutes or so had passed. Rose sat in a chair next to the man, while Leah stood along the wall, waiting for the doctor.

"Nurse Leah, what is the emergency?" Dr. Amal asked as he entered the room.

Leah pointed to Rose. "She is. She may be the man's mother, but she has questions and wants to speak to you."

Dr. Amal walked over to where Rose was sitting. "Ma'am, what can I help you with?"

Rose looked from the man in the bed to the doctor. "This kind lady here," she nodded her head at Leah, "Thinks that this is my son, Adam, but I need more proof than just looking at him and the scar on his back."

"Scar?"

"Yes, I wanted to see his birthmark, but there's a scar covering it up and we can't tell if there is a birthmark under it," Rose rambled on.

"I see, so what is it you want me to do? How can I assure you that he's your son, Adam? You say he isn't?" Dr. Amal questioned.

"Can you tell me what his blood type is? Adam has a rare blood type, AB negative. If you can show me this, then I'll believe that he is my Adam."

"Leah, could you retrieve the patient's file, please?"

Leah nodded and slipped out of the room. She searched the nurse's station for his chart and found it filed in a rack with the other patients. She opened the file and scanned over the sheet, stopping when she saw the blood type. Her eyes closed, and she fell back against the chair. She needed to collect herself before she walked back into the room to tell Rose.

34

Officer Moore held the photo in her hand as she sat in an empty stall of the women's restroom. For twenty-seven years she'd wanted nothing more than to see her daughter again. The daughter she'd regrettably given up.

She stared down at the picture Woods had given her an hour ago. She had no idea what he was up to when he had her sit in the interrogation room, then slid over a photo. She thought it was about the case, the accident, but once she looked down and saw the young woman in the photograph, she knew it was her child. They had the same smile. The curve of their eyes was the same. She could see Roland in her too.

As she sat there across from Woods, her mind flashed back to that day so many years ago and she quickly stood, knocking the chair to the floor, and ran out of the room with the picture still in her hand.

Oh my God, she said to herself. *I can't believe it's you. After all this time.* She'd been sitting in the stall for over an hour when she heard the knock on the women's restroom door.

"Adanya," Woods said. He never called her by her first name at work unless it was personal. "Can I please come in, so we can talk about this?"

Out of all the people she knew in this town of Edon, he was the only one she would want to know about her daughter. She stood and opened the door of the stall and walked to the mirror. She didn't want him to see her like this and wiped away the tears. Her eyes were beginning to puff up from all the crying. Well, she couldn't do anything about that now. She was just glad that she didn't wear much makeup. No mascara to smear beneath her eyes. She took in a deep breath and walked to the door. Her hand touched the cold metal knob. She hesitated, almost changing her mind, then opened the door. Their eyes met as if it were the first time they'd seen each other.

"Can we go some place quiet?" she asked.

He nodded. "I know just the place."

Moore followed him out to his car, keeping her head down as they walked. They drove off down the road, neither speaking a word. Woods entered the parking lot of the only park in Edon. He parked the patrol car facing toward Lake Erie and turned off the engine.

The silence was more than Moore could take. She had to say something, but silence wasn't always a bad thing. Two people can sit in the same space and not talk, but that wasn't why they were here. Woods deserved the truth if they were going to be in a relationship together. Although she hadn't talked to him about getting serious. Maybe he had changed his mind after the way she talked to him the other day. She didn't know, but they had to talk about everything today and get things out in the open once and for all.

She had never thought that after all these years, she'd be sitting here talking about the baby she'd given up. It was so long ago and such a heartbreaking day. One she didn't like remembering. "How did you know? How…"

Woods cut her off. "She came into the station yesterday right after you left for your appointment, which you haven't said what was wrong with you. What did the doctor say?"

"You grabbed me right when I walked into the station this morning; besides, I think we have another matter that we're discussing. I want to know how you know," Moore stated, hoping that she didn't sound too bossy, too demanding, like she always did. He started this, and she wanted to know what he knew. Then a thought came to her. *What if he talked to someone else about this? What if they saw her too?*

"Okay, you're right, but I want to know if there's something wrong with you. You'd tell me, wouldn't you?"

"Woods," she said a little too loudly, her words echoing inside the closed-up car. Their body heat together was making her more irritated. She placed her hand on the door and powered down the window, just enough to get some fresh air inside the car. She couldn't take this *not knowing* a second longer. She took in a deep breath and spoke as kindly as she could. "Yes, I would tell you, but I can't take more than one obstacle at a time."

Woods nodded. "Yesterday, I opened the door at the police station for her, she turned and smiled at me. I almost lost my footing and fell backwards down the stairs," he explained. "My God, I couldn't believe the resemblance. I wanted to ask her if you two were related, but I remember you saying that you had no more family since your father died."

Moore nodded in agreement, which now seemed to be a lie. "What did she come to the station for? Was she looking for me?" She sat waiting patiently for his answer. Wanting to know everything.

"She came in with questions about a man from the accident. You know, the accident on the Ohio Turnpike."

Moore knew which one, since it had been the only horrific accident they've had in all her years of being a police officer. She nodded for him to continue.

"She wanted help to find the family because the man is apparently brain-dead and will soon be taken off the ventilator. She said she'd gone to the Franklin Police, but no one there could help her, so she came to us."

"She wasn't looking for me?"

Woods shook his head.

"But what made you look into this?" She held up the picture she was still holding in her hand since they left the station.

"Well, I can't say that I wasn't acting weird about her looks. I mean, my God, she looks exactly like you, Adanya. I guess I made her feel uncomfortable because she practically ran out of the building like it was on fire," he said. "I went back to my desk and ran a search on her name. I found her address and where she works."

"Where does she live?"

"Franklin."

"She lives in Franklin?"

"Yes, she's lived there her whole life."

"What is her name?"

"Leah James."

"Leah James," Moore whispered into the car. Everything was coming at her too fast. First the tumor and now finding her baby girl, but if anything, Moore was shocked. This whole time she had lived one town away from her daughter. She wanted to scream. All this time when Moore thought that she'd never know where she was, her baby was only several miles away. "Does it say anything else? Like who her parents are?"

He nodded. "The mother lives in Naples, Florida and the father passed away when she was sixteen. Adanya, can you tell me who she is? Is she your daughter?"

Moore swallowed. She liked it when he said her name; it felt more intimate between them. She decided that she would just tell him and let it all out. No more secrets between them. She began telling Woods of her past and that she had made the decision to give up her baby because of her dreams and not being able to take care of her. "I couldn't take care of her and give her a good life. Trust me, I have tortured myself for what I've done, but I can't take it back. I can't change the past that I put in motion."

"What about the father? Did he agree to this adoption?"

This was the worst part of the whole story, telling him that she had never told the father about the baby. She could lie to him, but she didn't want to. She loved this man beside her and didn't want to start their relationship with any lies. So if she were going to start a relationship with Trevon Woods, the hottest man she'd ever met since Roland, then she had to tell him the truth and hope that he would still want her because she knew she wanted him. "He died," she whispered.

"Oh, no. You never had a chance to tell him?"

She wished that was how it happened. "Trevon," she said as she looked into his eyes. The same eyes that she dreamt of every night when she went to sleep. "I never told him because he was leaving to go to college and eventually play in the NBA. He was killed two years after making the cut to play for the Chicago Bulls. The bus that he and his teammates were on hit a sheet of ice and only four survived. Roland wasn't one of them."

"Wait one second," Woods said, holding up his hand. "Are you talking about Roland Hayes?" Woods asked. "*Thee* Roland Hayes who was awarded the most valuable player for the Chicago Bulls in 1997?"

Moore nodded. "How did you know?"

"I'm a big Chicago Bulls fan, and I remember when he made the team. You know I moved from Chicago, right? Came here ten years ago."

She nodded. "Yes, I do recall when you transferred here." She'd never forget that day. The day she fell in love with him.

"But why didn't you tell him? He had a right to know he had a daughter."

"I told you why. Roland had a life to live. Dreams to fulfill. He didn't have a home here. His father abused him all through his childhood, and his mother didn't give two shits what Roland did. Don't you see? He had talked about leaving since we started dating in high school. I couldn't be the one to hold him back. To live here and what? Work at some factory just so he could raise our child?" she explained, then began to cry into her hands. This is what she didn't want to happen. She didn't want to cry like a baby in front of Woods.

Trevon touched her shoulder. "I'm sorry. I didn't mean to criticize the choice you made. You did what you thought was right and now…now you have a second chance."

Moore looked up at him. "Second chance?"

"Yes, you can have a relationship with your daughter."

She hadn't thought about that. Could she really get to know her child? She wasn't a child anymore. She was twenty-seven years old. Then the fear of what Leah would ask came at her full speed. The questions she'd want to know. How would Moore answer them? It wasn't the same as talking to Woods. This was her daughter, the baby that she chose to give up, and Leah would want to know the truth of why Moore had done it. She'd read books about people being reconnected with their birth child after giving them up, and the one question they always asked was, *"Why didn't you want me?"* What would she tell her? Because in all honesty, Moore had wanted her and loved her; that was why she'd given her away. "But…I can't. What if she doesn't want anything to do with me?"

"How will you know if you don't find out? People still have dreams that they want. Just because yours was to be a police officer doesn't mean that you have never dreamed of finding your child one day, right?" he questioned.

Yes, it was true, she'd always wanted to find her, but with God's strength, she had plowed through those times when she was fragile and in a blink of an eye twenty-seven years had passed her by. "Yes," she said, and she meant it. She did want to be a part of Leah's life, but the question was, did Leah want Moore to be a part of hers?

35

Kaitlyn's mind was reeling since breakfast. Ben had acted different, strange in a way she'd never seen him. Although he'd been in a terrible car accident, she felt there had to be some of the old Ben she knew still inside him. The Ben that abused her and had raped her if she didn't give him what he wanted, especially when he was angry. The Ben who had written letters to break her and Adam up. This man, in this house with her right now, wasn't the same man from five days ago or from the days and weeks before that. She couldn't imagine him not wanting to hit her or belittle her for whatever reason. *Poached eggs,* she questioned herself. Since when didn't he like them? It's what he had for breakfast every morning since they'd been married.

Then seeing that mark on his lower back, which to her looked like a birthmark—she didn't recall Ben having a dark brown birthmark there. Maybe a few scars, but a birthmark? No, she would know the difference. Placing the thoughts to the back of her mind, she focused on the other things that were bothering her.

After they had their breakfast, Ben went back to the bedroom to lay down. He was complaining of his leg hurting him and took a pain pill. He never in their life together complained of pain, at least not around her. Probably because he didn't want to seem weak or fragile. He needed to feel empowered around her.

She'd kept herself busy and cleaned up the dishes. She scrubbed the countertop until her arm ached, making sure that all crumbs and splatters were cleaned, just in case her husband remembered who he was. Though this was more out of habit and fear than it was anything else.

Once she was done, she tiptoed down the hall to the bedroom and peeked in on Ben. His head was tilted and facing the wall. She could hear him breathing. The rising of the sheets told her that he was in a deep sleep. She turned to leave, her eyes catching a glimpse of something sticking out from under her dresser.

She slinked over to the dresser and grabbed it. It was one of the pictures she had taken of herself after one of the beatings Ben had given her. She'd taken them as evidence against him just in case she decided to go to the police. But how did the photo get on the floor? She thought back before her drive to Ohio. She hadn't opened the drawer since she left to meet Ben for dinner on that Friday. So, unless... She looked at Ben lying in bed. Had he found the photos since they'd been home? And if he did, why hadn't he said anything to her? She didn't know, but she needed to find a better hiding place for them.

She quietly opened the drawer and placed a hand under it. The white envelope was still there. Her shoulders relaxed, feeling relieved. She quietly removed the envelope and left the room. There was a tingling in her chest as adrenaline raced through her body, something she'd felt many times before when she tried to run from Ben. She went straight to the den and closed the door, locking it behind her before sitting in the chair. She closed her eyes, her hands trembling as she held the envelope. When she looked down, she saw that the tape she'd placed over the seal was detached and her heart raced. Ben had found the envelope and she knew for certain he would make her pay for taking pictures of herself. But the question was, when did he find them? Weeks ago? Would that be why he wanted to talk to her? No! She was sure that if he had found them, he certainly wouldn't take her to a restaurant and confront her. He'd either lock her up in the house or kill her for taking these.

She opened the envelope and gathered the stack of pictures in her hand. She looked at every one of them. Her stomach dropped at the sight of the black and dark purple bruises. She stood and ran over to the garbage can beside the desk and threw up all the contents in her stomach.

"Kaitlyn," Ben hollered as he turned the doorknob. "Are you in there?" His fist knocked on the door.

Kaitlyn wiped her face with a Kleenex from the desk. "Just a minute," she said back, trying to keep the panic out of her voice. She shoved the photos back inside the envelope and opened the bottom drawer. No, she wouldn't hide them in there; he would find them. She stood and looked around the room. She spotted an area high up on the top shelf. Yes, she would hide them behind one of the books. He wouldn't look there; Ben hated to read.

Once she was done and composed herself, she walked to the door and opened it. "Hi," she said, slapping a smile on her face. She saw that his face was flushed. Was he angry with her?

"Is everything okay?" He tilted himself toward her. "What is that smell?"

Kaitlyn's face fell. She forgot with the sudden panic of him at the door that she'd thrown up. "Oh God." She turned and grabbed the wastebasket. "I guess breakfast didn't sit well," she replied as she grabbed the pail and moved past him and into the bathroom by the kitchen. After all these years together, she hadn't been more scared than she was at this moment. Ben wasn't stupid. If he did see the pictures that she'd taken, then he knew for a fact that she was going to leave him. The Ben she knew wouldn't allow that to happen and she needed to be prepared. *But he's not the same Ben that I married. He is different and that thought scares me even more.*

"Do you want to get out of the house for a while?" Ben asked.

Kaitlyn held the rinsed-out garbage can in her hands, looking bewildered. What was he going to do to her?

"Is everything okay? Did I say something wrong?" he asked.

She could tell he seemed concerned, not like someone who wanted to hurt her. She slowly shook her head and swallowed. "No, it's just… I mean are you sure you're up to it?" She nodded her head toward his leg.

"I feel fine. Pain pill is working well," he smiled. "I don't feel a thing," he chuckled.

At least one of us isn't, she thought. "Okay, but only if you're sure."

"Yes, I would like to see the town we live in. Maybe it'll trigger a memory from my past."

Kaitlyn smiled, but inside she was fearful. She didn't want him to remember and be who he was. "Let me freshen up a bit before we go."

"Of course, and I'll find a spray to eliminate the odor," he said, smiling back at her.

Kaitlyn walked to the bathroom in their bedroom and brushed her teeth, then changed her shirt. She was moving fast, afraid that Ben would yell at her for making him wait for her.

Once she was done, she helped him into the car. They drove down Broad Street then turned onto Meadows Drive. She wasn't driving to anywhere in particular, just around the block and through the local business area. She stopped at a stop sign across from the church they had been married in. She looked over at Ben, who was looking past her.

"That church beside us."

She swallowed. He remembered?

"I've seen that church before."

"You have?"

"Yes, but I can't recall why."

"It was the church we were married in four years ago."

Ben shook his head. "No, I don't recall that part. It's something else."

Her heart ached from what he said. She didn't know why it made her feel sad inside. This was a man she despised for abusing her. Why would she feel hurt by his words? Why would she even care that he didn't remember that day? She set aside her thoughts and asked, "What do you remember?"

"I was almost in an accident at this intersection. I can't recall when, but I do remember driving off in a hurry."

36

"So, if he isn't my son, then who is he? And where's Adam?" Rose questioned.

Leah looked from Rose to Dr. Amal, hoping against all hope that Dr. Amal would take the lead, but he just stood there. She could see the tension in his jaw as the muscles pulsated beneath the five o'clock shadow that was already appearing. He was pissed, but she knew that he wouldn't show it in front of Mrs. Tucker. No, he'd wait until they were alone and scream at her for making such a mess of everything when she should've left well enough alone.

Leah swallowed, holding the panic out of her voice. "I'm not sure who he is, Mrs. Tucker. I'm so sorry for the mix-up. I mean they look so much alike from the picture you showed me."

"Some resemblance, but clearly not enough to make me believe it's Adam. And you have proof now because the blood type shows O positive not AB negative."

Leah was flabbergasted when she saw that the blood type was different. It took her over five minutes before she came back into the room to tell both Dr. Amal and Mrs. Tucker that he wasn't her son. Leah wanted to run out of the hospital and hide from her horrible mistake, but how was she to know that he wasn't her son? She saw the photo and *assumed* that he was because of the similarities of the two men. *Never assume*, her father had always told her. And yet, that was exactly what she did. She couldn't feel any less irresponsible for making this mistake, and she prayed that she wouldn't lose her job. She loved it here, but maybe it was for the best if that's what it came down to, but she hoped not. She'd probably go live with her mother in Naples, Florida, and find a job down there.

"Who should I talk to about my son missing? If he wasn't in the accident, then where is he?" Rose asked.

"I will call the authorities and have someone come here and help you with this problem," Dr. Amal replied. "I'm sure he's out there, maybe on a vacation or something. He could have told you, and you don't remember?"

"No, school just started. He's a teacher. He wouldn't miss work when school started weeks ago," Rose insisted.

Leah could see that Rose looked flushed and offered her a chair. "Please sit down and I will call the Franklin Police Department."

"No, I want to deal with the Edon Police Department. That's where we're from, and they know Adam. They know who we are and can help."

Leah nodded and left the room. She fought hard to keep the tears at bay, but once she was out of the room they came flooding out. Each time she wiped them away more came sliding down her face. She didn't want or need anyone asking what was wrong with her. She had done this all by herself. Why didn't she just leave the man for others to take care of? Well, she knew why. She cared too much for people and had to always take them under her wing and try to take care of them. Who did she think she was trying to be, God, like the other nurse had told her a couple of days ago?

She sat down in the chair in front of the computer and Googled the Edon Police Department. When the site came up, she dialed the phone number. She prayed that they wouldn't transfer her to Officer Woods. The thought made her shiver in her seat as images of the other day came crashing back to her.

Two rings later a woman answered. "Hello, Edon Police Department, how may I direct your call?"

"Yes, hi, I need to speak to someone about a missing person."

"Hold one second, please."

Soft violin music played through the receiver as she waited for someone to pick up. She sat back in the chair, her thoughts dazed as she replayed the last thirty minutes.

"Hello, this is Officer Moore. How can I help you?"

Leah snapped forward in her seat. "Hi, I have a missing person to report."

"What's the person's name?"

"Adam Tucker. He lives in Edon and his mother Rose is looking for him."

"Adam is missing?"

“Yes, apparently so. Wait, you know who I’m talking about?”

“Yes. Adam is well known throughout Edon. When was the last time he was seen?” Moore asked.

“The accident last Friday. The ten-car pile-up,” Leah replied.

“Where is Rose now? I can come to her.”

“We’re at Franklin Hospital, fifth floor, room # 501.”

“I’ll be there in fifteen minutes, give or take. Tell Rose I’m coming,” Moore said before disconnecting the call.

Leah hung up the phone and used the restroom before returning to the room Rose was waiting in. Leah felt relieved when she saw that Dr. Amal was nowhere in sight. *Thank you, God,* she said to herself. But she knew that there were going to be repercussions for what had occurred in this room today. Dr. Amal had told her to leave it alone, but she didn’t and now she was paying for it.

“I’m so sorry for the misunderstanding, here today. I didn’t mean to cause you any heartache.”

“I know, my dear, and I thought about what may have gone through your head at that moment when you saw the photograph. Dr. Amal said that you have been trying to locate the family for this poor, poor man,” Rose shook her head. “That’s such a nice thing for you to do.”

Leah was shocked that Dr. Amal had said anything about what she had been doing. He seemed so cold and heartless, but she wouldn't let herself get soft for the guy. She knew how quickly he could change and just because he said nice things to this woman Rose, didn't mean he would when they had their meeting, which she knew would come.

Twenty minutes later, Woods and Moore showed up at the hospital. Woods was the first to walk into the room, making Leah jump where she stood. Her heart hammered in her chest. *What is he doing here? Why did they have to send him?* she thought.

"I'm sorry, I didn't mean to frighten you the other day," Woods said, walking toward Leah.

Leah stood at the edge of the bed, her eyes sketching over him, but before she could say anything, Moore stepped through the door and their eyes met.

37

Eleven Years Ago

Leah James sat at the kitchen table reading a piece of paper—a folded piece of paper she had found hidden inside her father's dresser drawer when she went looking for a certain t-shirt of his to wear. He never minded that she wore his shirts; in fact, he loved it when she did. He said it made him feel closer to her even though she was the one wearing the shirt. Though, he had always been the one to get the shirt for her. Now she knew why.

An hour had passed, yet she didn't move from the chair in the kitchen. She sat as if she were slapped in the face or punched in the gut.

Adoption papers.

She had been adopted, and they had never told her. Her parents of sixteen years had never mentioned once that she wasn't theirs, and it broke her heart. No, it shattered her heart. She didn't know who they were anymore. Two people that raised her since birth and now she felt like a stranger. She had wondered why they were so much older than most of the other parents of friends her age. How was she supposed to act around them now? How was she supposed to still love them as her parents? This couldn't be happening to her. Her life was perfect in every way, until now.

In the next room, she heard the front door open and then close. The wooden floorboards creaked under the heavy boots that moved toward the kitchen where she sat.

"Pumpkin," her father said when he appeared in the doorway.

But he wasn't her father, was he? She looked up and into his face. His eyes sparkled back at her; a smile spread across his face, but changed when she didn't respond. What would she say to him? How could she sit here and pretend that everything was true and real between them? She couldn't. She wasn't the type of girl to let things be. She had to know why they were the way they were. She had to know who she really was and where she came from. If she wasn't their daughter, then whose daughter was she?

"Is everything okay? Are you all right?" he asked.

His words registered in her head. Of course, she wanted to be okay, but she wasn't. Without saying a word, she slid the piece of paper across the table. He didn't reach for it. It was as if he knew what it was without reading it. The big bold words stared back at him.

She watched the expression on his face crumple in front of her. This was all too much. Now she knew why she didn't look exactly like them in the family pictures. Her friend Loretta had said that she didn't look like anyone in her family either, but Leah knew she'd said that just to make her feel better.

"Leah," her father said as he placed his large hand on the table and sat down across from her. "Your mother and I were going to tell you."

"When?" Leah's voice croaked. Tears threatened to escape.

"When you turned eighteen. That way if you wanted to find her, you could."

"Find her? She gave me up! Why would I look for her?" But Leah didn't know for sure what had happened the day she was born—why her real mother gave her up and didn't want her. Though she had already thought about looking for her real mother the moment she read that she was adopted. She couldn't imagine why she wanted to find her, but she did. Who would give up their baby? And why? What did she do that was so bad? Leah had so many questions, but no answers. Leah wouldn't rest until she found the answers.

"Your mother and I—well, we couldn't have any children of our own. Your mother's sister, who works for the state, suggested that we adopt. She knew people that worked in children's services. So, one day we called and scheduled an appointment. Three months later, we had you," he said with a smile on his face. "You were the most beautiful baby that I had ever laid my eyes on," he whispered as tears streamed down his face and disappeared in his graying black beard.

Leah wiped away the tears that cascaded down her cheeks. “Why didn’t you just tell me?”

“We were afraid of losing you,” he said as his eyes grew sadder.

“Losing me? How could you lose me? I’m your daughter, but I deserve not to be lied to by my own parents.” She raised her voice, which she knew better than to do.

He nodded. “I know, Pumpkin, and I’m sorry that we did. Please forgive me. Forgive us for keeping such a secret from you,” he pleaded, tears leaking from his eyes.

She had never seen him cry before. Why did she do this to him? Leah stood and walked over to him. Although she was sixteen years old, she still loved to sit on his lap as if she were a child. “Oh, Daddy,” she said. “I’m not angry with you or Momma. I’m just hurt that you couldn’t tell me the truth.”

He nodded. “I’m sorry, Pumpkin.” He squeezed her into his chest.

She loved it when he called her Pumpkin. They had a bond the moment she laid eyes on him. She would do anything for him. “What do I do now? Do I look for her or pretend I don’t know about being adopted?”

“Leah, you can do whatever your heart wants. If you feel you need to find her, then we won’t stop you. We’re here for you no matter what you decide. We understand because she was the one that gave birth to you.”

Leah turned and hugged her father for a long time before she stood and left the room, leaving the adoption paper on the table. She didn't need it anymore, but she would have to think about what she was going to do.

She slipped the cell phone out from her back pocket and called Loretta. Loretta was her best friend, someone she told everything to. There wasn't anything Loretta didn't know about Leah. Well, except for what she was about to tell her best friend. If they put their heads together, they both could figure out what she should do.

Negative thoughts continued to weave their way into her mind. If her real mom gave her up, then why should she go looking for her? Apparently, her real mom didn't want her, otherwise she would have kept her, right? She knew that she'd never give up her child when she became pregnant, no matter what the reason was. Or had she died giving birth? Leah didn't know, but she wanted to find out. She needed to know what happened that day.

Leah had returned to the kitchen after calling her friend and found her father slumped over the kitchen table. At first, she thought that he had fallen asleep but when she nudged his shoulder he fell off the chair and slumped to the floor. Leah screamed and dropped to the ground, rolling her father onto his back. "Daddy," she called out through her tears. "Daddy, please, wake up. I'm sorry for everything. I shouldn't have gone snooping in your dresser drawer," she pleaded, but she knew that he was already gone before she had found him. Leah sat on the kitchen floor with his head in her lap, tears cascading down her face. She knew she had to call for an ambulance and call her momma, but she didn't want to leave him. She didn't want them to take her daddy away because she'd never see him again. She'd done this to him. If she hadn't found the paper, then he'd still be alive.

Weeks had passed since the funeral, leaving Leah alone and heartbroken from the loss of her father. She wasn't sure what she should do about finding her real mom. It almost felt like a betrayal against her father, who had died because she had found out about the adoption. At least that's what she believed. If she hadn't found the papers, then she wouldn't have confronted her dad and he would still be here with her. Maybe it was too soon. Sixteen years had already passed; what would another week or month matter if she waited?

Several months later, Leah decided that she would try and find her biological mother with the help of her best friend Loretta. Questions surfaced in her mind that she wanted —no, needed—to find the answers to. She just prayed that her real mom wouldn't be disappointed in her. Disappointed in the way she was raised, but why should Leah care what her real mom thought? She was the one that gave her up, not the other way around.

Leah went to the county office and was then directed to child services. The woman there told her that the records were sealed and that she couldn't for any reason unlock them and give Leah her mother's name. Feeling defeated, she drove over to Edon and asked the same questions and received the same answers. The files were sealed. End of story! Then a thought came to her. Maybe her mother didn't live in this state, but the adoption papers did say Ohio on them. She felt at a loss and pushed the thoughts to the back of her mind.

As time went by, Leah decided to leave the past in the past, but found herself searching the faces of every black woman she met, only to walk away disappointed. Sometimes she would ask the unthinkable question, "Did you ever give your baby up for adoption?" Some women answered back, "*NO!*" But some asked her why she'd ask such a question to a total stranger. Once she explained herself, they would apologize and go on their way.

After she graduated high school, her time was filled with college classes, and she put the adoption to the back of her mind. Though she would allow herself to think of her real mother from time to time, still looking at the faces when a black woman walked by her. Maybe one day she would finally find her when she wasn't looking.

38

Five Days after the Accident

Late Afternoon

Later that day, as Ben slept his mind began putting his life back together. His subconscious had a way of organizing the things that happened in his life. Things that he had once done and had long forgotten, so he thought. His time in the war hadn't been that long ago, but there were things he let slip to the back of his mind. The battle he fought and the injuries he sustained, the Dear John letter he received from a loved one back home. Someone that he chose to let go because of his foolishness without even trying. But she had written the letter that said goodbye, not him. He knew deep inside himself that he truly loved her. This his heart knew to be true.

He could see himself in combat and with other men in his unit. He could hear guns going off and men screaming in pain as bullets entered their bodies, leaving them immobilized. Then he himself flew through the air and his face was covered with small shards of metal and glass. His mind went black and then his mind flicked to images of Kaitlyn in her wedding dress. Her laughing and smiling. He could see it all so clearly, but it wasn't him beside her holding her hand because he was standing off in the distance, watching from afar. Who was the man next to Kaitlyn if it wasn't him? He had brown hair like himself. Possibly even the same height, but it wasn't him. Kaitlyn and the man kissed and then got into a car beside the road. That's when he drove off and almost caused an accident.

Ben jolted awake, the sweat rolling down his face and neck. The sheets under him felt sopping wet. He blinked as he stared up at the ceiling. The dream seemed so real, but he knew it wasn't a dream, but memories of his life coming back to him. He wasn't sure if he was Ben Gordon; if not then who was he? Should he tell Kaitlyn of these thoughts that were coming to him? She could help him. Would she help him? Yes, of course, she would; why would he even think that she wouldn't? *The photos*. If he were her husband, this Ben guy, he had beaten her, and she probably despised him, was afraid of him.

He threw his leg over the edge of the bed and placed his good foot on the floor. He couldn't wait to get this cast off, but six weeks was a long time away. Maybe it wouldn't be so bad if it weren't his right leg. Driving wasn't something he'd be doing anytime soon.

He grabbed the crutches and went into the bathroom. He gave himself a sponge bath, because taking a shower would be a two-person job with his leg like this. He threw some water on his face and somewhat washed his hair. He undressed and threw his wet clothes in the hamper and grabbed some fresh ones from the dresser drawer. He felt exposed walking around naked with his junk freely swaying. What if Kaitlyn walked in and saw him like this? He couldn't very well run and hide, but why would he? They were married. Husband and wife. Besides, it wasn't like she hadn't seen him naked before, right?

He struggled into the boxers, that he *apparently* wore, by sitting on the edge of the bed. He realized that he needed to put the broken leg in first because bending the knee in a cast was impossible. By the time he was finished, he'd worked up another sweat. He wiped off his forehead and neck with a washcloth before leaving the bedroom. He made his way into the kitchen, in search of Kaitlyn. He saw her sitting at the dining room table. The late afternoon light glowed around her as it poured through the window beside her. She looked like an angel.

He wanted to, but he couldn't tell her that he didn't think he was her husband, but some stranger she'd brought home instead. The dreams, he knew, came from someone other than her husband, but he could be wrong. He didn't know the life that Ben had before the accident. He didn't know what their life was like. In his heart, he didn't want to tell her because he didn't want to lose her. But how could he lose her if he never had her to begin with? It was all too much to think about.

He went to take a step toward her when his crutch slipped on something and he went flying forward. The crutch dropped to the floor with a clatter and he grabbed the counter with his free hand, keeping his bad foot from hitting the floor. Kaitlyn quickly scooped the letters on the table toward her before running to help keep Ben from falling.

"Are you all right?" she asked.

"Yeah, there must have been something on the floor that caught the rubber end of my crutch," he half chuckled, feeling stupid for being such a klutz.

He watched as she bent down and grabbed the metal crutch and handed it to him. He could tell that there was something wrong. Then he remembered that she was holding her cell phone at the table. "Are you okay?" he asked.

"What?"

"I asked if you were okay? Weren't you just on the phone?"

She nodded. "Do you remember Officer Moore? She was the officer who came and asked you questions after you woke up."

"Yes. Was that her on the phone?" He leaned against the counter to rest his back. Kaitlyn must have noticed that he was uncomfortable.

"Let's go sit on the sofa where you'll be more comfortable. I don't need you hurting yourself again."

Once they were seated on the sofa, or he should say, she was sitting, and he was lying against the arm of the sofa after she had propped his leg up with pillows.

"So, you were saying…" he said.

"Yes, right. Officer Moore called and said that we need to be back in Ohio tomorrow."

"Tomorrow?"

"Yes," she said, brushing a few strands away from her face and tucking them behind her ear. "It seems that there has been some new evidence in the case."

"What's the new evidence?"

"She didn't say, only that we need to be in Ohio by tomorrow around noon. She said to go straight to Franklin Hospital. Said I would know as soon as we got there."

He nodded, but inside he wondered if he should be worried. What could this new evidence be that they had to drive all the way back to Ohio? Did Officer Moore know that he might not be this Ben guy they had thought he was? Or maybe it was about the accident. Was he involved somehow in the crash? Was he the cause of it? A chill ran through his body. He didn't know answers to any of these questions but would soon find out.

39

Officer Moore sat in the fake leather-upholstered wooden chair in the lobby down the hall from where the brain-dead patient was. She'd just gotten off the phone with Kaitlyn, telling her that she needed to return to Ohio at once, and nothing more. She couldn't tell her over the phone that the man in her house might not be Ben Gordon, her husband. Moore didn't want to frighten Kaitlyn that there was some man, some stranger in her house. Moore knew and would bet her life that it was Adam Tucker with Kaitlyn and that Kaitlyn had nothing to worry about. Adam was a great guy; the whole town loved and cherished him. He was polite, sweet, and the nicest man she'd met. He fought in the war and came back in one piece, which was more than Moore could say about the other men and women who fought in the war. So that's why she didn't tell Kaitlyn to run or get to Ohio this evening.

Moore had one more thing she needed to do, and that was to talk to the young woman who was standing in the doorway right now. Moore looked up at Leah and motioned for her to sit down beside her. She wasn't sure how this was going to go or what words would come out of her mouth. She hadn't had time to prepare a speech because she didn't think this day would ever come. She had given up all hope of ever finding her daughter.

Leah walked over and sat down next to her. She could smell the fresh scent of perfume lingering from Leah. "Leah, that's such a pretty name," Moore said, controlling her excitement at finally meeting her daughter.

"Yes, my mother and father gave it to me," Leah replied bitterly.

Moore recoiled in her seat, feeling the sting of Leah's words. She knew this wouldn't be easy and prayed that she wouldn't lose her daughter again after finally finding her. "I'd like to meet them sometime," Moore said, "but only if you want me to."

"My dad passed away and my mother lives in Naples, Florida, now. Besides, what makes you think you can just waltz into my life after all these years? What makes you think that we will have any kind of relationship?" Leah snapped.

She was angrier than Moore thought she'd be. Moore felt as if a knife had punctured her heart from the words Leah had just said. Not that she didn't deserve it, but she wanted to explain. Explain why she did what she did and that she was sorry for giving her up. But she knew Leah was angry at her for what she did so many years ago.

"Why? Why did you not want me?" Leah asked. "What did I do that was so terrible that you didn't want me?"

And there it was. The same questions Moore knew her daughter would one day ask her. "You didn't do anything wrong. Please don't ever think that you did," Moore pleaded. "I was young, and it was a decision I've had to live with for twenty-seven years."

"Did you ever come looking for me?"

Moore smiled. "Yes, every day from when you were a baby and as you grew up, I looked at the faces of young women your age, but I wasn't sure what you looked like."

"I apparently look like you," Leah hissed back.

"Yeah, I can see that. So…" Moore hesitated. "So, you've lived in Franklin this whole time?" *God, I can't believe she was an arm's length away and I didn't know,* Moore thought. The more she looked at Leah the more she could see Roland in her too. Leah's eyes were more like his than Moore's eyes, but she definitely had Moore's smile and the curve of her face. Leah was slim like Roland, with long, thin legs. *Thank God she doesn't have my hips,* Moore thought and almost laughed out loud at the thoughts running through her head.

"Yes."

"I don't go to Franklin much since my dad died. Your grandfather," Moore said.

"Oh, I'm sorry to hear that. What about your mom? My grandmother?" Leah asked.

"She passed away when I was young. Never had the chance to know her."

“I guess we have something in common then.”

More bitter words shot through the air. She knew this wasn’t going to be easy, but the day arrived, and she needed to face it head on. No more running away from the choices she’d put in motion all those years ago. Moore looked up from her hands that were resting in her lap. She always had the tendency to wring her hands together when she was in a situation that was uncomfortable or new to her. It was like she had to have something to do while she was waiting for the matter at hand to be resolved. She heard the hurt in the words Leah just said and it pained her, making her rub her hands more aggressively. She wanted to get out of here because she needed time to think things through. Leah needed time to register all that had happened within the past hour, too.

“Moore,” Woods said from the door. “We have to get back to the station. Chief wants to have a meeting with the department.”

Moore nodded. “Okay, be right there,” she said before she looked back at Leah.

“Guess you have to leave?”

“Yeah, but I want to get together with you, but only if you want to. I don’t want to be a nuisance. I know you have a life and a job, and I’m not anyone important,” Moore said. “Take as much time as you need.”

“Don’t you think twenty-seven years is long enough?” Leah replied.

Moore nodded. "I guess you're right."

Leah reached out and placed her hand on Moore's. "I would like to talk with you more. Let me give you my number, and we'll get in touch in a day or two," Leah said. "I do need time to process all that has happened; besides, right now, we need to find out who that man is in the room and pray I don't lose my job over it."

"What do you mean?" Moore asked. "How will you lose your job?"

"That's something we can talk about later. Go and do what cops do."

Moore gave a faint smile. She wasn't sure after all these years that she could go through with getting to know her daughter. Did she deserve to spend time with her? She didn't think so. But she wasn't going to walk away or run. Woods would make sure that Moore was there when Leah called to get together. He would be her shoulder to lean on through all of this, and she appreciated his compassion and loving kind heart, even though he was a big strong man.

They both stood at the same time. Moore wondered if Leah was going to hug her but didn't give her any sign of doing so. Moore stepped back to give them space.

"I'll call you soon," Moore said before leaving the room.

40

Before the call came from Officer Moore telling Kaitlyn that she needed to come back to Ohio with Ben, Kaitlyn sat at the kitchen table, going through the letters from the envelope Ben had hidden. She sat there just after Ben had gone to lie down in bed.

She couldn't shake the words that he had said when they were driving around, and she stopped in front of the church where they had been married. What did he mean when he said he was almost in an accident? Was it on that day? Well, she didn't think so because they were at the church together. Was it before the wedding? It was possible. They weren't together in the morning or the day before.

She closed her eyes and searched into her past. The day of their wedding came into focus. She scanned over the things she did up to the moment she'd walked down the aisle. Her family and friends around her before she got dressed in her wedding dress. She remembered crying and wishing for just one split second, maybe two, that it was Adam she was about to marry and give her life to. She loved him so much, but knew it was time to let him go and be Mrs. Ben Gordon. She did love Ben, but she couldn't fully love him unless she closed her heart off from the memories of Adam that she held so tightly in her heart. She couldn't let herself remain in the past, wanting him to return and say that he was sorry for letting her go. That he loved her with everything that he had. Everything that he was.

After they had said their '*I do's'*, Ben and Kaitlyn walked down the aisle and out the front doors of the church. In her mind, she stood there on those steps looking around her. It was supposed to be the happiest day of her life. Well, she was happy, but she also felt unsure of the decision she'd just made. If this were true, then why did she go through with the wedding? Why didn't she just say, *I can't do this because you're not the man for me and because I love someone else.* Because that wasn't Kaitlyn. She did love Ben, but in her heart, he'd never be Adam, her true love who understood her and loved her in a way that no other man could ever love her. She had never felt so complete with someone as she had with Adam. He was her stability. He made her whole. Without him she felt like a lost child trapped in the dark woods, not knowing which way to go. But she did marry Ben and she'd have to live with her decision. She did love him, she just wasn't in love with him. She was young and yet she settled for the first man that replaced her Adam when there were so many other men in the world, but even those men wouldn't and couldn't add up to her Adam.

As her mind went deeper into that day, that moment when she was standing on the steps at the church, she looked out at all the faces in the crowd of family and friends. But it wasn't them she was hoping to see. She was looking for only one person, and he wasn't there. Why would she think that he would be? He hadn't known that she was getting married today. She hadn't seen him in three years.

Kaitlyn and Ben walked down the cement steps to the sidewalk leading them to the awaiting limo. She was smiling and laughing because this was supposed to be the best day of her whole life—well, until she had kids. Then her children would be her life.

She turned away from the car and gazed at all the people behind them, then turned back to get inside the car. It was in that small almost imperceptible moment that she had missed him. A man sitting on his motorcycle across the street, looking straight at her. Then he took off through the intersection right in front of an oncoming car.

Kaitlyn's eyes sprang open. "It couldn't be," she whispered. "Had he been there after all? And seen me with Ben?" A tear slid down her cheek. Her Adam was there, she was sure of it, but… Her thoughts were hazy, still unsure if she'd really seen Adam on the day of her wedding. She knew the mind could make you think and believe things that weren't there. She shook her head. No, it had to be real. She wanted it to be real.

The more she thought about that day the more questions surfaced. Had he known and had to see it with his own eyes?

No, she was sure that wasn't the case. But then why? How? Had one of her best friends called him and told him to come? She knew that Lisa, her best friend from college, didn't really care for Ben, but would she have contacted Adam to come to Illinois to stop the wedding? If so, then why wasn't he in the church? Why didn't he stop the wedding from happening? She wanted to scream into the room. "Why didn't he stop the wedding?" She whispered the words again and again.

Her eyes welled up with tears. Tears she didn't know she had inside her. She knew why she was crying, but four years ago, she didn't know that she would be married to a man who would abuse her. Hit her anytime he felt like it. Otherwise, she wouldn't have said yes. She was sure her mind was overthinking the whole scenario and the man she thought was Adam was someone else altogether. Yes, of course, that's exactly what she was doing. Adam was never there. She was only making herself think that he was. A part of her wasn't so sure because it still didn't explain what Ben had said about the accident a couple of hours ago.

She rubbed her forehead. A headache was surfacing from all the thinking she was doing, but before she could retrieve some Tylenol, her phone buzzed. She picked it up from the table, recognizing the number as Officer Moore. She quickly wiped the wetness from her face before answering the phone, then realized that Officer Moore couldn't see that she was crying.

Kaitlyn breathed in a breath to help calm herself before answering the call. “Hello.”

“Hi, Mrs. Gordon?”

“Yes,” Kaitlyn replied, wondering what the call was about.

“How is everything going over there?”

Kaitlyn swallowed, nervous that Officer Moore could hear the stress in her voice. “Everything is fine. We’re doing fine,” she said, though it felt like a lie.

“Good. That’s good.”

“Is that why you called, to ask how we are doing?”

“Oh, um, no, not exactly. I’m calling because I need you to come back to Ohio as soon as possible.”

Silence fell between them.

Kaitlyn wasn’t sure why they needed to go back to Ohio, but then remembered that Ben was in an accident. The police probably found something against him and needed him to be in the state when they arrested him because two people had died in that crash and others were severely injured. A small visible smile appeared on her face. Ben would be arrested and couldn’t hurt her anymore. This was good news! But she couldn’t get her hopes up and placed a hand on her belly. This would be a dream come true if he were arrested. She and the baby would be fine. She should feel awful for thinking such a thing. She shook her head. No, she had every right to feel the way she did.

“Mrs. Gordon are you there?” Moore asked.

"Yes, I'm still here."

"Can you be here by noon tomorrow?"

"Sure, we can be there at that time," Kaitlyn replied. "May I ask what this is about?"

"I think it's better if we talk when you get here."

"Oh, okay," Kaitlyn replied, wariness setting in.

"See you tomorrow," Moore said.

The line went dead.

Kaitlyn held the phone out in front of her. "That was a strange call," she mumbled under her breath, then nearly jumped out of her chair when she heard something hit the kitchen floor behind her. She whipped her head around and saw that it was Ben and that he was falling. She quickly slid the letters on the table toward her before running over to him. She grabbed his crutch that had somehow fallen from under his arm and handed it to him.

After helping him to the sofa, she propped his leg up to help keep the swelling down. When she finished, she sat in the chair across from him. They looked at each other for a few seconds before she looked away. She felt uncomfortable sitting in the same room with him. She knew if it were the old Ben, the Ben before the accident, he wouldn't have allowed her to be more than a few inches from him, even in their own home. He was possessive like that.

It wasn't the first time that she had wondered why she lived like this. Letting Ben order her around like she was some child, someone he owned. She could only blame herself for letting him control her, abuse her, but she was afraid of what he would do to her. To her family. The family she hadn't seen in months, thanks to him. Each time her mother called, she had to lie and say that she was busy with schoolwork and couldn't come visit. When her parents suggested that they could come to her, she would tell them that they were going out of town and wouldn't be home on that day. One excuse after another. That's what her life had been like these past four years, and now she had a chance to escape.

41

Six Days after the Accident

The morning light filtered through the creases of the curtains that hung from the copper rods above the bedroom window. Leah and her mother had picked them out together after Leah had rented the place several years ago. They had always loved going to the consignment store in Edon, one of the few stores that remained open in that small town. Sometimes they bought things; other times they just browsed.

Leah laid in bed, looking up at the ceiling, her thoughts a shambled mess on yesterday's events. She couldn't believe she had finally found her real mother after all these years.

Edon.

She'd lived in Edon the whole time and she didn't even know it. Although Leah didn't spend all that much time in Edon, it still blew her mind that Officer Moore lived just a town away for twenty-seven years.

She laughed at herself. She didn't even know what Officer Moore's name was. She couldn't go around calling her Moore like her partner did, or Officer Moore. And she sure wasn't going to call her mom because she didn't deserve that name even if she were her mother. At least not yet.

She couldn't believe that it took one person coming to the hospital to bring them together. She knew she'd have to tell her real mother eventually, but she had to get through this day first; the rest could wait.

She let out a sigh, then tossed the blankets to the side and climbed out of bed. She should be more excited about today because she would finally find out who the brain-dead man was. She would know his name and meet his family. Now she knew where her detective traits came from, she laughed into the room.

She still couldn't believe what she did when Rose showed her the picture of her son, Adam. Rose was hysterical when she identified the man as not being her son. Dr. Amal had left the room and she hadn't seen him the rest of the day. God, she had to worry about him too?

Leah padded to the bathroom and turned on the shower. This is the very thing she needed right now. A hot steamy shower to wash away her stress and worries of the day to come. She would allow herself to forget for ten minutes or maybe she would splurge and take fifteen minutes in the shower. What difference did it really matter anyway? She would still have to face the demons that were waiting for her at work.

~~~

The morning flew by as Leah kept herself busy with the patients in the ICU. She changed the bedding after some of the
~~~

patients were transferred to a different room and tended to the ill still in critical condition.

Officer Moore had phoned the ICU, leaving Leah a message to meet her in the hallway in the coma ward at noon. Leah looked at her watch; it was five minutes till twelve. She placed her chart in the rack at the nurse's station and left, making her way to meet Moore. She wiped her hands on her scrubs, something she did when she was nervous, whether they were sweaty or not.

She turned the corner and saw three people standing near the room where she was headed. One of them she knew, Officer Moore, but didn't have a clue who the other two people were. Was it the man's family? Yes, that's exactly who they were. The man turned and looked at her as she approached, her heart stopped. Was her brain-dead patient alive? No, that couldn't be, he wouldn't be able to stand with all the broken bones in his body. So, then who was this man standing here with Officer Moore? Maybe it was his twin brother. They looked similar in appearance, at least from afar.

"Leah," Moore said, smiling. "I have some people I want you to meet. This is Kaitlyn Gordon and her husband."

Leah was a little confused. Why didn't she say the man's name? "Hi," she replied, spreading a smile across her face.

"Shall we all go into the lobby?" Moore instructed as she led the way. "Since we're waiting on the results of his bloodwork," Officer Moore nodded in the direction of the man next to Kaitlyn. “Which…” she looked at the clock on the wall. “Should be here any minute now. Then we’ll go from there; besides, we’re still waiting on Rose to show up.”

“I’m sorry, but I don’t understand what this has to do with the man in the room?” Leah asked as she walked beside Moore. “I thought that’s why you wanted me here.”

“It is, and you’ll know soon enough.”

Leah followed Moore into the lobby. She was exhausted, and it was only noon. How would she make it through the rest of the day? Coffee. She needed coffee. Leah walked over to the coffee maker. She placed a k-cup into the machine and pushed the button. Time seemed to stand still as the coffee brewed and filled her cup, gurgling as it finished seconds later. She closed her eyes, breathing in the aroma of fresh brewed coffee.

“Leah, could you please remove the gauze from this man’s face?”

“Are you sure it’s healed enough?” Kaitlyn asked. “It’s only been a couple of days.”

“Won’t know until we’ve removed the bandage,” Officer Moore replied.

“Yes, but…”

“Leah here is a nurse. She’ll be more than careful when she removes it.”

“I’m sure she is, but shouldn’t the doctor be present?” Kaitlyn said.

"No, most doctors won't even touch the bandages," Leah said from across the room, her back facing them. "I'll go get the first-aid kit." She left her coffee where it was and bolted out the door. She needed to get out of the room. She didn't know what was going on, but Moore was acting very strange. Granted, she didn't know her all that well. Okay, she didn't know her at all, but what did those two people have to do with the man in the room? Her head hurt from thinking so much. If they were related wouldn't they be in there visiting and deciding what needed to be done?

She grabbed a few things from the cart down the hall and went back to the lobby. She placed the items on the table and started cutting away the bandage. She couldn't believe how much this man looked like the brain-dead patient. She was afraid to ask questions. She had already caused enough trouble and heartache with Rose.

She unwrapped the gauze and tossed it in the wastebasket next to the chair. She placed two fingers under his chin and moved his head up and to the side. "The burns look to be very minor and you should begin to let them air out, it'll help them heal faster," Leah said. "I'll put on a light coat of cream and a fresh bandage, but when you get home tonight, take the bandage off."

He nodded at her.

As she spread the cream over a small area on the right side of his face, she noticed scars that ran along the outer area along his face near his ear. He seemed to have had surgery sometime in his life, which looked relatively new since they were still a shade of pink in some areas. She wanted to ask, but decided it wasn't any of her business. She cleaned up the wrappers and threw everything in the wastebasket and went to retrieve her coffee. No sooner had she sipped from the cup that a dark-haired nurse walked into the room.

"Here are the results you've been waiting on, Officer Moore."

"Oh, great! Thank you," Moore replied as she reached out and took the papers from the nurse and began reading them. She had talked to Dr. Meadde this morning about what she needed to look for on the results.

The silence in the room was nerve-racking to Leah, but she didn't want to interrupt or be rude by making any kind of noise while Officer Moore was reading.

"Just what I thought," Moore said.

"What is it?" Kaitlyn asked, looking from Moore to her husband.

Leah stood back, listening to the story she had shared with Moore yesterday. Moore told Kaitlyn and the man sitting in the chair that there was a mix-up on the day of the accident when she'd found the wallet. She went on to tell them that the license in the wallet looked like the man that she had just helped rescue. The man that was sitting in this room right now, but she had been wrong.

"What do you mean, you were wrong?" Kaitlyn asked. "I saw the wallet you gave me; it was the exact one I had bought for Ben," she replied, looking at the man sitting next to her.

"I know and it's a terrible and unforgivable mistake on my own part. I had no other evidence. No other photos but the one in the wallet to go by. I hadn't thought to check the other hospitals in the area. When I went to Edon Hospital and talked to the nurses one of them suggested I go to the ICU because a couple of the survivors from the wreck had been taken there. So I did and that's when I saw him. The photo looked so much like him, it could have been anyone's mistake if they were in my shoes. Who knew that there would be two men that looked almost alike in some way?"

"What are you saying?" Kaitlyn asked again.

"I'm saying that he," Moore pointed at the man beside Kaitlyn, "is not your Ben. This man is not your husband, although they look somewhat alike."

Kaitlyn looked from the man to Moore and back at the man again. Her mouth fell open and then closed before speaking. "Then who is he if he's not my husband?" she asked.

All heads turned toward the doorway when they heard a woman speak.

"Adam," Rose gasped.

42

Images slammed inside his mind, one right after another. His years as a child and then graduating from high school. When he had enlisted into the Army and then he had seen her for the first time. She was so beautiful. They had danced, talked, and spent all their waking hours together when he wasn't working on the Army base in Chicago. Then an explosion appeared, and he fell to the ground, shielding his body. He couldn't see, and his face felt like it was on fire from the cuts and burns of the bomb that went off twenty yards in front of him. Half of his unit had died that day, and he was left with scars and images of what had happened. Although he had the choice to be discharged, he stayed in the Army and was transferred to Texas to finish his remaining years. Then he was home and started teaching students at the same school he graduated from.

He felt a hand touch his left arm. He turned to see who and what it was. It was her. The girl from his past. "Kaitlyn," he whispered.

She stared at him in shock.

"You're here?" Adam asked.

Kaitlyn nodded.

He sat in the chair as the memory of a letter came into view. She had written him a letter to say goodbye because she didn't want to wait for him any longer. That she had met someone else. He longed to see her again. To hold her again. But she was married to someone else.

Rose walked over to Adam and hugged him. "I was so worried about you, son. I thought I'd lost you like I did your father."

"Oh, Mom, I'm fine. I'm not going anywhere," he said, placing his hand on Rose's arm.

"Adam," Officer Moore said. "Do you remember the accident? What happened six days ago?"

"Parts of it, anyway."

"Do you mind sharing them?"

He shook his head. "Scott and I were on our crotch rockets. We got onto the turnpike, heading toward Indiana. We always like riding on the country roads. Scott sped up and took the curve before I did. It all seemed to happen rather quickly after he crashed his bike and flew through the air and then he was gone," Adam choked back the tears threatening his eyes. "He… he hit a semi-truck on the other side of the highway." Adam pressed on his eyes, wiping the tears away. "He didn't make it, did he?"

Officer Moore shook her head. "No, I'm sorry."

"I tried to slow down my bike, but then out of nowhere a car tire came at me, hitting my front wheel. I flew off my motorcycle and hit the car in front of me. I saw another vehicle coming toward where I was. Somehow, I managed to hide inside an area between the other cars. It was the only thing that I could think to do, or I would have been crushed." Adam stopped talking, as if waiting for more of the accident to come barreling back to him.

"Do you remember anything else?" Moore asked.

"No, I sort of blacked out until… until you found me," he whispered.

Officer Moore nodded.

From the other side of the room Leah spoke. "So, if he's not Ben Gordon, then the man in the room down the hall is our Ben Gordon?" she questioned.

"Ben's here?" Kaitlyn whispered as disappointment and dread ran through her.

"Yes," Leah shouted out before Moore could interject.

"Well," Moore looked at Leah. "He's not—well, it's hard to explain, Kaitlyn."

"He's brain-dead," Rose said. "Just tell her the truth."

43

Kaitlyn fell against the back of the chair, her mind whirling. *Ben is here. He is brain-dead? What does that mean exactly? Is he dead? Alive? Stuck in between worlds?* She wasn't sure what it meant or what she was supposed to do now. Should she run to him like a wife would do? Well, maybe a loving wife would run to her husband lying in the hospital. Of course, she had to go see him. She had to make sure that it was him, right? God, she felt sick to her stomach. Her thoughts were spinning in her head. This couldn't be happening.

"Kaitlyn," Officer Moore muttered. "I need you to come with me. I need you to identify the man and confirm that he is indeed your husband, Ben Gordon."

Kaitlyn couldn't move. She didn't want to move. Her eyes looked over at Adam sitting next to her. How hadn't she known that it was Adam and not Ben? They were similar, but she should have known that he wasn't Ben. Was she too worried about him hurting her, hurting the baby that she refused to really see the man she'd brought home? In all these years she had wished for this day to come. To be with Adam again, but it all felt like a dream. She wanted to pinch herself, but she felt all eyes on her. Adam, Rose, Leah, and Officer Moore were all watching her—for what, she didn't know.

Kaitlyn looked up at Officer Moore. Her lips were moving, but she wasn't sure what she was saying.

"Kaitlyn, are you all right?" Officer Moore asked.

"I think she's going to pass out," Rose chimed in.

Adam reached out and put his hand on her arm. "Kaitlyn."

Kaitlyn flinched from his touch, something she always did with Ben. She looked from Moore to Adam. Her ears felt clogged as if she had a head cold, then the nurse named Leah appeared at her side. Leah touched Kaitlyn's face. Her hands felt soft and gentle against her skin.

"Kaitlyn," Leah said, snapping her fingers in front of Kaitlyn's face. "Snap out of it."

Kaitlyn blinked, and the sounds of their voices made their way into her head.

"Hey, Kat," Adam whispered; this time he didn't touch her.

The words made her smile. It was what Adam had always called her when they were together nine years ago. Adam, her one true love, was here. He was alive, and she didn't know what to do. It was all too much, Ben was brain-dead, and Adam was here, alive.

"Kaitlyn, I know it feels like you've been hit off balance with the news of your husband, but we need for you to come with me and identify the man in the room down the hall. There are decisions that need to be made if he is your husband," Leah said.

Kaitlyn nodded and stood. Part of her was afraid to leave the room. Afraid that when she returned, Adam would be gone. It would be wrong to ask him to come with her. Should she ask him to stay? To wait for her like she would've done for him all those years ago?

Officer Moore and Leah led the way down the hall. Kaitlyn hadn't noticed how alike the two of them looked, as if they were related. By the age difference, Kaitlyn would say that they were mother and daughter, but it wasn't any of her business, and at this moment it wasn't important.

Kaitlyn heard the hum of the fluorescent lights as she walked down the narrow hallway. She stopped behind Moore and Leah, who stood in the doorway that led her to Ben. She felt nauseous. Not from the baby but being near Ben. She willed herself to walk past them and entered the room. She could see even from afar that it was him. It was Ben.

She stood beside the bed and looked down at him. Even in the state he was in, he still gave her the chills. "You said he's brain-dead?"

"Yes," Leah replied, standing across from Kaitlyn. "I was his nurse for a day and a half. When he was moved from the ICU to a different room, I came to see him and talk to him. I promised him that I would find his family, so they could say good-bye to him." She smiled at Kaitlyn. "He didn't have any identification on him, as you know, so he was our John Doe," Leah concluded.

Kaitlyn looked from Leah and then back down at Ben, replaying what Officer Moore had said in the lobby. She had found Ben's wallet, but the wallet wasn't with Ben, it was on the ground. Officer Moore had just found Adam and since their features looked somewhat alike, she had assumed with no other body to compare the two men, that Adam was the man on the driver's license. Anyone could have made that mistake. She herself had thought when she saw Ben for the very first time that he was Adam, but seeing them just minutes apart, their faces didn't look the same. There was gauze covering the same right side on Ben's face as there was on Adam's. By what she could see of him, it was and could be an easy mistake on anyone's part.

Kaitlyn let out a weighted sigh. A weight she had held onto for far too long. Ben couldn't hurt her anymore. He couldn't hurt the baby. Their baby. She had at one time loved this man, but he had taken that all away when he hit her. She didn't feel any remorse for him. Inside herself for the first time in over seven years since she'd met Ben, she felt happy. Safe. Relieved that he was gone from her life, and she could finally be free of him without any worry that he would come for her. "What happens now?" Kaitlyn asked, glad that her thoughts were hers, and no one knew what she was thinking as she looked down at this man she called her husband.

"So, you're identifying him as your husband, Ben Gordon?" Officer Moore asked.

Kaitlyn nodded.

"Well," Leah said, answering Kaitlyn's question, "I can go get the doctor and he can talk with you about what's next."

"Next?" Kaitlyn questioned. "He's brain-dead, what could be next?" she replied in an exasperated voice.

Leah looked from Kaitlyn to Officer Moore, back to Kaitlyn. "You can choose to keep him alive on the ventilator or you can have the machine turned off, and he will be pronounced dead."

Keep him alive? Why would she do that? Kaitlyn hadn't known the word *dead* would sound so…so good. God, she felt like a horrible person standing here thinking these things, but he had done this to her. He had made her into this person who wanted nothing more than to see him gone! Dead! "I don't need to see the doctor. Turn off the machine," Kaitlyn said with an added hiss in her words. She looked at Leah and then at Officer Moore.

"I still need a doctor in here to pronounce him," Leah added, taking a step back, as if Kaitlyn was about to attack her.

Without raising her voice, Kaitlyn said, "then please go get him."

Leah nodded and quickly left the room.

Officer Moore cleared her throat. "How long has he been hitting you?"

Kaitlyn looked up; their eyes met. "How? Who?"

"When I saw you flinch the second Adam touched you and by watching you standing here. Your emotions are turned off and your expressions gave you away."

"I guess that's why you're a police officer," Kaitlyn noted with a garbled laugh. "He started a couple of months after we were married, four years ago."

Officer Moore's body stiffened as her mouth dropped open and then closed. "Why…"

Kaitlyn held up her hand. "You were about to ask me why I stayed."

Moore nodded.

"Because he made me afraid to leave. He threatened that he would hurt my family. He would kill me. He promised he would stop after he hit me each time. I believed him. Then he killed my baby." Kaitlyn's anger was rising with each word.

Officer Moore came and stood beside her, reaching a hand out and touching Kaitlyn's arm and squeezing gently. "I'm so sorry."

"Thank you, but as much as you probably mean it, I will feel more relieved once I know he can't hurt me anymore, or my baby."

"Baby?" Moore questioned.

"Yes, three weeks ago, I found out that I'm pregnant and was planning on leaving him for good, then the accident happened. Now I don't need to be afraid. My baby and I can be safe. Will be safe now that he can't hurt us anymore." A tear ran down her face, not from sadness, but from relief. Her shoulders and back had always felt tense with fear, but right now she felt the weight begin to lift from her body.

Leah returned a few minutes later with Dr. Amal at her side. "Kaitlyn, this is Dr. Amal. He's been the doctor treating Ben."

Dr. Amal held out his hand. "Mrs. Gordon, I'm so sorry we have to meet under these circumstances," he said as Kaitlyn shook his hand. "Leah has informed me that you are giving us permission to turn off the life support?"

"Yes," Kaitlyn replied.

Dr. Amal handed Kaitlyn a clipboard. "Please sign at the bottom giving us permission and then I will turn off the machine. The ventilator will stop and then this machine," he pointed to the one tracking Ben's heart rate, "will tell us when his heart stops and will produce a thin, straight line."

Kaitlyn nodded.

"There is one other thing," Dr. Amal said before continuing. "When he was brought in and taken for a CT scan…" he paused as if waiting for some kind of reaction from Kaitlyn. When there wasn't one, he continued. "He has a brain tumor, one that can't be removed because of its location." Before he had a chance to ask her if she'd known, he saw her mouth drop open. "You didn't know, did you?"

Kaitlyn shook her head.

"Well, like I said before, it's inoperable. The surgery alone would have killed him."

Kaitlyn stood there in shock. Questions began to form in her head. "How long has it been there?"

"It could have been growing for quite some time, but if I were to take a guess, two, maybe three years."

"And what symptoms would it give a person with this kind of tumor?" Why…? Did she care? She wanted him gone. What difference would it make knowing what the symptoms were?

"Headaches for sure, maybe even make him more aggressive with certain things. Angrier even. Some people deal with their pain in different ways than others. Some may have no pain at all."

Kaitlyn sucked in a breath. So this tumor could have made him want to hit her? Made him angry? Irritable? She hadn't done anything wrong. He made her think that she was the problem, but she knew now that it wasn't her fault. She closed her eyes, letting go of everything, and breathed in deeply.

"Everyone deals with pain in a different way," the doctor said again as if she hadn't heard him.

Kaitlyn raised her hand. "I don't want to know any more. I'm ready to let him go." She did the math in her head. If it were only three years ago, his beatings started after they were married. The tumor had nothing to do with how he treated her. He knew what he was doing before he got sick. It would be stupid to believe that she was to blame so she decided '**NO**

MORE.' She wouldn't let him hurt her anymore. She signed the paper and handed to back to Dr. Amal.

Dr. Amal reached over and flicked off the switch on the machine. Leah removed the ventilator from Ben's mouth. Kaitlyn took in a breath and exhaled, waiting for the machine to inform them all that he was gone. Gone from this world he so desperately needed to get out of.

As silence filled the room, Kaitlyn only heard the *tick, tick* of the second hand moving on the clock out in the hall. Kaitlyn looked from Ben to Dr. Amal, waiting for the machine to sound, letting her know that he was dead.

Tick, tick, tick. Five minutes passed, then ten. Her thoughts were beginning to run wild. *They said he was brain-dead, so why hasn't he died yet? God, I can't take this any longer.* She wanted to wrap her hands around his neck and squeeze the life out of him as he had done to her more times than she could remember. Her mind screamed and told her that he wasn't going to die. That he would stay alive only to torture her until he killed her. A gurgle deep inside her started to move its way up, making her almost laugh out loud at the thought of Ben surviving after being pronounced brain-dead. Kaitlyn stilled as the alarm sounded, and a straight line appeared on the screen.

Dr. Amal clicked off the machine and placed his stethoscope on Ben's chest. "Time of death is 1:12 p.m."

44

Ben's body was transported back to Illinois, where Kaitlyn had him cremated. She told the morgue to do whatever they wanted with his remains; she didn't want them. Ben hadn't told her about his family. She only knew that he was in foster care and that was all he had said. She didn't dare ask him any more questions about his childhood life, knowing what the end result would be.

Kaitlyn knew she had a lot to do. She wasn't going to remain in the house they shared. The house that only reminded her of the abuse she lived with for five long years. No, she had already spoken to a realtor on her drive back from Ohio and set up an appointment for the man to see the house the minute she got home.

She'd spent the past week going through their things. She had taken two car loads of Ben's clothes and belongings to the local Goodwill store. There was nothing he had that she wanted. She packed everything else that she needed and put all the boxes in the garage.

She lifted and placed the last box of her things on top of another box when pain coursed through her abdomen. She doubled over, squeezing her eyes shut. Loud, piercing sounds came from deep inside her, as she screamed bloody murder.

The sounds of her screams echoing off the walls of the garage. Then blood exploded down her legs and onto the floor. She was losing the baby.

~ ~ ~

Three days later, Kaitlyn's friend Judy came over to visit and to see if she needed any help. Judy was the one who took her to the hospital. She had stopped by on her way home from work to see if Kaitlyn needed any more boxes for her move. Judy had told the EMTs that she heard the screams coming from the garage the moment she opened the car door. She had been thankful that the front door was unlocked.

Kaitlyn was ordered to stay off her feet for a few days after the miscarriage. The doctor said that she had probably overdone it, but not to blame herself. These things happened, especially since she had a miscarriage in the past. The doctor hadn't known that Ben had caused her to lose the baby the first time, after he used her as a punching bag.

There were two scenarios that could have been a factor: damage to her uterus from Ben's punches to her abdomen all these years or a weakened cervix. When the fetus started growing it became too heavy, causing her to lose the baby. The doctor told her that she could still try to get pregnant after a couple of months.

Within a week, Kaitlyn felt more like herself and although she was still sad from her loss, she knew that it was for the best. She had thoughts about the baby being like Ben and knew that God had his reasons for taking the baby before it was born. Though it didn't change the sadness she felt inside at losing her second child.

With all that had happened and since she had missed so much work, she decided to give the school her resignation without a two-week notice, but said she wanted to say goodbye to her students. The principal told her that if she needed anything to just call. Kaitlyn was moving to Ohio. She had been away from Adam for far too long and no matter what it took, she would be with him again; he just didn't know it.

She had put the house on the market the day she returned home from Ohio and sold it within two weeks, along with all the furniture inside the house. She didn't want any of it. She said goodbye to her family and friends, promising to visit often. Then she packed her car and left Illinois behind. At one time she thought she couldn't live anywhere else in the world, but she was wrong. Illinois wasn't the state she needed to live in. She needed to be wherever her true love was, and that's the way it should've been nine years ago.

Yes, she'd been in college, but her life without Adam in it didn't mean anything to her. She was lost without him and she wouldn't lose him again, which she knew now was because of Ben, thanks to the letters he had kept all these years. What was that saying? *"If you love something, set it free. If it comes back to you, it's yours; if it doesn't, it wasn't meant to be."* Adam had come back to her and she would do whatever she had to to keep him. She just hoped that he felt the same way.

45

Three Weeks Later

Adam had decided after another week off from teaching he needed to go back to work. He couldn't stand sitting at home not being able to do anything with the cast still on his leg. He couldn't drive or ride his motorcycle, which had been totaled in the crash. With his best friend Scott dying, he wasn't so sure he wanted to get another bike. Maybe it was time to close that chapter in his life, but what else did he have to do?

The silence alone in the house was nerve-racking, although his mother had suggested he stay at her house. He refused to have her take care of him. He was a grown military man who was taught to take care of himself, but it was lonely in his three-bedroom house, and the weather outside had begun to turn cold. October was here, bringing the cold winter weather with it. There were things he needed to do but couldn't with his leg the way it was. Scott had always been his right-hand man and with him gone, Adam felt even more alone.

He would have had his mom drive him to the cemetery to visit his friend, but was informed that Scott had been cremated and that there was no funeral or services to attend. Adam had gone to see Gilda, Scott's grandmother, to pay his respects and give her the American flag that Scott so deserved from his service in the Army.

The rest of his memories came back a couple of days later. He remembered everything that he shared with Kaitlyn before he went for Afghanistan. The letter. The bomb, and even the day of her wedding when he watched from across the street. Kaitlyn, after her husband Ben died, had gone back to Illinois to take care of the funeral and, he assumed, to live her life. He hadn't heard from her since she'd left three weeks ago. He didn't think his heart could break again after losing her the first time so many years ago, but he was wrong. It was breaking and crushing him worse than the first time he'd lost her. That's another reason why he had finally decided to go back to work.

The days seemed to drag, his thoughts only of Kaitlyn. His students were beyond thrilled to have him back as their teacher. The bell rang, and the students grabbed their things and walked out of the room, heading home for the day. Adam grabbed his satchel and placed his things inside, then positioned it around his neck so he could use the crutches. Once outside he waited for his mother to pick him up since he couldn't drive legally with the cast still on his leg. In two weeks it would come off. God, he couldn't wait to be able to do the things he used to do.

A few minutes later, a black Audi pulled up along the curb, blocking the handicap zone. He stood there, but the car didn't move. He looked around to see if anyone was waiting for a ride, but no one showed. After five minutes, he made his way over to the car to tell the person that he was waiting for his ride and ask if they could please park somewhere else.

He tapped on the window. It began to lower. "Excuse me, but could you maybe park in a different spot," he said before looking inside the car at the person in the driver's seat. "Kaitlyn?" he murmured, nearly losing his balance. "What are you—? I mean why are you here?"

"Do you want me to get the door for you, or can you get in on your own?" Kaitlyn asked.

"My mom will be here…" he was cut off.

"We talked, and she suggested that I should pick you up from the school," she smiled.

"Oh." His insides were melting from the sight of her. He thought he would never see her again. He hoped he would, but when she left, she never said she'd be back. Of course, a lot had happened with her husband dying, and she needed to go back to Illinois to take care of the funeral or whatever needed to be done.

"Do you need help getting in?"

He shook his head. "I got this," he said, puffing out his chest. He didn't want to seem like a wimp around her. He opened the door and lowered himself inside. There was so much he wanted to say to her, but he wasn't sure what her intentions were, and his heart couldn't take any more heartache.

Kaitlyn pulled away from the curb and drove out of the parking lot. "Where would you like to go?" she asked.

"Um, how about my house," he said. "I'd like to get out of these clothes and put my leg up. Is that okay?"

"Sure, just lead the way."

The ride seemed longer than the ten minutes that it took to get to his place. Neither had spoken another word since he had gotten in the car. It wasn't as if he knew she was coming. He would have been ready for her and had questions, or at least something to talk about, but he was scared to tell the woman beside him how he felt.

"Wow, nice place," Kaitlyn said, looking out the windshield. "Did you build it yourself?"

"No, but I have done some renovations to the inside. I've always wanted to live near Lake Erie, and I guess I was just lucky the house was for sale when I got out of the Army," Adam said as he opened the door and maneuvered his way out. His mother had a small SUV, which was higher off the ground; Kaitlyn's car was closer to the ground, making it harder for him to get out.

Once standing, Adam slammed the car door behind him and made his way toward the house. Kaitlyn followed behind him.

"Sit wherever you want, I'm just going to put on some shorts," Adam said as he slipped into his bedroom and closed the door. Once the door was closed, he rested his back against it. What was he going to do? Or say to her? He couldn't believe how nervous he was around her. He felt like a teenager who was having a crush on a girl for the first time. *Get a grip, dude,* his mind shouted. *You can do this. First, find out what her intentions are and go from there. Don't look like an idiot. Be yourself.* "Be myself," he mumbled into the room. He'd try; that was all he could do was try. He hadn't been with a girl since, well, since Kaitlyn. He didn't date while in the Army or when he came home. He was always busy doing things. Things that kept him occupied. God, he was pathetic. Kaitlyn had gotten married, and he hadn't done anything with himself. He felt like prey ready to get eaten up by coyotes.

He grabbed the pair of sweats from the chair beside the dresser and sat on the edge of the bed. He had cut the right leg into shorts and kept the left leg as it was. He had gotten pretty good at changing his clothes lately; it only took him a few seconds.

Back in the living room, he didn't see her anywhere, then spotted her outside on the deck. He opened the slider and stepped outside.

She turned and looked at him, her eyes sparkling in the late afternoon sunlight. God, she was breathtaking and so beautiful. He had never loved anyone as much as he loved her.

Always had and always would. But did she feel the same way about him?

46

The results from Moore's bloodwork came back showing that she did indeed have ovarian cancer like her mother. Surgery was scheduled immediately for a full hysterectomy. Moore knew it was too late for her to have any more children. She'd adopt if it came down to wanting children with Trevon, which was another thing she had done the minute she left the hospital.

After leaving the hospital on the day she had reunited Rose with her son Adam and Kaitlyn with her now dead husband Ben, she called Woods the second she was in her truck. "I need to see you," she said when she heard him answer the phone, not giving him a chance to talk. They met at the park he'd taken her to days ago, when she told him about her daughter, Leah.

He parked beside her vehicle and climbed into her truck. "What's the urgency?" he asked. "Are you all right?"

She laughed, then said, "Trevon, I have waited far too long to tell you this."

"Tell me what?"

"That I love you and want to be with you," she said quickly, her heart beating fast. "I don't want to put us off any longer." She sat there waiting for him to say something, anything, but he didn't say a word. She waited too long and now he didn't feel the same. "Well, are you going to say anything?" she finally asked. "I'm too late, aren't I?"

"I don't know what to say, except…" he paused.

Except what? her thoughts were screaming at her. *Answer the question,* she wanted to shout at him. She watched as his lips parted, then closed. Her heart sank, and her shoulders drooped. She was too late. He didn't want her any more. He didn't love her the way she loved him.

"Except that I love you too, Moore. And it's about damn' time you got your head out of your ass and told me how you feel," he howled, laughter filling the truck.

Moore looked over at him. "You love me?"

"Ever since the first day I met you." He reached over and wrapped his muscular arms around her and pulled her into him. "I've been waiting for this day for far too long, Adanya Moore. You're a foolish girl for waiting as long as you have been," he said, then kissed her.

They kissed, unlike any kiss she'd ever had—well, since Roland because she'd loved him too. When they parted, she looked into eyes. "I am foolish for waiting so long."

"Yes, you are," he laughed again.

They spent another hour at the park, holding one another, and making plans for their future. Most police stations didn't allow dating among coworkers. Woods said he would transfer to another shift at Edon police station or put in a transfer to

Franklin police station—somewhere close to Moore. Moore was overwhelmed with happiness and wondered why she had waited so long to let herself be loved. Woods had been her knight in shining armor. She didn't know what the future held for them, but she would stay and find out.

~ ~ ~

The memory of that day three weeks ago made her smile as Officer Moore sat in a booth near the back corner of the diner. She was nervous for her first date with her daughter, Leah. They had agreed to meet and have lunch at Moore's favorite diner that she and Trevon began coming to since they *officially* started dating. With all that had happened in the past month, she didn't want to waste any more time sitting around waiting for God knows what to come trotting into her life. She needed to live life to its fullest, not wait to be buried in the ground next to her dad.

The bell on the diner door rang. Moore looked up to see Leah walking in. Moore raised her hand and waved. She hoped she didn't look stupid sitting here waving her hand in the air, *"like you just don't care"*, the lyrics to the song entered her mind. A song she hadn't heard since it came out in 1986. She had no clue why it entered her mind at that moment either. She hadn't heard it on the radio before coming here.

Leah slid out of her coat and tossed it beside her in the booth. She smiled. "Hi."

"Hey, how are you doing?" Moore asked. *Hey.* What was that? Maybe she was more nervous than she thought she was.

"I'm doing good—no, actually great!" Leah said.

"Please, tell."

"Do you remember Dr. Amal? The doctor I said would probably fire me because of what happened with the patient Ben Gordon?"

"Yes." Moore frowned. She wasn't sure if she liked that doctor much.

"Well, he did."

"He did?" *What an asshole,* Moore thought. "I'm so sorry."

"That's not all," Leah said, a smile appearing.

"Oh?"

"After he fired me, I collected my things and went home." She sipped some water. "A couple of days ago, I received a call from a Dr. Meadde and she wants me to come work for her at her clinic."

Moore's eyes widened. Dr. Meadde gave Moore's daughter a job? Her heart swelled with happiness. "This is wonderful news, Leah. I'm so proud of you." Moore said. "Will you take the job?"

Leah nodded. "Thank you. I agree so that's why I told her I'd take the position."

Moore smiled as her heart filled with excitement. She was so proud of her daughter. Moore took a sip of her water. "This is a celebration lunch now, and it's on me," Moore said. "You've worked very hard to get that job." Moore was so happy. She couldn't believe after all these years, she finally found her daughter and she was successful. Not that Moore thought that she'd be living on the streets or uneducated, though she'd had thoughts and worries that maybe she did the wrong thing by letting her go and having someone else raise her. She was beyond glad that she was well taken care of and had a great home with two loving parents.

"I don't know if I worked that hard, but it's definitely something new for me."

"It looks like things are going great for you," Moore smiled.

"I guess so and I did finally find you after all these years too," Leah smiled. "I still can't believe it was all because of Ben Gordon. What were the chances of that happening and everything falling into place the way it did?"

Moore nodded her head. "I know. I can't believe everything that's happened." She took another sip of her water, her throat feeling dry. "I also heard that Kaitlyn, Ben's wife, is back in town. It seems that Adam and Kaitlyn were long-lost lovers from nine years ago. It's strange how the events fell into place the moment the accident happened. Although, tragic, of course." Moore tended to ramble when she was nervous.

"Oh my God, that's wonderful," Leah said cheerfully. "Long-lost lovers. Sounds like a fairy tale."

"Yeah, I mean I heard Ben wasn't that great of a husband. Abusive toward Kaitlyn," Moore stated as if she were trying to get Leah's approval, even if it wasn't her relationship, or was she just trying to avoid the conversation they were here to have? She was waiting to have this conversation the past twenty some years, but she honestly didn't think she'd ever be sitting here with her daughter. Maybe she was dreaming all of this up and she really wasn't here. Maybe the whole accident was a dream and she just didn't know it yet? No, there was no way this was something her mind made up. She was really here, and she wouldn't mess it up.

"I'm sorry that I haven't contacted you earlier with all that has happened," Leah said.

Moore waved a hand in the air, the lyrics coming back to her again. "You have been busy. And I'm sure you needed time to think about everything."

"What's your first name?" Leah spat out. "I'm not going to go around calling you Moore, and I'm so not ready to call you Mom," she smirked.

"Adanya." Although the words Leah said had hurt, she understood.

"That's a pretty name. Was there a reason why your mother named you that?"

Moore shook her head. "None that I know of."

"What about my father? Is he still around?"

Moore shook her head. "He died around the time you were five years old."

"Oh," Leah replied, lowering her head. "What was his name?"

Moore didn't know how this part was going to go, but she knew she had to tell her. "Roland. Roland Hayes."

"Wait. What?" Leah said, shocked. "You're sitting here telling me that I'm Roland Hayes' daughter? You're shitting me, right?" Leah swore, then looked around the room to see if there were any children around. "The basketball player from Chicago? There's no way!" Leah questioned. "He's my father?"

Moore nodded. "How did you know he played basketball?"

"I love watching basketball and who hadn't heard about Roland making it big when he started playing for them? My father was a big fan of his and well, he's the one who taught me all about the game," Leah said then fell silent.

Moore saw a change come over Leah's face. "I'm sorry you have to find out this way. You know, about you father and me. About everything," Moore said. "Roland was a great guy."

"Is that why he didn't want me? He went off to play basketball?" Leah asked bitterly.

Moore's face froze with the question and she heard the hurt in Leah's voice. She knew that Leah would ask, and she thought she was prepared to tell her the truth, but she couldn't tell her that she'd never told Roland about her, could she? No, she'd lose her forever, and she couldn't do that; she just found her. Moore swallowed the bile rising in her throat. She needed to get control of herself before she lost it. She didn't have to lie to Leah; she just didn't need to tell her the whole truth. She would have to keep this secret to herself. Leah could never find out what Moore never did. How she made the decision without discussing it with Roland. Would he be here now if she had told him? Would they have been a family? "No, that's not why. It was more my decision than his," Moore said.

Tears ran down Leah's face. "So why didn't you want me?"

"I…" Moore began to stutter. She had replayed this answer in her head many of times. "I was young, and my dad and I didn't have a lot of money to take care of you. I wanted you to have a good life. It's the only thing I knew to do. I just…" her voice cracked. "I just wanted you to have a better life than the one I could give you. A chance to make something of yourself. And you did." Moore took in a breath and exhaled. There, she said it and now she'd wait for Leah to yell at her and stomp out of the diner and not ever see her again.

"There wasn't a day in my life that I didn't think about you or wonder what you were doing and if you were in a good place. The files were locked, so I didn't know who you lived with," she sort of lied. She meant everything she said. She had never stopped searching for her face in the crowd or stopped loving her daughter.

Moore looked across the table at Leah, who sat there staring down at the table, or maybe it was her hands; Moore couldn't tell. She only wished she'd say something, anything. The silence was deafening. Had she made a mistake telling her?

47

Leah was a nervous wreck about having lunch with Officer Moore. She'd phoned her mom in Naples and told her all that had happened lately. The patient that was brain-dead, who turned out to be Ben Gordon from Illinois who apparently was passing through on his way to some meeting in Ohio. He had gone back to his hometown after the ventilator was turned off and he was finally at peace, although he really hadn't been suffering.

Then meeting her biological mother for the first time in twenty-seven years because of this man, Ben. And she had lost her job at the hospital. This had all happened because of *the accident* on the Ohio Turnpike. This, she knew, was a new beginning in her life, one that she would work hard at. Leah had accepted a job with a Dr. Meadde that worked in a clinic near Franklin hospital, working as a nurse. She hadn't heard of the woman, but she was thrilled to have been given the job.

On the way to the diner, Leah had several panic attacks. She almost talked herself out of going because seriously, the thought of sitting across from the woman who gave her up was beyond stressful. *What good would come out of this lunch with Moore?* she thought on more than one occasion.

She stood outside the door of the restaurant and saw Moore sitting in a booth, staring off into space. She looked as nervous as Leah felt. She needed to do this and be done with it. She needed to close this part of her life and start a new chapter, either with Moore or without. She wasn't sure which she preferred. Her mom in Naples said to give Moore a chance. Let her explain what happened and go from there. That Leah didn't have to make any decisions right at this moment. She could take as long as she needed.

Twenty minutes into the conversation, after Moore, no Adanya, told her the reason why she gave her up, she wanted to cry. Of course, Adanya would use the excuse that she only wanted the best for her; it's what all the websites that Leah Googled said. The thing was, Leah wanted to know anyway. She needed to hear the words come out of her biological mother's mouth, and she wanted to get to know this woman sitting across from her no matter what the excuse was, because she was her blood. Leah would sit there and listen with an open mind, as her mom in Naples said to do.

"I thought about you too," Leah finally said. "I wondered if you were alive or if maybe you died giving birth to me. I tried looking for you for years after I found out that I was adopted."

"They told you?"

"No, I *accidentally,*" Leah made air quotes, "found them in my dad's dresser drawer." The sting of that day pierced her heart as the memory replayed in her head. For so long she had hated herself for killing her father by finding the adoption papers. The doctor had said it was a massive heart attack possibly caused by blocked arteries, but she believed the stress of her confronting him was the real cause of his sudden death. Maybe in time she would forgive herself and accept that she had no control over what had happened eleven years ago.

Moore nodded.

Leah swallowed, trying to keep her composure. "He said that they were going to tell me when I turned eighteen, but I found out when I was sixteen. I started searching and going to the hospitals, but they all said the same thing. The files were locked. Every time I passed a black woman of your age—and I didn't even know that either—I looked at them for any resemblances to me."

Moore nodded. "Me too. Every time I saw a young woman your age, but I didn't even know you were in Ohio, much less the town of Franklin."

Leah nodded, looking down at her hands, then back up again. Tears cascaded down her face. She didn't want to cry but how could she not? The day she had waited her whole life for had arrived and she didn't know what to do from here. Would they continue to meet and get to know each other? Or would Leah decide Adanya wasn't worth her time?

"All I know, is that it's going to take some time. I can't sit here and say that I'm glad that I finally found you. I am, but

I'm also hurt," Leah said, wiping away the tears from her cheek. "I want to take it slow, maybe meet once a week and talk," Leah said. "We can get to know each other. I want to know more about my father when he was younger. Will that be all right?" Leah asked.

Moore looked at Leah through her tears. "I'd like that, too. I want you to have this," she said, sliding a thick manila envelope across the table.

"What's in it?"

"Everything that I saved over the years about your father, Roland. There're newspaper clippings in there and a few other things," Moore said, then added. "They're yours to keep. You deserve to have them."

Leah wiped away the tears as more came pouring out. "I'm not sure what to say but thank you."

"That's all there is to say," Moore said. "I wish he were here with us now. To see how beautiful and smart you are."

"He can, just like my dad," Leah replied.

48

Kaitlyn was surprised when Adam took her in his arms and kissed her on the deck overlooking Lake Erie. The sun reflected off the lake, making the moment even more romantic. She was breathless when the kiss ended. She forgot how good he kissed. “Adam,” she whispered. He put a finger against her lips. She hadn’t noticed when she picked him up at the school that the side of his face had healed with minimal scarring, but he was still as handsome as she had remembered.

“Don’t say anything. Kaitlyn, I love you more than anything, but before we go on, I need to know what your intentions are. Why did you write me that letter saying goodbye eight years ago?”

She had wanted to explain to him about the letter. All the letters that Ben had kept from her. “I never wrote that letter to you, Ben did, and he wrote one to me that was supposed to be from you, saying goodbye. That you didn’t want to be with me anymore. I think he stole my mail when we were in college, way before he and I actually met. It’s the only scenario I can come up with. I found the letters last month, a week before the accident,” she explained. “I didn’t get a chance to ask him about them.”

Adam looked confused, yet relieved. "That would explain a lot."

"I have them with me, all the letters you sent that I never got," she said. "I looked for you that day I got married to Ben. It wasn't until last month when you were at my house that I realized it was you standing there watching me. I remember someone, a man staring at me from across the street on his motorcycle. You were there, weren't you?"

Adam nodded.

"Why?" she questioned. "Why didn't you say something? Or stop the wedding?" She swallowed to get rid of the dryness in her throat. She had dreamt of the day she would be with him again but had thought it would never happen.

"I'm sorry, I thought that...Well, I thought you didn't want to be with me just like the letter said. And I saw you with him."

"I waited for you to come back even after I received that letter. I want to know everything that has happened to you in our time away from one another," Kaitlyn said.

"A lot happened, and I would love to tell you everything, if you stay."

"I'm not going anywhere," she replied. "I had made the decision to marry Ben, but I didn't know what I had done until…" She stopped talking, her mind going back to last month. "When you were in Illinois last month, did you find the photos in my bedroom?"

Adam's face grew tense. "He hurt you, didn't he? That man, Ben," Adam grew angry. "He hit you? Beat you?" The bitter, angry words flew out of his mouth.

She closed her eyes as the images flicked like a slideshow in her mind. It felt like it was happening as she stood there, but she knew that Ben was gone, and she didn't have to be scared or frightened anymore. She was safe with Adam. She had always been safe with Adam. "Yes," she whispered.

"That bastard," Adam snarled. "If he weren't already dead, I'd kill him myself."

She put a hand to his face. "Thank you for that, but he can't hurt me any longer. There's so much I need to tell you."

"Me too," he said as he pulled her into him and kissed her deeply, then whispered against her lips, "I want nothing more than to live my life with you," he said. "But only if that's what you want."

She smiled. "I want that too."

49

The Morning of the Accident

The morning Ben left his home in Illinois, he drove onto Interstate 80/90. He had a meeting at a bank in Toledo, Ohio. His plans were to drive there and be home by five that night. It was to be the last business trip he would attend because he was quitting his job. He made plans to meet his wife Kaitlyn at their favorite restaurant and tell her that he was dying. That he was diagnosed with an inoperable brain tumor. He was going to tell her that he was sorry for everything. But he wouldn't tell her that he was leaving that night and taking her with him.

He'd thought about his plan nonstop since the doctor's appointment when he was told that he had a few weeks to a month to live. He would have to tell Kaitlyn and then kill them both because he wasn't going to leave her here. No, she had to be with him, if not in life, in death. He knew she'd fight him, but he had that all figured out too. They'd have their last meal at his favorite restaurant and then go back to their house. He would close off the bedroom after drugging her with sleeping pills and fill the room with carbon monoxide from a generator that he'd purchased after finding out the results. He would then lie beside her on the bed, and they would die together, the way it was meant to be.

The morning rain had finally stopped, leaving the highway slick and wet. Ben crossed the state line entering Ohio. Once through the tollbooth, he accelerated, passing several cars. He had forty-five minutes to get to the bank and once again he was going to be late, but this time he couldn't blame Kaitlyn. This time it was due to the stupid ass morons on the road this morning. Ben, his usual self, was fuming behind the wheel of his Chevy Malibu. One of the symptoms caused by his brain tumor, so the doctor had told him. He had always been angry since he was abused by his mother when he was little and then put into foster care, but the doctor had said the tumor started three years ago. He couldn't pinpoint the exact day he started to feel different, but he had realized the change inside of himself and that he'd become more violent toward Kaitlyn, more aggressive, especially when the headaches surfaced.

"Come on, asshole, move it," he yelled as if the person in the other vehicle could hear him. The car beside him finally moved forward, giving him the room to pass. He pressed on the gas, zooming in and out of traffic as if he were in a race to the finish line. The two-lane highway turned into three. Ben checked his surroundings before moving into the far-left lane to drive around the semi-truck that was blocking his view.

He sped up to 85 then 90 mph and moved into the left lane. As he accelerated around the truck, pain shot through his head. He closed his eyes for a split second then opened them. Sunlight ricocheted off the chrome-plated mud flaps on the semi-truck beside him, blinding him instantly.

He jerked the wheel, causing the car to swerve on the wet pavement. He tightened his grip on the steering wheel his knuckles turning white. The car hit the cement dividers separating the highway. His heart pounded in his chest, causing sweat to form along his brow and hairline, which then ran down the back of his neck. Ben felt the car move in slow motion as it slowly somersaulted into the air, standing straight up like a ballerina on her toes. A cold chill ran through him, as if the blood had drained out of his body.

Pockets of sunlight beamed down to the ground as his car stopped in mid-air. With bulging eyes, he peered out the windshield. His only thought was of Kaitlyn and what she had once said to him. They were driving through town after the rain had stopped, just like this very moment. She had pointed to the rays of sunlight beaming through the clouds and said, "God was taking new souls up to the heavens." But he knew as he stared out the windshield, looking at the beautiful rays of sunlight streaming through the clouds, he wasn't going to heaven like she said people do when they die. He didn't deserve to go there.

His body jolted forward against the steering wheel and then slammed back against the seat. The car spun in the air, over the concrete wall, and into the westbound traffic, crashing upside down on the hood of his car.

He heard tires screeching and horns honking around him before they collided into his car. His body was broken, and the pain was worse than he'd ever imagined as he was pinned inside the vehicle. Airbags deployed, sending white powdered dust through the air and landing all around him. The sounds of metal crunching and glass shattering were the last things Ben heard before everything went black around him.

Acknowledgements

Here's where I get to say thank you to all the people that mean so much to me and helped make my dream as a published author come true. First and foremost, I want to thank my readers for reading my books. I don't know what I'd do without your support.

I would like to express my many thanks and appreciation to Steve Talaski for answering my many questions about firefighters and what happens at the scene of an accident. The procedures when arriving to an accident and at the hospital. I hoped that I didn't annoy you too much with all the questions. Thank you again for all your help with writing this book. I greatly appreciate your input.

I want to thank Deborah Bowman Stevens for reading through my synopsis and summary and critiquing my small flaws and missing commas. I can't seem to ever get them right.

I want to thank my parents for believing in me and wanting nothing but the best for me. I love you both so much! Thank you to my daughter who has to live with my insane conversations about my work and the characters I create and have actual conversations with from time to time. I love you, sweetie; you'll always be my baby bird.

The Accident was something that came to me when I was driving to Ohio to visit my family. The magic of the book came together like a puzzle, and in the end, it became a masterpiece.

About the Author

Donna M. Zadunajsky published her first novel, *Broken Promises*, in June 2012. She since has written several more novels and her first novella, *HELP ME!* Book 1 in the series, which is about teen suicide and bullying.

HELP ME!, won Awards in:

The Great Northwest Book Festival- **Winner** Global eBook Awards- **Gold Medal Winner** The Great Southeast Book Festival-**Winner** IPA Award- **Winner in Grief Category**
Reader Views Awards- In 3 different categories:

***Children-Teen 12-16-year-old**

***Children-Young Adult 16-18 years old**

***Best Teen/YA Book of the Year**

eLit Awards- **Silver Winner**

Talk To Me, Book 2 was a **Finalist in the Author U unpublished contest**, 2016 and later published in 2017.
IPA Award- **Winner in Death and Dying**

She is currently working on YA mystery series. To find out more about the author and her books go to:
http://www.donnazadunajsky.com

www.ingramcontent.com/pod-product-compliance
Lightning Source LLC
Chambersburg PA
CBHW030548310726
48979CB00010B/2073/J

* 9 7 8 1 9 3 8 0 3 7 7 6 4 *